## BELLE OF PEACHAM

Before she knew what was happening, Mirabelle was flung upon Charles Carlton's lap with her silk skirt riding high at her waist and her snowy white petticoats a froth of lace over her dimpled shoulders.

'What are you doing?' she cried as she felt his fingers tugging at the band of her drawers. 'How dare you?'

In truth, her displeasure was pretended – his masterful behaviour was most exciting.

A ripping sound heralded the baring of Mirabelle's full bottom, followed by a loud slapping sound as a strong hand descended upon her delectable pouting peach-halves . . .

*Also available from Headline Delta*

Peacham Place
Fair Ladies of Peacham Place
Naked in Paradise
Passion in Paradise
Amour Encore
The Blue Lantern
Good Vibrations
Groupies
Groupies II
In the Mood
Sex and Mrs Saxon
Sin and Mrs Saxon
Love Italian Style
Ecstasy Italian Style
Rapture Italian Style
Amorous Liaisons
Lustful Liaisons
Reckless Liaisons
Carnal Days
Carnal Nights
The Delicious Daughter
Hidden Rapture
A Lady of Quality
Hot Type
Playtime
The Sensual Mirror

# Belle of Peacham Place

Bethany Amber

**Delta**

Copyright © 1997 Bethany Amber

The right of Bethany Amber to be identified as the Author of the Work has been asserted by her in accordance with the Copyright, Designs and Patents Act 1988.

First Published in 1997
by HEADLINE BOOK PUBLISHING

A HEADLINE DELTA paperback

10 9 8 7 6 5 4 3 2 1

All rights reserved. No part of this publication may be reproduced, stored in a retrieval system, or transmitted, in any form or by any means without the prior written permission of the publisher, nor be otherwise circulated in any form of binding or cover other than that in which it is published and without a similar condition being imposed on the subsequent purchaser.

All characters in this publication are fictitious and any resemblance to real persons, living or dead, is purely coincidental.

ISBN 0 7472 5669 1

Typeset at The Spartan Press Ltd
Lymington, Hampshire

Printed and bound in Great Britain by
Mackays of Chatham plc,
Chatham, Kent

HEADLINE BOOK PUBLISHING
A division of Hodder Headline PLC
338 Euston Road
London NW1 3BH

# Belle of Peacham Place

# Chapter 1

Mirabelle Washington fluttered her fan furiously.

A large round housemaid bustled into the drawing room, a beaming smile wreathing her dark chubby cheeks.

'Mister Charles Carlton here to see you, Miss Mirabelle,' said the maid, dabbing her face against the heat.

A sigh whispered from Mirabelle's rosebud lips. 'I suppose I must see him,' she said adjusting her *décolletage* to show the upper ivory slopes of her lovely breasts to the best of advantage.

Diddy, the maid, tutted loudly and bustled over to the lovely Southern belle. 'What y'all doing, showing your titties like that?' She pulled up the low neckline of the cream silk dress with strong, dark fingers to a more modest position. 'You'm gonna give yo' poor daddy a heart attack, way you carry on with your beaux!'

'They all so tedious, Diddy!' complained Mirabelle, looking down at her neckline. 'And you makin' it more tedious!'

Diddy tutted again, louder this time as she bent with considerable puffing and panting to adjust her charge's skirts about slim, but immodest ankles.

'Showin' all you got to your beaux!' Diddy wagged a finger at Mirabelle. 'Now you behave like a lady, a real Southern belle, to Mister Carlton!'

Gleaming jet lashes fluttered over periwinkle-blue eyes and the softest of rosebud lips curved in a mischievous smile. 'And what if I don't?'

Diddy placed her hands on her more than ample hips and

glared at Mirabelle. 'Then Ah'll git yo' daddy to tan yo' hide!' The maid shook her turbanned head, making her chubby dark cheeks wobble crossly. 'Jest yo' see if Ah don't!'

A shudder ran through Mirabelle's shapely body. It was a shudder of sheer delight, she admitted to herself. Her beautifully proportioned buttocks fairly rippled with anticipation at the thought of castigation of her bottom, and yet she had no idea why.

With that final threat the large maid turned on her heel and flounced from the room.

The lovely Miss Washington sat very straight in her damask chair and covered her perfect ivory features with her lace fan ready to receive Mr Charles Carlton.

'Is she in a sunny mood?' she heard from beyond the door.

'Ain't bad as she could be,' she heard Diddy reply.

A slight teasing smile again curved the rosebud lips, but it was gone in a trice as the door opened to allow Charles Carlton entry.

'I've come to pledge my troth!' said Mr Carlton dramatically, throwing himself to his knees before Mirabelle.

A peep over her fan told her that he was surely one of the most handsome young men in Atlanta, Georgia. Broad shoulders tapered down to a slender waist. Firm, chiselled features were bronzed by wind and sun. All in all, he had a ruggedness and vital power which attracted her.

Mirabelle dipped her blue-black curls to the side as she thought. 'Perhaps—' she began.

'You'll marry me?' The handsome features were set in a radiant glow.

'I said perhaps!' Mirabelle said sharply, tapping his bended knee with her closed fan. 'You got to join the competition.'

The handsome face looked up at her, puzzled. 'I don't understand, Miss Mirabelle.'

'No! 'Cos I've sworn the competitors to secrecy! I don't want my reputation ruined!'

The pert Miss allowed her gaze to drift down to that part of Mr Carlton's body where his long, muscular legs joined his trunk. It looked promising, she thought, peeping at it over a fluttering fan.

'Stand up, Mr Carlton.' The melodious voice dripped honey at the command.

Mr Carlton stood. Mirabelle quivered with delight. In a leisurely manner he stretched his long legs and she could see his muscles rippling under the fine cloth of his trousers.

'Now what, Miss Mirabelle?'

'Lock the door,' she said, her voice husky, barely audible.

Watching him stride, with gloriously fluid movements, to the door made Mirabelle's lacey, cotton drawers damp about her cunney.

'Oh, I do hope—' she breathed.

'You hope what, Miss Mirabelle?' asked Mr Carlton, suddenly standing over her, his hands thrust deep in his pockets.

A whispered sigh escaped Mirabelle's pretty mouth and she felt the need to run her pink tongue tip around her lips.

'I hope you're the one!' she managed. 'So far my beaux have been so disappointing and you'm so handsome!'

Charles Carlton thrust out his loins. Yes, thought Mirabelle, that bulge certainly looked like the one for which she was searching.

'Open your trousers!' she gasped. 'Quickly!' She couldn't wait. There was an uncontainable urgency inside her pretty drawers.

'My trousers, Miss Mirabelle?'

Had he heard right? He gulped, feeling his cock fairly leap in readiness.

Mirabelle tutted impatiently. 'You deaf?' she gasped. 'I want to marry the man with the biggest and most upstanding cock . . .'

A long shiny length, pulsing with vitality, shot from Mr Carlton's trousers.

'And so far my beaux have sorely disappointed me,' continued Mirabelle. This, though, seemed to be the one.

Dainty fingers gracefully stroked the convulsing shaft. 'So smooth,' Mirabelle sighed, tracing the silky skin, beneath which were thickly engorged veins.

The lithe hips thrust forward eagerly and the lovely, although inquisitive, Southern belle slipped her slender fingers into the trousers to cup the heaviness of Mr Carlton's ballsack.

The young suitor could do nought else but groan, throwing back his handsome head in ecstatic appreciation of the action. On his way to the immensely rich Washington Plantation he had been more than a little apprehensive, for Miss Mirabelle's pettish, spoilt ways were well-known, not only in Atlanta, but in the whole of the State of Georgia.

'Oh, Miss Mirabelle . . .' he sighed, 'could it be that I am successful in my suit for your hand?'

He thrust back and forth, allowing the dainty fingers to brush the moistness of the swollen plum which was the peak of his shaft.

'I got to admit that y'all got a cock like no others I've seen!' whispered Mirabelle, before lapping out a beautifully agile tongue to stroke it up and down the rigid darkness of Mr Carlton's shaft.

'It tastes nice too!' the investigating Miss admitted.

Mr Carlton ventured a peek at the bobbing jet curls which were Mirabelle's perfectly groomed tresses. Was he truly going to be lucky enough to have this gorgeous, talented creature for his wife? His cock beat with pleasure.

The daintiest of index fingers smoothed across Mister Carlton's plum and touched the pearly dew of pre-issue which shimmered there. He clenched his muscular buttocks in a supreme effort for control.

'Drop your trousers to your ankles,' whispered Mirabelle silkily.

'Drop . . . ?'

A finger and thumb grasped the very root of the swain's cock, making him fight for breath, so wondrous was the sensation. The slim trousers were suddenly in a wrinkled heap at his feet and his cock, pulsing and shiny with turgidity, shuddered from his underdrawers.

'Now your drawers,' sighed Mirabelle.

'My drawers?'

'Must you repeat everything I say?' said the lovely daughter of Georgia.

'It's just that it seems a strange request...' Mister Carlton's beautifully honed legs seemed suddenly weak at the thought of being naked from the waist down before this glorious young creature.

'Don't be so old-fashioned!' snapped Mirabelle, grasping the band of his underdrawers and ripping them from his legs. 'We're at the beginning of the twentieth century. Things are different!'

With his balls full to bursting and his cock fairly drooling with pleasure, Mister Carlton had to admit Miss Mirabelle did appear to be right.

'Now the competition!' said Mirabelle happily, slicking both little hands up and down the considerable girth of his cock.

'But I thought—'

'You thought I just wanted to compare your length and width with my other beaux?' Mirabelle slid one little hand into the dark cleft of his bottom, searching for the tightness of his most intimate pit.

Gulping hard in his effort to hold back his joy, Mister Carlton nodded.

The pretty blue-black curls shook as Mirabelle negated his theory. 'Huh-huh!' She planted a soft, pecking kiss upon the muscular flatness of his belly. 'The competition is to see who can hold back his spunk the longest!'

Mister Carlton gasped partly that such a crude word should issue from such a sweet mouth and partly because he was sure that his spunk was about to spurt all over the Washington drawing room carpet.

'You ready?' asked Mirabelle, looking up at him with those limpid periwinkle-blue eyes.

The hapless young swain nodded apprehensively. He looked down and saw a sight which made his young heart sink. Miss Mirabelle was moistening her lips with the dearest of pink tongues and was pursing them into the sweetest of rosebuds.

'Oh, Miss Mirabelle . . .' he groaned.

His fine, handsome legs were shaking in earnest. A gloss of perspiration, not entirely due to the Atlanta heat, made his broad forehead gleam. His balls popped up and his cock shook with eagerness.

'Hush up, now Charles!' commanded Mirabelle, not looking up at him, but focusing the lovely blue eyes upon her quarry. 'This part is very important for the contest.'

Charles Carlton was more than aware of this fact and he was sure that he was not going to pass the first hurdle. The thrusting thickness of his turgidity was becoming unbearably painful.

'Oh, Charles!' sighed the eager Miss. 'Your plum is so pretty! It's little skirt is drawn back and I can see it all shiny and ready for my lips!'

The most refined of tongues lapped out to lick away another drop of pre-issue which hovered so prettily upon the purple globe. This was followed by a polishing finger which slipped over the sensitive knob with the lightest of touches.

Charles Carlton moaned, throwing back his head as the knowledge dawned upon him that he could hold back no longer. The soft lips closed around his silky firmness.

'I'm truly sorry, Miss Mirabelle . . .' he began.

He felt a surge from his vitals which he knew heralded the evidence of his excitement. It was as though all of his innards had turned to white hot spunk which he could not control. His large hands drove into the jet curls, pressing the loveliness of the sucking lips into his manliness.

'I feel my whole length in your mouth, Miss Mirabelle, honey!' he panted. 'I am in heaven!'

Mirabelle, although vastly enjoying the flood of cream pouring into her throat, mentally dismissed Charles Carlton from her list of suitors. Papa would just have to go on looking for beaux with staying power.

Lordy, she thought crossly, what was she going to do? She was eighteen, for heaven's sake, and if she didn't find a beau with staying power, she was going to stay an old maid. She swore she was!

Mirabelle bobbed up and looked at Charles with anger in the periwinkle-blues. For all she was joyously savouring the flavour of his copious spunk Mr Carlton was not the man she could marry.

'Git!' she commanded, pointing to the locked door.

'But I thought you admired the size . . .' Mr Carlton bent to pull up his underdrawers. He could feel his length, still firm and solid, oozing the last of his spunk down his muscular legs.

'I do!' exclaimed Mirabelle, fluttering her fan about her pretty features as she took a last, lingering, but regretful, look at the length in question. 'Indeed I do!'

'And you liked the feel of my plum in—' he persisted.

'It felt wonderful between my lips,' she assured him, giving the tip a final glance. 'It's a mighty fine plum and felt so big in my mouth.'

'Then what,' demanded Mr Carlton, fastening the button at the waist of his underdrawers, 'in tarnation did I do to displease you, Miss Mirabelle?'

He could feel his pecker rising within the fine home-grown Atlanta cotton of his underdrawers and knew that there could not be many young men in the State of Gerogia who could be as vigorous.

'You didn't do anything to displease me,' she assured

him. 'My lips fairly gloried in the silkiness of your cock, but...'

Mirabelle lowered her eyes to her lap. Beneath the silken folds of her skirt, between the milk-white flesh of her thighs was a cunney which dripped with longing.

Mister Carlton drew his trousers up over his muscular legs and looked at the lovely Miss Washington.

'But what?' he asked eagerly.

The hard flesh of her clitty fairly grated against the cotton and lace of her drawers. Diddy seemed to have laced her corset far too tightly, way beyond its normal seventeen inches and she felt overly confined. There was a deep yearning to throw herself at Mister Carlton's feet but she could not.

'You got no staying power!' she confessed. 'Your cock is beautiful. It's large and thick, but it's too eager to spill its contents!'

Mirabelle glared at the handsome young man, challenging him to refute her knowledge.

'It's your lips!' he gasped, allowing his trousers to slither swiftly back to the expensive carpet. His much maligned pecker was thrusting once more from the convenient slot at the front of his drawers.

Mirabelle looked petulant. 'What's wrong with my lips?' she asked angrily.

Charles Carlton stood over her, his expression threatening and his jutting length more so. 'Nothing wrong with them,' he assured her. 'They're just overly experienced. They're too clever. No man could withstand their practised caresses.' He was breathing hard, rapid and deep, as though he had run a long way. A hard hand reached out and grasped her wrist.

The periwinkle-blue eyes widened with fear, although Mister Carlton was grinning mischievously. 'What y'all doing?' she said nervously, her voice husky.

The finely cut trousers were kicked aside. 'You are a prick tease, Miss Mirabelle,' he said in a dangerously measured tone. He clasped her to him, pressing the firm, full breasts against his broad chest. One hand was hard against her bottom, clutching the shapely pillows of flesh through the silk of her gown and the several layers of her petticoats.

'Very shortly,' he murmured, still with that teasing smile upon his wide lips, 'you will discover what I am doing, but first . . .'

He paused and his dark, smouldering eyes stared into her frightened blue ones. Fearful though she was, she was also excited. The hard cherry stones of her nipples chafed against the silk of her gown and her breasts pouted heavily over the upper margin of her corset. The plump lips of her sex seemed swollen, brushing sensuously over the cotton of her drawers.

'Let me go!' she whispered weakly, but she did not struggle in the strong clasp of his arms.

'You don't mean that!' he said with a chuckle.

The very next moment his hot lips were upon her cool ones, still slick with the remains of his spunk. She felt his tongue sink into the willing openness of her mouth, invading her as, if she had judged him suitable, his cock would have invaded her cunney, given half a chance.

After long moments she broke away from him. 'You wretch! Didn't I tell you to git!'

Mister Carlton's arms clasped her yet tighter. 'My dear Miss Mirabelle,' he said, a sardonic grin upon his firm and sensual lips, 'I must tell you that I have absolutely no intention of going until I have finished what I intend to do.'

'You're going to rape me?' Mirabelle sounded excited rather than frightened. 'I'll cry for help! I'll cry for Papa.'

Mister Carlton threw back his head and let out a great peal of laughter, his hand tightening his hold upon the fleshy pillows of her buttocks.

'And he'll pepper your hide with buckshot!'

'Now that is where you are entirely wrong!'

Mirabelle frowned. 'I don't understand,' she murmured.

Charles Carlton ran a finger softly down the line of her

lovely neck. It was a caress which sent frissons of supreme pleasure down to her eager cunney.

'Your Papa gave me strict instructions to tame you!' he informed her, laughter hovering on every teasing word.

'He did what?' Mirabelle stiffened in his arms and tried to tear her shapely body away from him, but he was more than ready for such an action.

Before she knew what was happening she was flung upon Mister Carlton's lap with her silk skirt high at her waist and her snowy white cotton petticoats a froth of lace over her smooth shoulders.

'What are you doing, you devil?' she gasped.

She felt the cool touch of his strong fingers at the band of her drawers. When the cotton resisted his tugs, he tore at it roughly.

'How dare you!' she panted, but her cry of anguish was pretended. His very roughness was exciting and her little cunney had never felt so stimulated. However, as a lady, and a Southern lady at that, she must keep up her pretence of torment. She kicked her little feet up and down, giving Mister Carlton a gloriously moving display of silk stocking.

A loud ripping sound heralded the baring of Mirabelle's full bottom.

'Oooh! You wretch!' she cried, but she gloried in the display of her ivory hillocks and, surreptitiously, parted the milk-white thighs to show him yet more of her person.

A broad strong hand, palm flat and hard, slapped down upon the pouting peach-halves.

'Your father . . .' panted Mister Carlton, 'informs me . . .' Another slap followed the first bringing a cry from Mirabelle. 'That you are a disobedient young lady who he cannot control.'

Bottom cheeks fairly stinging with the strength of the slaps, the young Miss felt obliged to open her lovely thighs yet further, for a great heat seemed to suffuse the castigated part.

'And I can quite see what he means!' said Charles Carlton. At the lewd action of the pretty Miss, the punishing beau felt forced to administer a third blow, ten times harder than the first two.

'Your bottom is scarlet,' murmured Mister Carlton, 'and I can see the outline of my hand.'

'Stop crowing!' mewed Mirabelle. 'I'm only too aware of what you can see.' At this admission the naughty Miss Mirabelle made her bottom cheeks rise from Mister Carlton's lap. She was fairly offering him the burning cheeks and the deep valley between them.

'Oh, Miss Mirabelle!' groaned the young beau. 'I fear that the wonderful sights beneath my eyes are too much for a poor weak-willed soul such as myself.'

His touch was heated from the swift abrasions which he had given her buttocks. A soft mew escaped her lips as his fingers parted the burning cheeks of her bottom. Feeling a fleshy hardness press into the pliancy of her belly, Mirabelle bore her mons down upon it such as the many layers of her clothing would allow.

'Such delicious wetness!' sighed Mister Carlton. A stiff finger was now sliding up and down the silky cleft below her bottom valley. The mischievous Miss wriggled delightedly as the tip of the finger glanced moistly over the tiny bud hidden between her maidenly folds.

'Oooh!' she sighed in sheer ecstasy. 'Stroke that part once again, Charles Carlton. Please!'

Mirabelle bounced up and down upon his lap, abrading his finger upon her erect clitty. The finger rubbed several more times and the heated hillocks of her bottom began to bounce more wildly.

'Oh, Mister Carlton! I surely don't know what you're doing to me, but I declare that it is quite the nicest feeling I've ever had!'

Mirabelle crossed her little fingers, as she often did when she told an untruth. She knew exactly what the young swain was doing, having done it to herself before the mirror in her bedroom many times a week.

'Called finger fucking, Miss Mirabelle,' panted the young man knowledgeably.

The naughty minx bit the rosebud lips to prevent him hearing her subdued chuckle. 'Is it truly?' she said innocently. 'I like those words. Can I tell Mama?'

Mister Carlton coughed, almost choking at the thought. 'Better not,' he advised. 'It's a phrase only used between man and wife.' Or man and whore, he thought to himself.

'Well, that finger fucking is making the most glorious feelings come upon me!' admitted Mirabelle, her voice rising as she came.

'Oh, my love!' gasped Charles Carlton, feeling the lovely young woman's breasts quiver upon his lap. 'Would you allow me to—?'

He paused, pressing three fingers gently at the beauty's entrance, feeling her love sap pour over his digits and feeling her spongy walls pulse at the pads of his fingers.

'Would I allow you to what?' sighed Mirabelle, feeling herself shake from head to toe as her peak passed.

Cock fairly throbbing with eagerness against the pliancy of Mirabelle's stomach, Mister Carlton cleared his throat, wanting to pledge his needs with a firm voice. This time he would not take 'no' for an answer.

'Would you allow me to fuck you?' he said quickly.

'With your fingers?' frowned Mirabelle, over the creamy smoothness of her shoulder.

'Er-no,' stammered the young man.

Mirabelle could feel the hard thickness probing her flesh and knew exactly what he required.

'With what then?' Mirabelle made her voice small and sweetly curious.

Charles Carlton's patience was at an end and he pushed the half-naked tease from his lap, standing up with a springy bounce, waving his freshly turgid and dripping brute about her, like some magic wand.

'I'll show you who has the staying power!' he promised.

Mirabelle, her blue eyes dewy and her lips parted, smiled up at him. Teasingly, she kicked her shapely legs and spread them wide, deliberately increasing the gap in her ripped drawers.

'Aaagh!' groaned Mister Carlton, his hands flying, panic-stricken to his upright cock. His dark, smouldering eyes were drawn to her pink and shining little cunney.

'Come!' she mocked playfully.

'No!' he gasped, his hands clutching his length as though he would strangle it. It began to throb. 'I'm trying so hard not to spume, Miss Mirabelle!'

With dainty index fingers she spread her plump cunney lips which were so gorgeously sprinkled with tight jet curls. 'I do so want you to take me,' she purred. She pointed delicately to the tightness of her darkly flushed entrance.

'Oh Miss Mir—'

No sooner had he started to speak than his spume began to spurt.

Mirabelle was furious. 'You had your last chance!' Leaping to her feet she threw his discarded trousers into his arms. 'Git! I don't want to see you ever again!'

'But your Papa—'

'I don't give a fig about my Papa and I care even less for you!' Her little hands were placed firmly upon the swell of her hip and she glared at him, allowing her gaze to drift down to the limp contents of his underdrawers.

'One more chance . . .' pleaded Mister Carlton.

'I told you to git!'

For a dainty Southern lady Miss Mirabelle packed a hefty kick upon her beau's backside, propelling him through the drawing room door to the gracious hall, much to the amusement of Diddy.

# Chapter 2

'Fiddle-de-dee!' exclaimed Mirabelle, admiring her image in the mirror. 'There must be somebody else suitable.'

Diddy thrust her young mistress to the bed post and indicated that she should hold tight as she pulled her corset laces. 'No, Miss Mirabelle,' puffed Diddy. 'Ain't no-one!'

Mirabelle thrust her handsome backside rearwards and held the post tighter. 'Is that what Papa said? That Mister Charles Carlton was the very last eligible bachelor in Atlanta?'

Puffing and panting, Diddy tugged at the corset laces, her large, round face glowing darkly with the effort. 'He the last one in the whole of the State of Georgia!'

'They can't all be milk sops!' Mirabelle felt her waist being whittled to the required seventeen inches. In the mirror by the bed she could see her hips and buttocks flaring from the tininess of her waist. Fine, full breasts pouted pertly over the upper margin of her corset, covered only lightly by the finest of lawn bodices.

'You worrying your poor daddy to death, Miss Mirabelle!' exclaimed Diddy.

The young Miss allowed her large maid to help her into her lace-trimmed, long cotton drawers. 'Don't be melodramatic, Diddy!' she chided, slipping her small feet into dainty leather boots and watching as the maid bent, panting heavily, to fasten the tiny buttons.

'It's true!' exclaimed Diddy, looking up with worried brown eyes. 'Why you so fussy 'bout who you choose for a husband? All those boys were handsome.'

'They had no staying power, Diddy,' said Mirabelle, stretching up her long pale arms to allow her several petticoats to be slipped over her head.

'What you mean? Staying power?' The maid tied the satin ribbons which held the pretty petticoats about her mistress's waist.

Mirabelle closed her eyes, seeing again the parade of fine, upstanding young cocks which withered and wilted at the touch of her lips or the sight of her cunney. She sighed wearily.

'I shall not marry a man that I cannot love to the full,' she declared staunchly.

Diddy huffed in disgust. 'Y'all thinking about sex again, Miss Mirabelle.'

Wide periwinkle-blue eyes turned upon Diddy, flashing blue fire. 'You damned right, I am!'

'T'ain't right!' protested Diddy, shaking her turbanned head. 'T'ain't right at all. Ladies shouldn't be thinking about sex. They should lie back when their husband comes to them and think about their family and their nation.' She pursed her lips angrily and shook her head making her fat cheeks wobble furiously.

Mirabelle laughed, her dear dimpled hands resting on the flare of her hips. 'Is that what you do with your husband?'

The servant took a simple white dress from the huge wardrobe and walked crossly to her young charge. 'T'ain't the same!' she hissed.

'Why not?' persisted Mirabelle. The soft, gossamer folds of the dress fell softly over her head and her long, slender arms were slipped into the sleeves. 'Why isn't sex the same for you? Why must I suffer boring sex which doesn't last a moment while you can enjoy it?'

Diddy tugged the dress into place rather more forcefully than was absolutely necessary.

'Don't be rough, Diddy!'

'You know very well why, Miss Mirabelle,' said Diddy as she began the tedious business of fastening the tiny buttons which ran from neck to waist. 'Y'all don't need me to tell you.'

The dress was one of Mirabelle's prettiest. High-necked with a neat bodice, ruffled to emphasise her full breasts, it fell straight at the front but was cut on the bias at the rear to fall into a short train. Mirabelle sighed. Lord only knew why she chose this, she thought. There were no callers expected and she wasn't going anywhere except perhaps for a stroll around the Washington Plantation.

The rosebud mouth pursed in determination. 'Come on, Diddy,' Mirabelle persisted. 'Why can you enjoy sex and I can't?'

'Good job yo' poor daddy can't hear you!' chided Diddy. 'Ah can enjoy sex 'cos Ah got a good, big husband who's got a good, big cock and Ah'm a servant, that's why!' The explanation came out all in a rush, leaving poor Diddy breathless and embarrassed.

'So that's the answer!' said Mirabelle, dancing away from Diddy. 'That's what I need!'

'A servant?' exclaimed Diddy. Her big, plump hands flew to her mouth in horror. 'Oh, no, Miss Mirabelle! Please! Forget what Ah told you!'

The pert young miss picked up the parasol which matched her dress and flew, giggling, to the door. 'Maybe I'm only teasing you, Diddy,' she said with a playful chuckle.

'And maybe you ain't!' said Diddy, beginning to tidy her young mistress's room. 'Don't you dare do anything to upset yo' poor daddy!'

Mirabelle danced from the room and flew down the gracious staircase which curved from the first floor to the grand entrance hall. The smile still hovered about her pretty features when her father, Colonel Rhett Washington, strode from the library.

'Oh, Mirabelle!' he said, a smile taking away the seriousness from his distinguished features. 'You look radiant, my dear!'

'Thank you, Papa,' replied Mirabelle, with a toss of her lustrous blue-black curls.

'Is there a beau of which I am unaware?' he said hopefully, taking his daughter's hand.

'No, Daddy,' she said, leaning forward to peck her father on his tanned cheek. 'I'm just taking a walk around the plantation.'

Her father smiled, trying not to show his disappointment. Mirabelle was eighteen. It was time plans were made for a wedding. It was giving him a great deal of concern. He watched her, pretty head held high and parasol twirling as she stepped out into the Atlanta sunshine.

There was the sweet scent of magnolia blossom in the air. The sky was the deepest of blues and birds sang in the trees. It was a perfect day, and Mirabelle should have been happy, but she was not. What if she never found her dream man, she thought. What if she was destined to be a dried-up old maid? She shuddered. She couldn't bare that. She knew her special place between her shapely, milk-white thighs needed attention. Her cunney. The very name made her quiver with delighted excitement and she felt the place begin to ooze the love sap which was so ready for the right man.

So deep was she in thought that she failed to notice that she had reached the edge of the carefully tended lawns of the Washington Plantation and was on the road leading to the fields.

It was hot and dusty and she had left her fan in the coolness of the house. The parasol, although affording some shade, did not shelter her from the blistering heat of the Atlanta summer. The heat made her become cross and out of sorts.

'Why, good morning, Miss Mirabelle!' said a deep voice.

Startled, Mirabelle, braving the heat of the sun, looked up beneath the frilled edge of her parasol.

It was Joshua Hackensack, the overseer of the plantation. It was strange, but the sight of him made Mirabelle's heart do a little dance.

'Good morning, Joshua.' It was hard, she noticed, to keep her heart still beneath her full breasts. She was sure he would notice the flutter beneath her pretty bodice.

The periwinkle-blue eyes looked up at him, it seemed for the first time, seeing how handsome and rugged he was. The realisation made her shudder pleasurably.

'Mighty pretty dress you're wearing this fine morning,' he offered.

He sat on his horse so straight and tall, his muscular legs so relaxed about the chestnut mount's flanks that the sight made her own shapely legs go quite weak. Mirabelle felt her cunny lips swell deliciously.

'You going anywhere in particular?' asked Joshua.

'Just walking,' said Mirabelle, trying to keep her soft voice steady.

She never had this problem, she mused, when talking to the beaux Papa picked out for her. She was confident as can be with them, but with Joshua, who was, after all, a mere servant like Diddy, she was nervous and fluttery. The realisation hit her like a thunderbolt.

The blue eyes, so thickly fringed with black lashes, gleamed with excitement as they attempted to scan, quite surreptitiously, any bulge which might be hiding beneath the Southern grey of Joshua's pants.

Joshua's own eyes, which were as green as the dark forest, twinkled merrily as he watched her strain her elegant white neck to peer between his muscular thighs.

'Something wrong, Miss Mirabelle?' he asked, a chuckle making his deep voice catch.

Mirabelle, sure that she had found the answer to her problem, did not answer immediately, but slowly, with tiny steps, edged closer to the chestnut horse, staring, quite blatantly now, between Mr Hackensack's thighs.

Joshua, realising her quest, moved his feet in his stirrups, parting his finely honed legs to allow her to see between them more clearly.

Blushing, Mirabelle lowered her eyes, devastated that he had realised the significance of her curiosity. Slowly, she turned away, head bent and not caring that her dress swished the dusty road.

'Miss Mirabelle . . .'

Joshua's voice was husky, beckoning, and she turned, a soft smile on her lovely features.

'Don't go,' he added. He was reaching down, holding out his hand.

Placing her small hand in his, she allowed him to swing her up behind him. She straddled the horse in a most unladylike manner. The full breasts brushed against his back and his closeness made a new flowage of dew from her cunney moisten her drawers.

'It's too hot for a lady to be walking so far from the house,' he said softly. 'I'll take you back.'

'Oh, no!' The exclamation, although brief, told of her disappointment. She didn't want to be taken back to the house. Why hadn't she ever noticed Joshua's fine physique before? She was sure he was the very man she sought.

'No?' he echoed. She heard him chuckle again. 'Well, now, if you don't want me to take you to the house, where do you wish to go?' His voice was mocking, as though he knew quite well the answer.

The heat cloaked Mirabelle like a blanket. The corsets which Diddy had laced so tightly earlier in the morning confined her and she felt that she would swoon from the strange feelings in her head. She leaned against him, feeling his power and strength and the slight moistness of his muscular back through the fine lawn of his shirt.

'Well, Miss Mirabelle?' he prompted her.

'To your house,' she said boldly.

He reined the horse in and turned to look at her. He took

off his broad-brimmed hat and wiped a sheen of perspiration from his forehead with his billowing sleeve. Mirabelle had only to look into those dark green eyes set in the handsome chiselled features tanned by the summer sun and she felt an overwhelming longing.

'You sure, Miss Mirabelle?' he said, the smile fading and his features becoming deadly serious.

'I'm very sure,' she said, sitting very straight and determined upon the horse's back. 'I've never been so sure about anything in my whole life.'

'But your father—'

'My father wants the best for me,' Mirabelle finished. 'Well, I think you're the best, after all, if you and I were to marry he would have an overseer and a son-in-law all rolled into one!'

Joshua Hackensack smiled at Mirabelle's over-simplified logic and then pressed his spurs into the horse's flanks. They set off at a gallop and as the wind scurried her blue-black curls she knew that she had made the right decision.

Minutes later Joshua reined in the horse outside a white-washed house only slightly larger than its neighbours. Mirabelle gasped. It was the first time she had been to this part of the plantation.

'What's wrong, Miss Mirabelle?' Joshua said, jumping down lithely and looking at her with a wry smile as he turned to help her down.

'Just nothing at all!' she said brightly, holding out her arms for him to catch her as she slid into his.

'You didn't realise how poor I was,' he offered. 'Didn't realise how little your father paid me.'

A blush suffused Mirabelle's creamy face, but she shook her head. She was anxious to be close to Joshua, close as Diddy was to her husband. Naked as the day they were born.

'Come on,' she chivied, taking Joshua's hand in her small one.

21

The cottage was no more than one large room, roughly furnished with a homemade bed, table and chair. Never mind, thought Mirabelle, when she and Joshua were married he could sleep next to her in her bed with satin sheets.

The blue eyes, glistening with excitement, went straight to the hugely bulging part between Joshua's parted legs. The Southern grey breeches only served to emphasise the overseer's attributes.

'Oh, Joshua!' she sighed, standing close and placing her slender arms around his neck. The bulge was rock hard and pressed between her own soft thighs, already invading her.

His big hands spanned her tiny waist and she felt him shudder with need. His long fingers slid upwards along her corsetted ribs until they reached the perfect globes of her breasts. They cupped each rounded mound and index fingers teased the hardness of each nipple, making Mirabelle almost swoon with delight.

'I've got to be sure that you really want this,' he said, his voice so low and husky that Mirabelle could barely hear it.

'I want you, Joshua,' she told him. 'You don't know how much.'

He grinned, hurriedly pushing up her skirt and petticoats and feeling the hot dampness in her drawers; feeling the thrusting bud of her clitty between the plump lips.

'I know!' he said, with his grin widening.

'Take off my clothes, Joshua,' she murmured. Her mouth felt parched and her tongue felt clumsy within it.

His arms dropped to his side and she thought, just for a moment, that she had been too bold. Pleadingly, she stretched out her hands, begging him to hold her once more, but her concern was unfounded. He merely paused in his caresses to bolt the door.

Mirabelle smiled, enjoying the dimly lit little world which he had created for them. He strode towards her, already unbuttoning the lawn shirt, baring his broad chest. Watching him with eager eyes she found her desire growing by the second.

He sat on the narrow bed, the bed upon which they would, very soon, fuck. Her use of the crude word to herself made her quiver with a deep passion. He held out a booted and spurred leg.

'Take off my spurs and boots,' he said. His voice was no longer husky with passion; no longer subservient. It was strong and commanding. Mirabelle loved it, even though she had never had to do anything so servile in her whole life.

'My trousers,' he said as he stood up. He stood over her, his face expressionless, carved in stone.

Fingers trembling, Mirabelle popped each button and slid the Southern grey breeches over his slim hips. She gasped. He wore no drawers and his cock was hard and thick, probing from a bush of lush brown curls.

'Are you afraid?' he asked, sliding a finger and thumb along his length. The globe was dark, Mirabelle noticed, although not as purple as Mister Carlton's. There was no little skirt behind the globe. It was naked, gleaming with pre-issue and shining as though polished.

'No,' she said softly. 'I'm not afraid. I'm excited,' she admitted, 'but I'm not afraid.'

'But you are a virgin?' She watched him slide his big palm over the shining globe, spreading the smear of liquid and then watched him encompass the girth of his cock with his fingers. They barely touched, he was so thick.

'Yes,' she admitted. 'I'm a virgin.'

A sudden heated flowage wet the fine cotton of her drawers and her clitty jerked so hard that it startled her, making her give a tiny mew of excitement.

'Shouldn't you wait for your husband?'

Looking at him, so handsomely naked, his muscular legs straddled wide apart, his stomach flat and hard, his chest broad and expanded, she wanted him more than ever. Why was he making her wait so long?

'I want you to be my husband,' she said softly, sliding her

fingers to her breasts, tantalising the hot nipples, hard as stones, thrusting against her bodice.

He threw back his head and laughed. The laugh was dry and scornful. 'And do you really think that Colonel Rhett will allow that?'

'Papa always gives me what I want,' she said, lifting her arms to take out the pins which held her curls in place.

'Not in this case!' He picked up his shirt, beginning to shrug into it.

'No!' cried Mirabelle in anguish. 'Don't! What are you doing?'

His face was stern as he looked at her. The soft folds of his shirt fell from one broad shoulder, brushing the fullness of his balls and the stiff hardness of his cock.

'He'll horsewhip me if I touch you!' It wasn't fear in his voice, but something else. Maybe Joshua was thinking how he, himself, would react if he was punished in such a manner. Mirabelle shuddered and closed her eyes, hearing in her imagination the report of a gun.

'I need you, Joshua,' she said, her voice steady now in her determination.

'Very well,' he said in a voice equally firm. 'If you're sure.'

Nodding, she turned her back to his magnificent nakedness and pointed to the row of tiny buttons, indicating that he should slip them free, one by one. She felt him open one, his hands on her neck amazingly gentle, her hair falling in a glorious inky black cascade over the slope of her shoulders.

'Damn it all, Mirabelle!' he exclaimed suddenly. 'My hands weren't made for such fiddly woman's work.' The gentleness was gone and she gasped as her gorgeous gown was ripped roughly from neck to below the waist.

'Oh, yes, Joshua!' she sighed. 'Take me, like that. Free me from all restraint.'

Her beautiful body felt limp, on the verge of collapse, in a state of wonderful lethargy. She turned to him, her full breasts lifted, her lips parted, offering herself to him.

The flimsy cloth of her bodice was no barrier to his strong hands and that, too, fluttered to the rough dirt floor of the shack, in shreds. His dark eyes were slitted, obsidian in their glitter and she lost herself in their depths.

Within moments she felt herself lifted, naked, in strong arms, cradled for a moment, as he laid her gently on the low truckle bed. She had no memory of him relieving her of the constraint of her corsets or her drawers, but since she felt so deliciously free, he must have done so.

'It will hurt,' he warned her, kneeling by the bed, cupping the plumpness of her heated mound in his big hand.

'I don't care, Joshua,' she murmured, neither did she. All she knew was that this man was here to take her as he wished.

'Never thought that you could be so pliant,' he said, spreading the young plump labia to bare the jutting hardness of her clitty.

'For you and you alone,' she said huskily. Her body arched upwards, urging his caresses. She felt her seepage ooze over his fingers as he delved into her softness. The urgent tip protruded from its little hood, the nerve endings aching for his touch.

A glorious languor spread through her when his lips replaced his fingers. In the whole of her young life no-one had touched her in that private place with lips and tongue. She bore down to the oral caress, spreading herself, offering all of herself, knowing that she would reach the ultimate peak within seconds. She was there!

'Oh, Joshua!' she cried. 'Take me now! How wonderful you have made me feel!'

His magnificent body straddled her, pressing her into the thin mattress and the rough blankets. His arms wrapped around her slender, but voluptuous, body, holding it tight as the convulsions of her climax faded.

'Don't ever let me go, Joshua,' she sighed.

He kissed the delicate skin where her long neck joined the curve of her shoulder. The kiss slid down until his lips enclosed her nipple, lapping at it with his tongue.

'Will you stay with me whatever happens?' He arched up, pressing the hardness of his loins into her, looking down at her with sad, serious eyes.

'How can you ask such a thing?'

Mirabelle looked at him almost crossly. She could feel his cock nudging its bare tip at her entrance and she urged him to tear into her.

'I have to be sure before . . .' he said hesitantly, but then his need seemed to overpower him and Mirabelle felt the first searing pain.

Should she ask him to be gentle with her, she wondered, but didn't she want him to take her roughly?

'Oooh!' she moaned, her lips forming a perfect 'O' of the sigh being drawn out. The pain came again as he thrust deeper. He was big, thick and long.

'Bear with me,' he begged softly.

'It's wonderful,' she told him, 'even though it hurts!'

Finally, he pushed all the way into her moist softness and they lay still for a moment, enjoying the closeness of the naked bodies, enjoying the blending of their juices. He grasped each breast, kneading the pliant flesh, pressing the firm mounds together.

Mirabelle could feel the hardness of his mound grating against hers, feel the ripples of his stomach muscles echoing hers. She discovered that the soft walls of her female passage could pamper his cock by closing around him. She squeezed and he chuckled happily.

'Fuck me, Joshua,' she said at last, not in any crude way, but the way one lover speaks to the other.

'Whatever you wish, my darling,' he replied, drawing his thickness from her until she was about to cry out in distress. Slowly, he pushed back into her and she felt her passage welcome him, flooding him with warm juices. The slow withdrawal was repeated many times and Mirabelle reached her peak time and again.

'Staying power,' she murmured.

'What?' Close to his own climax, he murmured the question absently.

'Nothing, my darling. Nothing.'

# Chapter 3

The sun was low in the sky when Mirabelle awoke. For a moment she could not discern where she was.

She was not in her own bed, of that she was certain. The rough blanket thrown over her, chafing her naked, tender skin was unfamiliar and then she remembered.

Her heart leapt wildly in her breast as she turned to the warm male body beside her. Joshua was still asleep, looking younger and more vulnerable in sleep than in waking moments. Lifting a long slim arm she touched his smooth forehead very lightly, wondering that this handsome man should have bestowed his love upon her. She felt a stirring against the soft swell of her belly and smiled eagerly.

'Joshua.' She murmured his name, enjoying each letter and each syllable as they fell from her lips.

'Hm,' he murmured in his sleep. A big, deeply tanned hand strayed across her breast, startling against the paleness of her skin.

Mirabelle urged his movements, persuading him to knead the breast in his hand cruelly, to dig his fingers into its pliancy. She could feel his thickness rising more strongly against her, probing against her belly and the shelf of her hip.

'Would you like me to suck your cock?' she asked softly.

Dark, thick brown lashes fluttered against his weathered cheeks, but still he did not wake. His breathing though, she noticed, had quickened and become deeper. 'Hm,' he murmured again.

Chuckling mischievously, Mirabelle threw back the rough blanket, baring the nakedness of both of them. The low sun beat upon the closed wooden door and she could feel its heat on her skin. Stopping only for a moment to look at Joshua's magnificent body, she leapt lithely to the dirt floor of the shack and opened the door, letting in the warm rays to light the little room.

Eagerly, she returned to the bed and, gently, spread Joshua's splendid legs. Settling herself between the straddled limbs with her gloriously plump buttocks raised high into the air and her head low, she set to her task. She examined the heaviness of her lover's ballsack, marvelling at the smooth tautness.

Joshua opened his eyes, but remained perfectly still, allowing a small smile to play about his strong mouth. Enjoying the light touch of Mirabelle's fingers as she cupped the fullness of his balls though he was, he wished also that he could be at the other end of the bed. He wished that he could view the delights between those milk-white thighs; the plump, swollen outer lips so lightly dusted with jet curls; the scarlet inner folds which made such a pretty bed for the clitty which, he knew, would be fully exposed. Most of all he wished that he could see the newly opened gateway to the heavenly passage. This latter thought made his thickness pulse and Mirabelle giggle softly.

Joshua watched the tumbled blue-black curls bobbing between his thighs. He watched her open her own legs as if to give her swelling sex more space to expand. He watched the twin and perfect hillocks which were her buttocks and wished that he could plant a kiss upon each of them. Even more, perhaps, he wished that he could place his tongue in the deep valley to invade the tightness of her dainty rear entrance. These thoughts were playing havoc upon his spearing thickness.

Mirabelle, having finished the finger caresses of Joshua's magnificent balls, began to trace the tortuous path of the veins which pulsed from the base to just below the tip of his globe.

'Oh, Joshua!' she sighed, snaking out the tip of her pink tongue to taste his saltiness. 'You don't know how much I want you inside me.'

'My darling girl,' he whispered, 'I know only too well.' He grasped her thick black hair and arched her neck, forcing her to look at him with those startlingly bright blue eyes.

'You're awake!' she gasped happily, aware that now his gaze was focused upon the straining fullness of her breasts. This awareness made the nipples spring to pip hardness, flushing to scarlet heat at the same time.

'Kiss my globe again, my darling,' she urged, pressing her soft, parted lips to that silky peak.

'You don't know how wonderful I find that,' she murmured, slipping her mouth over the summit of his cock. She heard him groan pleasurably as her lips caressed the bare and sensitive part. Her tongue tip slipped into the oozing pore and he groaned again, pressing her mouth further along his thickness.

To add to his pleasure Mirabelle probed the spot between balls and rear hole, making Joshua groan more loudly. She tasted a trickle of love juice, a tiny trail of salty cream upon her tongue.

Only vaguely did Mirabelle realise that the warmth of the sun streaming through the open doorway was blocked. Joshua, however, was more than aware that there was something seriously amiss.

'I'll hog tie you, sir!' Her father's voice was strangled with fury. 'And that's after I've had you flogged within an inch of your life.'

Mirabelle continued to suck greedily upon Joshua, for the overseer, despite the sudden and considerable problems, was spurting his renewed store of love juice.

'I didn't force her, Colonel,' said Joshua calmly.

That same calmness made Mirabelle's heart flutter afresh. Any of those milk sops which her father was so determined she would marry would be grovelling at his feet in the same circumstances.

'And it's well that you didn't, sir!' spat Colonel Rhett. 'For if that had been the case I would have you shot!'

Joshua's spume stopped and, reluctantly, Mirabelle knelt up and turned to her father. 'I want to marry Joshua,' she said, smiling and taking dainty little laps at the remainder of her lover's spunk.

Colonel Rhett Washington stepped into the shack, taking in the scattered heaps of clothing abandoned in such haste hours before. 'Cover yourself, girl!' he snarled. 'Have you no shame?'

Jumping up with effortless grace, Mirabelle stood, shapely legs straddled and hands on her hips, glaring at her father.

'I don't think you heard me!' she snapped.

'I heard you right enough!' snapped Colonel Rhett, throwing her a torn petticoat which she refused to catch to cover herself. 'And if you think I'm going to give you permission to marry this rubbishy piece of white trash who keeps his brains in his bull pen—'

'Papa!' interrupted Mirabelle, looking at Joshua anxiously. 'If that's what you think why did you hire him?'

'You git some clothes on, my girl!' commanded Colonel Rhett. 'I don't have to explain any reasons to a chit of a girl!'

Mirabelle saw Joshua sliding into his breeches and boots. A knot rose in her throat and she felt her pulse quicken at the sight of him, bare-chested, facing her father.

'Then explain them to me, sir!' said Joshua. The dark obsidian eyes flashed with anger as he squared up to his employer.

Colonel Rhett allowed a sly smile to crease his weather-beaten features. 'Very well then,' he said slowly, but Mirabelle, in spite of the smile, saw a slight grimace of pain across her father's face. 'You were cheap, Mister Hackensack. That's the truth of it. The Washington Plantation is struggling and I have to save every penny I can.'

Joshua had a fiery, angry look which was unfamiliar to Mirabelle. Tiny muscles twitched at each side of the square jaw. The nostrils in his long nose were flared as though he was fighting for breath. 'Allow me to marry your daughter and I'll make the estate pay.' He spoke in a matter-of-fact tone as though that was the only answer to the problem.

Mirabelle was not at all sure that she was keen on being used as a barter bride, but what did it matter so long as she and Joshua were together?

'Damned if I will!' snarled Colonel Rhett. His summer tan, Mirabelle noticed, had paled to an unhealthy parchment colour and a hand was flattened against the left side of his chest. 'Why do you think I was introducing Mirabelle to the most eligible and richest young men in Georgia?' He clutched his chest, his long fingers plucking uselessly at his white jacket. 'She . . . needed . . . to marry . . . money.'

Mirabelle rushed to her father's side as he slid to the dirt floor. His face was contorted with pain and the colour had turned from parchment to grey. She sank, naked, beside the fallen man who was trying, desperately, to tell her something.

'Look . . . after . . . your . . . mother,' were her father's last words.

Joshua tried to lift Mirabelle, to comfort her, but she threw herself across her father's body, giving herself up to wracking sobs. He shrugged, walking away, angrily throwing a few items into a carpet bag.

Hearing the sounds of activity, Mirabelle looked up, her face streaked with tears and dust. 'What are you doing?'

'Got to go,' said Joshua roughly. 'If I know your mother, she'll have me shot.'

'But I need you, Joshua!'

Still naked she ran the few steps across the dirt floor of

the shack and threw herself against Joshua's chest. She flung her arms about his strong neck. He felt stiff and unyielding against her softness. His dark head was thrown back and he would not look into her pleading eyes.

He'd thrown on a faded black frock coat, so old that it seemed almost green in the light of the setting sun. Mirabelle thrust against him and she knew that her movement aroused him. She felt his cock jerk violently in his Southern grey breeches, hard and ready for her.

'You see!' she said triumphantly. 'You want me! You need me!'

'Damn your hide, girl!' he said, with a voice which held a rasp of excitement. 'Don't you know that any red-blooded man would react the same with a pretty, naked girl rubbing herself against his breeches. Don't matter who she was!' He was being deliberately cruel.

Tears stung her eyes, but she forced them back. 'You rat!' she hissed. 'My father was right in what he called you!' She stood back, glaring up at him, legs astride and lush mound thrust forward.

It was all Joshua could do not to groan aloud. Angry though she was, she looked so beautiful, so sexually tempting, that he had to thrust his hands deep into his pockets to prevent them reaching out to take her in his arms.

He shrugged, trying to keep the hurt from his eyes. 'Sure,' he murmured huskily. 'No doubt you're right.'

He managed to release his hands from his pockets and picked up his bag.

'And you're a coward!' she snapped at his back as he strode gingerly over her father's sprawled, fast cooling, body.

'No doubt you're right about that too,' he agreed.

Still naked, she ran after him, watching him swing onto the big chestnut horse. Her eyes flashed blue fire as she glared up at him. 'Do you have to agree with everything I say?' she hissed.

Slowly, he leaned forward in his saddle, his handsome face filling her vision. For a heart-stopping moment Mirabelle thought that he was relenting, was going to swing her up and carry her off to wherever he was going, but she was wrong. Their lips brushed, but then she heard the chink of his spurs as he touched the horse's flanks.

'No,' she heard, drifting on the evening breeze, 'I don't have to agree with you, but I do because I . . .' She thought she heard him say that he loved her. He agreed with everything she said because he loved her, but she couldn't be sure.

He was gone in a cloud of dust, leaving her before the shack which had been his home feeling very alone. In one afternoon she had lost the man she loved and her father.

'I hope you like wearing black, young lady,' said Mrs Amelia Jane Washington, Mirabelle's mama.

'I hate it!' the girl snapped. 'And why do I have to wear black drawers? No-one can see those.'

'To match your soul!' hissed Amelia Jane. She began to sob, touching her eyes with the merest snippet of lace. 'How could you do such a thing?'

Mirabelle joined her mother in the sobbing. 'I loved Papa so much,' she whimpered. 'Truly, I did. I would never have made him have a heart attack on purpose!'

'That I can forgive!' said Mrs Washington softly.

Mirabelle looked up sharply, making the hated black taffeta of her gown rustle. 'Can you?' she asked, unable to believe her ears.

'Of course,' went on Amelia Jane, 'your father and I have not enjoyed each other's bed for years.'

Mirabelle could not believe what she was hearing. 'No?' She gasped the word out, almost choking on it.

'But that isn't the problem.' Mrs Amelia Jane Washington stared sternly at her daughter.

'It isn't?' Mirabelle looked at her mama aghast. Where,

she wondered, was all this leading? Could it be that Joshua had an affair with her mother? It was all so confusing. Tears began to flow from her pretty blue eyes afresh.

'Stop snivelling, girl!' rapped her mother. 'It's a fine pickle you've got us into and you'll have to do something about it. With Joshua gone there is no-one to run the plantation and with your Papa six foot under Georgia soil there is no-one to look after our finances.'

Mirabelle brightened. 'I told Papa that if Joshua married me he would have a son-in-law and overseer all in one go!'

'Oh, fiddle-de-dee!' exclaimed Mrs Amelia Jane. 'We needed a rich son-in-law not that no account share cropper!'

'Joshua's good with figures, Mama!' argued Mirabelle.

'Good with your figure maybe!' snapped Mrs Washington. 'You got to go out into the world and find a rich husband, Mirabelle Washington and, while you're about it, find one for me!'

'Mama!'

Amelia Jane wagged a finger at her daughter. 'Don't you "Mama" me! You and your hot drawers got us into this mess, and you can darned well git us out!'

'But if we'd kept Joshua—'

A hard slap made Mirabelle's pretty head rock as her mother stood over her, shaking with anger. 'Don't you understand, girl?' she shouted. 'The Washington Plantation will be possessed by the bank if we don't find a rich husband or, better still, two!'

Feeling her cheek burn, Mirabelle hung her head unhappily. 'I don't know where to look for a husband,' she whispered.

'That's "husbands",' her mother hissed, emphasising the 's'. 'One for me as well.'

'Husbands,' repeated Mirabelle obediently, but with a deep frown marring her creamy forehead. 'Where shall I start?'

'You get Diddy to pack your trunks for a start,'

commanded Amelia Jane, flapping the snippet of lace about her handsome face for her sudden burst of anger had made her flush unbearably.

'You're sending me away?' Mirabelle could not believe that her life could have been upended so rapidly. And Joshua! She could not get the image of his magnificent body pounding into hers from her mind. She could feel the thickness of his smooth flesh opening her out, could feel it slicking the tip of her jutting clitty, could feel his spunk jetting warmly into her receptive body.

'Of course I'm sending you away, stupid girl!' hissed Amelia Jane. 'You have successfully managed to alienate every eligible man in the State of Georgia so I must send you somewhere where you are not known.'

'North Carolina?' suggested Mirabelle helpfully.

'England,' replied her mama.

'England!' gasped the girl, her dainty, dimpled hands flying, horrified, to her soft lips. 'But that's a foreign country.'

'Darned right!' said her mother, a smile of triumph making her handsome features glow. 'A foreign country full of rich men, with lands and titles.'

'Titles?' Mirabelle looked puzzled.

'The rich men in England don't get called just plain Mister,' explained Amelia Jane, 'but get called Earl or Duke or even . . .' Her voice lowered reverently. 'Prince. That's what I want,' she added dreamily. Her face took on an aristocratic expression. The nose tipped upwards to the ceiling. Her eyes looked disdainful. She sucked in her rather plump cheeks. 'For you, of course, my darling. Just a plain Baron will do for me.'

Mirabelle sighed, knowing that she would never see Joshua again and never feel the pleasure of his cock probing her depths.

'England's across the sea, isn't it?' she whispered, her soft voice full of melancholy.

'Sure is,' agreed Amelia Jane. 'I've pawned the last of my diamonds to send you there, so I hope you're grateful.'

Mirabelle nodded apathetically. 'Shall I go on my own, Mama?'

Mrs Amelia Jane Washington shook her head so vigorously that the dear little lace and flowered bonnet which kept her curls so neatly tucked away was almost dislodged.

'Your Aunt Hatty May will accompany you as your chaperone,' said Mama with a smile. 'Although I do believe she's after a husband herself.'

Mirabelle received this news with good grace, but had some misgivings. Nice as Aunt Hatty May was, and for all Mirabelle thought it a shame that she should have been made a widow at the tender age of twenty-two, she was quite sure that it would be Mirabelle herself who would be doing the looking after.

'I so wanted to marry Joshua,' sighed Mirabelle, her rosebud lips pursed prettily in a pout. 'I'm going to be mighty tetchy during this voyage, Aunt Hatty May, I promise you truly.'

The Statue of Liberty had long since faded into the distance and the beautiful liner ploughed the waves as they left the safe harbour and headed into the Atlantic.

Aunt Hatty May sighed, fluttering her fan in irritation and concern, although the stiff breeze far from warranted such agitation of the air.

'In England we'll find someone more fitting than that heap of poor white trash,' she soothed.

The air was brisk on the promenade deck of RMS Gloriana, the most luxurious vessel of the Edwardian era, and the two ladies were hard pressed to walk with their usual grace and stately elegance.

'Joshua fitted me very well!' Mirabelle smiled pertly, feeling her swain's thickness and length parting her love lips even in this most uncongenial of situations.

The promenade deck was busy with ladies and gentlemen all only too willing to display their respective charms. Although, it must be said, they oozed genteel sexuality with the utmost discretion.

Heads were bowed in greeting this way and that. Skirts trailed over lacey petticoats and parasols were twirled while walking sticks were thrust forward, phallus-like.

The large liner dipped into a precarious trough, hurtling Mirabelle into the arms of a grateful male passenger.

He grinned and stroked his moustaches in an upward direction. His dark eyes twinkled merrily, hinting that he had some naughty secret in his lusty breeches.

'I do beg your pardon!' he said in a very English voice.

He attempted to doff his hat at the same time as clasping a tiny waist. Delightedly, he found himself pressed hard against upthrust, tip-tilted breasts and his hand strayed down to hips which flared in a most enticing manner.

Inflamed by an enormous breakfast followed by a snifter of brandy the gentleman would have been unendingly grateful for immediate and further intimacy.

'Are you a lord, sir?' asked Aunt Hatty May bluntly, bustling up to rescue her charge.

'Er . . .' hesitated the passenger. His fingers were drawn to the under fullness of lightly clad breasts.

'If you are not, sir,' demanded Aunt Hatty, 'unhand my niece.'

The gentleman, although not young, was attractive, noticed Mirabelle, slanting the periwinkle-blue eyes at him mischievously. Her lips parted to show the tip of the dearest little tongue. The mouth was small, a mere rosebud, noticed he, in turn, but deliciously sensuous and promising.

'By jove!' he exclaimed, feeling his manhood take an upward jerk.

'An answer, sir!' demanded the companion, shielding her charge with her own lovely body.

Mirabelle did not take kindly to being pushed behind her

aunt and she jostled herself to centre stage once more.

Reluctantly, the gentleman allowed his hands to drop to his sides, grinning from one to the other of the two young ladies.

Such a shame, he thought, that he'd promised his wife complete faithfulness when they had days of luxurious First Class accommodation in front of them and the pleasure of such beauties on board. Still, he consoled himself, what the eye doesn't see, the heart cannot grieve upon!

'Have to admit,' he offered, 'I am a peer of the realm.'

Aunt Hatty May and Mirabelle allowed each other little smiles of triumph. Amelia Jane's diamonds were not sold for nought!

'Lord Carshalton of Carshalton Hall, Hertfordshire, at your service,' he said. 'Returning from business in your fair country.'

'Mrs Hatty May Chilton and Miss Mirabelle Washington,' introduced Mirabelle.

'Delighted to make your acquaintance,' said the peer, bending over each dainty dimpled hand in turn.

'Travelling to England on a big game hunt!' added Mirabelle mischievously.

His lordship's eyebrows shot upwards in amazement and his eyes perused the tight-lacing and tiny waist together with the well-covered prominences in front and behind. The padded coiffures and huge hats beneath which were the most glorious rosebud mouths and wide eyes; none of this spoke of anything so masculine as big game hunts.

'Really?' he managed, his face a picture of disbelief. 'Very creditable, I'm sure.'

After an angry glance at Mirabelle, Aunt Hatty gave a light laugh. 'My niece jests with you, sir. We are merely visiting friends.'

'Titled friends,' added Mirabelle with a meaningful glance at her aunt.

'By crikey!' exclaimed the peer. 'I'm sure they will be delighted to have you!'

'One hopes so!' murmured Mirabelle, lowering her lashes flirtatiously.

She thrust her arm through his lordship's tweedy one. 'Are there many spare lords in England?' she asked.

'Spares, m'dear?' He grinned at the lovely girl, admiring her forwardness. It was refreshing and made his manhood perk further in his tweeds.

'Unmarried,' she explained. 'My aunt and my mother would so love to be titled. In America, you see, the title became very *de mode*.'

Lord Carshalton patted the sweet hand which rested so lightly upon his arm. 'Dash it all, m'dear!' he blustered. 'The fellows will be falling over themselves, I'll warrant!'

As it was, his own need was such that his pecker was uncomfortably stiff within his tweeds and falling over would have been a most painful exercise.

Mirabelle moulded her curves to his and looked deep into his eyes. A smile curved her lips as she felt him shudder with longing.

'You flatter us, sir!' she purred. 'I am sure there are many beautiful women in England.'

Feeling ignored, Aunt Hatty made a startling proposal. 'What do you say to a friendly game of poker before lunch?' she said.

Lord Carshalton groomed his moustache once more. 'What-ho!' he said enthusiastically, his eyes glinting with the thought of such sport with such charming ladies.

'Strip poker,' added Mirabelle.

'Oh, I say!' His lordship's enthusiasm, not to mention his cock, was growing by the minute. 'What a ripping idea!'

Caressing his broad chest with the firm prominence of her bosom, Mirabelle whispered in his ear. 'Our quarters or yours?'

His lordship gulped with the luscious imaginings which filled his thoughts. It was all so glorious! How could he concentrate on poker when he would soon be ripping the drawers from these lovely creatures?

'Yours, I think,' he said with a voice a tone deeper than his normal. 'Not that poker is my game, but I'm sure I shall hold my own.'

Mirabelle giggled fetchingly. 'That won't be necessary, my lord,' she said, stroking his arm lovingly. 'Leave that to me!'

# Chapter 4

'The Captain's reception?' Mirabelle's honey voice hinted boredom. 'Don't want to go.' She lay, hands thrown languidly behind her dark head and wearing only a flimsy peignoir.

Aunt Hatty May's lace-mittened hand flew to her mouth in horror and her golden curls shook with fury at her niece's disobedience.

'You gotta go!'

Mirabelle closed her eyes and pursed her rosebud lips. 'Don't wanna do anything but lie here and dream of Joshua.'

Crossly, Hatty May stamped her little boot. 'Dreaming of that pesky share cropper ain't gonna get you a rich husband,' she warned sharply. 'And we ain't gonna find one for your mama . . .' She paused, sighing. 'Or me,' she added, 'unless we go to this party! I got myself all prettied up and you gotta do the same.'

Mirabelle sighed. She raised a dimpled knee allowing her peignor to fall open, fully revealing her luscious body.

'Cover yourself, girl!' fussed Aunt Hatty, pulling the gossamer of the peignoir across milk-white shoulders and breasts so gloriously ripe on a girl so young.

'Why?' asked Mirabelle wilfully. 'Ain't going nowhere!' The bright blue eyes flashed the sapphire fire of defiance at her aunt.

'You gotta go to the Captain's reception to meet all the Earls, Dukes and Princes to please your poor Mama!' insisted Aunt Hatty, stamping her foot once more.

'Fiddle-de-dee!' exclaimed Mirabelle, jumping up and tossing back the blue-black hair in a provocative gesture. 'Don't I have a right to be pleased?'

'How do you know the Earls and Dukes won't have a cock which will please you no end?' said Aunt Hatty pleading with Mirabelle's reasonable side. She dipped her blonde curls to one side in a quizical manner.

'Hm!' murmured Mirabelle, she thought deeply upon this for some seconds. 'Maybe . . .'

'Lord Carshalton had a splendid one,' added Hatty, noticing that she was claiming her niece's attention.

Mirabelle smiled excitedly, her eyes glinting and her tongue tip glancing over her parted lips. 'He surely had, hadn't he?' Her hand was raised to ring for her maid, but the sunny smile faded as quickly as it appeared. 'But he was married.'

'They ain't all married!' said Aunt Hatty May impatiently. 'Maybe there's even a King on board!'

Mirabelle was torn between her need to be fulfilled and pleasing her mama. 'It's all so difficult!' she sighed, throwing herself upon her bed and pummelling her pillows in frustration.

'Come on, honey!' soothed Aunt Hatty. 'You make yourself pretty and just maybe we'll find a Kingsize cock for you!'

Being so young and widowed so early in life, a cock of any size would have been eminently fulfilling for the pretty, blonde companion. Even as she soothed Mirabelle, her much neglected female parts fluttered and became inflamed with longing. Perhaps, she thought, the sea voyage was a good idea. A change of scene, a change of lifestyle . . .

Mirabelle sat up, her eyes wide with longing. 'Do you really think so? Do you really think I'll find what I need?'

'I'm sure of it!' Aunt Hatty crossed her fingers behind her back. The Captain's reception was the social event of the voyage and they had to go. Just had to! She sighed with relief as her niece rang for her maid.

'I hope I won't be disappointed!' Mirabelle's lovely face was marred by a warning expression which made Hatty May shudder. Not for nothing was Mirabelle's temper known throughout Georgia.

'I'll see you at the party,' said Aunt Hatty quickly, fleeing the stateroom and leaving Mirabelle to dress.

In the elegant walnut-panelled day cabin which was the venue of the Captain's reception, Aunt Hatty stood shyly by the door.

'Delighted!' said a rich English voice.

Hatty May's blonde head whipped round to peruse the owner of the voice. He was tall and pleasantly featured and, what was more, he was smiling down at her. She felt that same flutter in her drawers as she did when silently bemoaning the fact of her widowhood.

'King,' said the tall gentleman.

Hatty May fluttered her fan to cool her burning cheeks. 'King?' she queried, hardly able to believe her luck.

The gentleman nodded, taking Hatty May's mittened hand to brush the dimpled fingers with soft lips.

Dipping a deep curtsy she wondered whether kings were bothered about daring *décolletages*, one of which she was wearing.

'Travelling alone?' said the imperious personage, retaining her trembling hand.

It seemed dreadfully difficult to breathe in sufficient air and, having breathed it in, retain it. Her full breasts were heaving frantically up and down as she shook her head.

'Ah!' The handsome eyes lost their sparkle as he examined the gold band peeping beneath a lace mitten. 'Husband!' The owner of the eyes looked about the crowded room somewhat furtively.

The blonde curls shook even more vigorously and Hatty May attempted to force air into her lungs to enable her to speak. 'Widowed,' she managed.

'Ah!' The handsome rogue smiled broadly. 'Then we

must get to know each other better.' He had dark, almost mesmerising eyes, which seemed to be focussed upon the full upper swells of Hatty May's breasts.

A king, she thought. Mirabelle would be furious! Hm, her thoughts continued, serves her right for not arriving at the party promptly. She smiled at her suitor, fluttering her thick honey-coloured lashes.

'I say!' he crowed. 'You're awfully pretty!'

A thrill sang in Hatty May's very core at the compliment. 'And Ah just lo-o-ove to hear you talk!' she replied in her most Southern drawl.

'Do you really?' he exclaimed delightedly. 'How marvellous! Rather taken with your speech as a matter of fact.'

Hatty May looked at him admiringly. 'Are you really a king?' The very word made her pussy feel deliciously plump and pampered and she felt her heart give an extra beat. Mirabelle and Amelia Jane would be so envious of her luck!

The handsome suitor waved to someone across the room and then returned his gaze to her. 'Eh?' he asked, giving her an absent smile which to her seemed so very aristocratic and haughty.

'A king!' she reminded him, seeking his full attention.

'A king?' he repeated. 'Absolutely!' One of his long and, no doubt, aristocratic fingers traced the hillocks peeping above her low-cut gown.

'Oh, my gracious!' she whispered, urging his fingers to delve deeper. 'I declare I shall swoon. I've never met a king before.'

Her pussy fairly pouted beneath the lower margin of her tightly laced corset and her full buttocks seemed to flare beneath the rear hem. There was a dampening of the lacey cloth which fashioned her drawers.

'Haven't you really?' said the gentleman, his dark eyebrows rising in mild surprise. 'Don't see why? All over the dashed place.' He allowed one of his large hands to stroke the folds of silk which fell so elegantly about her thighs.

Hatty May shuddered joyously, but her own eyebrows raised. She had always been under the impression that kings were quite rare.

'I'm one of the Cornish Kings, actually,' he supplied, giving her a smile which made her cunney melt with its sensuality.

Of course, thought Hatty May. Wasn't that something to do with King Arthur? There were hundreds of kings in those days. She returned his smile. She felt that they were alone in the crowded room and she made no murmur of discontent as he guided her to a small sofa, the better to feel the shapeliness of her thighs beneath her silken gown.

'Going to England for pleasureable reasons, or perhaps you have some business in our green and pleasant land?' he asked softly.

The sensual touch of his hand was making Hatty May's thighs tremble apart until a finger actually grazed the plumpness of her mound. If only there was somewhere they could go to be alone. Looking around the room, her grey eyes flickering surreptitiously, she spoke in hushed tones.

'Is there somewhere we can go to be alone?'

'Ah!' he said, tapping the side of his nose. 'Understand! Confidential matter?'

Hatty May nodded eagerly.

His smile was rueful. 'Dear lady,' he whispered, 'would that we could, but you must understand my position. I am the—'

Hatty May blushed furiously at her own forwardness and she fluttered her fan in embarrassment. 'The King! Of course, how stupid of me!'

He looked at her curiously, almost as though he was puzzled at her exclamation. 'Ah! Absolutely!' He gave her another smile which some observers might have called uncertain.

Hatty May's nether regions were melting with need. Her curvaceous, if somewhat voluptuous, body trembled at his nearness. Let Mirabelle yearn for monstrous, working-class hugeness, but she wanted small high-quality, knowing organs like that of her dear, departed husband.

'It would only take a moment,' she said, her lips parted and prettily flushed.

A mere glance, she thought, was all that was needed. She would know whether or not he would suit her between the thighs. Perhaps a touch with finger and thumb, she mused, to feel the silky smoothness, even a caress with her lips.

Making a swift decision, he pulled her to her feet and pushed her through the bustling, chattering crowd. 'We must not be missed,' he warned.

Hatty May could barely breathe in her excitement as she was chivvied through to a room beyond. 'Of course!' she agreed, looking round at the cabin into which she had been hurried. It was small with a narrow bunk built into the walnut bulkhead. It occurred to her that it was not very luxurious for a king.

'Now, what is so confidential?' His gaze never strayed from the creamy hillocks soaring above her decolletage. His hands twitched as he backed against the bunk. She saw the twitch of a neat bundle in his dress trousers.

'I want you before Mirabelle or Amelia Jane see you!' cried Hatty May.

'Want me?'

She threw herself at his feet, clutching his thighs, burrowing her pretty features in the dress suiting.

'Say you want me!' she pleaded.

'Delighted, madam!' He was panting heavily, Hatty May noticed, and thrusting his loins towards her parted lips. His hands, too, were busy, flicking open buttons to release his masculine treasure.

As Hatty suspected the hidden hoard was small but of excellent quality. She could hardly wait to taste the darling creature.

'Aunt Hatty!' Mirabelle's voice was shrill in her anger.

'He's the King!' Hatty May tried to explain.

'No! No!' The gentleman sounded dismayed. 'Some mistake! Have to explain.'

Mirabelle, her temper flaring, beat upon his chest with small closed fists. 'Who are you?'

'Captain Peter King,' he said. 'Master of this vessel.

Mirabelle was furious. She knew this would happen and would continue to happen. Aunt Hatty always got things wrong. Mistaking the Captain for a monarch simply because of his name! How embarrassing! It was the talk of the ship and it had quite ruined her evening.

'Lost, Miss?' asked a rough voice in the gloom.

Mirabelle coughed at the pungent smell of Full Strength tobacco. She looked round. The surroundings were dreary and she realised, with horror, that she had strayed, in her anger, to the steerage decks.

'I suppose I am,' she said sharply, looking up at the speaker. With dark eyes set in a square, rugged face, he reminded her of Joshua.

'Can I escort you to the First Class gate?' He was very polite, she noted.

'I suppose so,' she said reluctantly, but she stayed by the rail, looking down into the grey water, sparkling in the moonlight.

He took her elbow and his touch was electric. His grip was firm and commanding, but at the same time sensual and tender.

'No!' she said suddenly. 'Stop!'

'Something wrong, miss?'

The hand around her waist rested on the curve of her hip and she knew he could feel her lack of under-garments. She didn't care. She felt reckless. This was what she desired. The strong roughness reminded her so much of Joshua.

'Nothing wrong,' she said, trying to stop the tremor in her voice. 'Nothing at all. In fact, everything is wonderful. Better now.' She smiled at him.

'I'm glad, Miss.' He returned her smile.

They leaned against the rail together in companionable silence.

'Are you a member of the crew?' she asked at last.

He grinned at her, showing white, even teeth and, she noticed, smears of coal dust on his rugged features.

'A stoker,' he admitted. It wasn't said defensively, or said with shame. He proclaimed his title with pride.

Mirabelle felt a flutter of excitement. He reminded her so much of Joshua. He had that same rough capability; a way of taking charge.

The steady hum of the engines seemed to be in tune with a throbbing within her own body. The swish of the waves against the sides of the ship was as inevitable as the stoker taking her in his arms.

Instinctively, she felt his eyes sweeping over her; taking in the splendid fullness of her breasts, the tininess of her waist. It made her feel deliciously vulnerable, just as she felt when Joshua looked her over so seductively. Her loins seemed to be melting, her legs felt weak and she stumbled against him as the ship took a sudden dip into a trough in the waves.

'Whoops!' he said, laughing as his arms swept around her.

He held her close and she could smell his maleness; his musk, the tobacco and the odour of the ship's furnaces. It was a heady mixture; one to send Mirabelle's senses reeling.

'Got to go below,' he said, still holding her close.

She raised her eyes, looking into his. 'No!' she breathed, a plea in her voice. It was like being with Joshua all over again. If he left her, there would be that dreadful sense of loss which she had experienced since Mama drove her from Atlanta.

'The chief'll have my guts for garters if I don't get below,' he told her, although his hands still pressed the fullness of her bottom close to his groin. She could feel his thickness, its urgency, its throbbing through his working trousers.

'Can I come with you?' she pleaded, circling her pale bare arms about his neck.

He laughed, his hands tracing the elegance of her figure. 'You?'

'I missed the tour of the engine rooms,' she excused. Her pussy felt dreadfully swollen, aching for the fulfilment which only someone like Joshua could provide.

'You like engines, Miss?' His grin was one of disbelief. He knew that it was his own piston in which her interest lay, but she didn't care.

'Yes,' she sighed. 'I'm very interested.'

One of his rough hands stroked her cheek and fell to the milk-white globes of her breasts, stroking them so lightly that she shuddered with pleasure. 'I'll show you the Golden Rivet, miss,' he said, his grin broadening. 'All pretty girls should see the Golden Rivet.' He released the hold upon her body and clutched her hand, tugging her hurriedly along the deck.

'What is it?' Mirabelle asked eagerly as he hurried her through the companionways. 'This Golden Rivet?'

'You'll see, miss,' he said with a chuckle, urging her to pick up her skirts as they entered the dimly lit bowels of the ship.

The noise and heat were like hell itself, she thought, but they excited her. The pounding of the huge pistons echoed the rhythm which she felt in her pussy. She watched, fascinated, as they slid so smoothly into the cylinders. She leaned against a greasy bulkhead, looking up at his tall figure looming over her.

'Name's Ernest,' he mouthed, for any speech was drowned out by the throb of machinery.

How marvellous were these modern inventions; these iron ships, she thought. 'Mirabelle,' she answered as he smoothed a damp curl from her forehead.

She lifted her face to his, her blue eyes beckoning and her lips parted. He had that same maddening hint of arrogance which she noticed in Joshua. Perhaps, she thought, that was an attraction; why her body ached to be tamed by him.

'This is madness!' she wanted to say, but it was useless to try and speak over the thunderous noise.

*The attraction I feel for you is perilous.* The thought drummed into her brain. *Surely, it can only end in unhappiness for both of us.* But she was compelled to try and quench the fire within her.

His breath was warm and moist against her cheek as he kissed the lobe of her ear, taking it between his lips and sucking it deeply. One of his big hands tore at her bodice, seeking to hold each heavy breast, delighting in the tremble of his fingers as they cupped each generous mound and lifted them upwards towards his questing lips.

His touch had that same sense of newness which she felt with Joshua. Eagerly, she offered herself to him, arching her body. Her skin tingled at every place he touched her and the heat and the noise of this hellish place only served to increase her delight in his embrace.

'Don't stop!' her mind screamed as the gown was ripped further. How glad she was that she had dressed so hurriedly that she wore no corsets or drawers to impede his view of her body!

She found herself smiling as she followed his smouldering gaze to the apex of her thighs and the lush triangle which glistened so darkly there.

The throb of the mighty engines enhanced the delight caused by the touch of Ernest's hand as it cupped the pouting pad of her pussy. The huge middle finger slipped inexorably into the moist cleft and she welcomed it with a soft gasp of breath.

She moved slowly against his touch, succumbing to the forceful domination of that digit. A large thumb gently slicked over her clitty and Mirabelle felt her body glow with a heat which had nothing to do with her surroundings.

His wide lips moved, but his words were lost in the steady

pounding of the engines. Mirabelle frowned. 'Chief...' she discerned, but his caresses continued and she gave herself up to them as he slid another finger into the soft wetness, gently violating her passage.

A tantalising kiss was planted in the hollow of her neck before her lips were forced open with his thrusting tongue. The movement of his fingers made her legs become as liquid and formless as her pussy. The delicious sensations culminated in a climax which threatened to bring her to a swoon. She sank down, weakly, to the grime and grease of the engine room floor.

His magnificent body covered her and she felt him enter her with the hardness of his piston. She felt his thickness opening her up and she screamed her pleasure above the noise of the mighty engines.

'The Golden Rivet!' he yelled, adding his noise to her own. 'Feel it?'

'Oh, yes!' she cried. 'Plunge it in!'

He rammed into her, like a hammer blow. He held her breasts to give himself full purchase as his slim hips thrust at hers. The roughness of the taking and the hardness of the steel deck beneath her enhanced the feeling of abandon. It was just as she had felt in Joshua's shack.

'Well, I declare!' There was no mistaking the shrill voice.

'Aunt Hatty!'

'So this is where your temper brought you!' Ernest was prodded with the toe of a contemptuous boot. 'I, meanwhile, am on an educational tour,' added Aunt Hatty. 'There is something most particular Captain King wishes to show me.'

Mirabelle couldn't resist a kiss upon Ernest's unshaven neck, delighting in the roughness of his skin.

'What's that, Aunt Hatty?' said Mirabelle, trying to show interest in her aunt's prattle, despite Ernest's insistent cossetting.

'It is, he says, the most important rivet in the ship. Isn't that correct, Captain, dear?'

The shadowy figure of the Captain could be seen above them tip-toeing up a companionway.

# Chapter 5

'Playful fillies!' exclaimed Lord Carshalton. 'Met them?'

It was the very last morning of the voyage. The ship was safely docked at Liverpool, but in the First Class breakfast lounge his lordship and an eminent Liberal MP were partaking of a leisurely meal.

'Can't say I have,' said George Lloyd, stroking the white moustache which made him unmistakeable. 'Any chance of it? Sound my sort.'

'Absolutely!' agreed his lordship. 'Invited them to the Hall.' He beckoned a hovering steward and pointed to his empty coffee cup. 'Meet them then,' he added. 'Although from what I understand they're on a husband hunt.'

George Lloyd looked put out and groomed his moustache nervously. 'Good grief, Tristham!' His hand had a noticeable tremor as he picked up his own cup to bring it to his lips. 'Got enough of that sort in London already. Don't want anymore.' His twinkling eyes renewed their sparkle as he added dreamily: 'Don't mind a few mistresses, but wives . . .' He shook his head unhappily.

'Specifically after titles,' supplied Lord Carshalton.

George Lloyd heaved a sigh of relief. 'That's all right then!' He turned a page of *The Times*, delivered earlier that morning.

'Not all right,' denied his lordship. 'Not all right at all. Be after young Rolstrum before we know where we are.'

'He's married!' exclaimed Mr Lloyd, reaching across the table and helping himself to hot, fresh toast newly delivered to the table by the hovering steward. 'Married that pretty young Geranium Field.'

'Lily,' corrected Lord Carshalton. 'No matter,' he added worriedly. 'Americans, so I've heard, take no quarters when it comes to divorce.'

'Ah!' George Lloyd nodded sagely.

His lordship looked around cautiously, ever mindful of the dangers of gossip on board ship even when it had docked. 'Can only hope that what I've heard is true.'

'What's that?' George Lloyd glanced about him, as wary of eavesdroppers as was his travelling companion.

'The beautiful Miss Mirabelle seems to have a penchant for the working class!'

George Lloyd leaned back in his dining chair, an expression of shock on his face. This was quickly replaced by one of triumph. 'In that case, I am sure I shall be able to find someone who would suit her down to the ground—' He paused, grinning widely. 'Or even under it!'

'Ah! One of your mining colleagues!'

'Got some lovely boys in the valleys!'

Lord Carshalton looked highly satisfied, feeling that the problem was solved and there would be no danger to Rolstrum's marriage, but his expression quickly changed. 'Title! The – er – boys from the valleys wouldn't have titles, would they?'

The white moustache bristled crossly. 'Good grief, man! Can't think of everything.' He rattled his *Times* and disappeared behind it. 'That's your department,' he added from behind the newsprint barrier. 'Have a word with old Bertie. The King'll sort it out.'

'Right-ho!'

The problem of the two beautiful Americans seemed to be amicably settled to the satisfaction of both chums and they settled down to finish their breakfast.

★ ★ ★

'Ernest!'

The caress of his mouth on her lips set Mirabelle's body aflame and she was hard pressed to catch her breath as he broke away.

'I'm being put off!'

'Sacked?' Mirabelle was horrified. 'Because of me?'

Ernest grinned ruefully. 'But it was worth it. Every minute of it!'

She looked doubtful. When Ernest caught her by the rail looking down on to the dockside, she had been searching for Aunt Hatty. In fact she had been searching for her for some time. It was too bad of her to disappear in this manner.

'Please, Mirabelle!' Ernest pressed against her and she could feel his need. It was as great as hers.

'I don't know,' she said doubtfully. 'I've lost Aunt Hatty May and—'

'For old times sake!'

'But Aunt Hatty—'

'Oh, blow Aunt Hatty!' The rough voice made it quite plain that he had things on his mind of far greater importance than Mirabelle's chaperone. Things which were pressing to the point of pain.

Ernest had somehow manoeuvred her between a stack of steamer chairs and a life boat to demonstrate just how pressing and painful it was. She felt his hand lifting her skirt to feel the silky band of naked skin atop of stockings. She sighed ecstatically.

'We'll be seen . . .' she warned, but the warning was said in a whisper and did not sound at all frantic. It was a whisper of passion.

'I don't care!' said Ernest, throwing caution to the winds. 'They've done their worst and I cannot resist the delights of your body!'

Mirabelle's tailored travelling skirt was lifted to her waist. The lushness of her dark bush was made available to Ernest by the convenient slit in her drawers.

'Nor I yours, Ernest!'

Her desire was wild as she flung back her jet curls in complete abandon. All thoughts of Aunt Hatty and, indeed, of Joshua and Atlanta, were dismissed from her mind as her cunney was pleasantly filled by Ernest's wayward piston.

'Ahhh!' she sighed as her slick companionway was opened up by her lover's fervent keel.

'Yes, Mirabelle! Yes! Tell me that the loss of my position is not for naught!' He thrust deeply into her, probing into her delicious depths.

'Oh, Ernest, how could you think such a thing!'

The two lovers, thrusting back and forth, oblivious to their surroundings sent an oar and a tin cannister containing emergency rations to the dock below.

Mirabelle could feel the silky smooth head of his turgid cock opening her out as it drove, straight and true, to the very entrance of her womb. Her hungry cunney flesh clutched him greedily and she heard him moan softly. His thrust became more urgent and rhythmic as she pulsed around him.

'Grrh!' heard Mirabelle.

'You roar your passion like the jungle king!' she sighed, feeling her clitty jerking upon the thickness of his thrusting cleat.

Ernest frowned, not fully understanding her statement, but this creasing of his puzzled forehead was quickly erased by the glory of a spend which could not be held back. A fountain of spunk spilled into Mirabelle at the very moment that they fell, jerking, and wrapped in each other's arms, upon the deck.

'You!' The roar was one of fury.

Mirabelle, whose eyes had been languidly closed, relishing the aftermath of a delightful spend, was brought roughly to her senses. She found herself looking upwards into one angry eye.

A broken oar was pummelling Ernest's still thrusting buttocks extracting groans of pain.

'Oh, Captain King!' intervened Mirabelle kindly. 'Don't! He has been punished enough! Losing his position and all!'

'Seems to me,' said the Captain, holding a piece of raw steak with one hand to a rapidly swelling and bleeding eye as he pummelled with the other, 'he has a most comfortable position upon you, madam, and cares little who or what was damaged in getting there!'

The Captain sat down heavily upon the stack of steamer chairs, nursing his aching head and groaning loudly.

Ernest, released at last from the Captain's furious beating, tucked his satisfied piston into his trousers and, looking somewhat shamefaced, stood, albeit shakily, and looked down at Mirabelle.

'I think I'd better be getting along,' he murmured in an agitated manner.

A pale hand reached out to him in a gesture of sympathy. 'But where will you go?'

'Another ship,' came the reply as Ernest cast a hurried glance at Captain King.

'Dashed if you will! Using my ship as a floating bordello! Ain't on and I'll make sure every gangway is closed against you if it's the last thing I do!'

Struggling to her feet in the most dignified manner possible and smoothing her crumpled travelling suit, Mirabelle spoke. 'Aren't you being a little hard?'

'No!' spat the Captain, nursing his damaged eye.

'Where will you go?' asked Mirabelle worriedly. 'What will you do?'

Ernest shrugged. 'Live on my wits, I suppose.' There was a rebellious, vengeful look upon the rugged, handsome features which somehow thrilled Mirabelle, making a heat flood the pussy so recently saturated by him.

'All you're fit for, you wretch!' hissed Captain King. 'Nothing but a thief and a rogue!'

'And you're not all that you should be!'

The two men sparred with their eyes, until she separated

them gesturing that the stoker should go before more damage was done.

Mirabelle, with some sadness marring her radiant beauty, watched Ernest walk proudly along the deck. A hand grasped her shoulder and she was compelled to turn into Captain King's embrace.

'You are a wicked girl!' But the accusation was said in a low, seductive manner.

Mirabelle frowned, her sweet rosebud lips pursed in a soft pout as she looked at him with defiant eyes.

He held her close with one arm and she could feel the push of his belaying pin, thickening swiftly, anxious for attention.

'The stoker is not your sort!' he said sharply.

An urge to struggle away from him was quickly prevented by his grip around her slender body tightening.

'Who are you to say who is my sort?' The periwinkle-blue eyes blazed up at him. Joshua's face suddenly occluded her vision. His body held her. 'Who are you to say?' she repeated, her voice becoming husky and low.

One hand touched the swiftly hardening nipples beneath her tight bodice. She shuddered and knew that her gaze softened as she looked up at him, but why, she wondered. This haughty being was not for her, she knew. He did not have the roughness of Joshua or the toughness of Ernest.

'Wicked girl!' he rasped. 'You deserve a thorough beating lusting after such a man.' The hand slid from the swell of her bosom to the handsome jut of her buttocks and Mirabelle trembled involuntarily.

'Would you relish that?' His good eye twinkled at her. 'A good, thorough beating?'

Mirabelle shuddered, shaking her head, the jet curls shaking loose from her high, wide coiffure.

'I think you would.' His voice was threatening, but somehow loving at one and the same time. 'Come.'

A gasp of anticipation drew breath from Mirabelle's

body, but she had no time to protest. She was hurried from the deck and led firmly to her own stateroom. Once there the Captain tossed her roughly upon her bed. His sudden aggressiveness caused her face to flush scarlet.

'Yes!' he said, his dark eyes blazing. 'This is what you like, isn't it? Violence?'

Mutely, lying propped up upon her elbows, Mirabelle shook her head. The position made her breasts thrust sharply against her tight bodice and she knew, without looking down, that her erect nipples were clearly etched against the silk cloth. The force with which he pushed her down upon the bed had opened her legs beneath her skirts. She could feel her pussy, open and vulnerable, beneath her petticoats.

'Don't deny it!' He looked devilish standing over her, his good eye blazing with the other black and partially closed. 'Take off your clothes.'

The sharpness of his commands made her skin prickle as if already beaten by a switch of thorns. Again she shook her head.

'Shall I tear them from you?' he hissed. 'Is that what you want?'

Looking at him quizically, she questioned herself. Was it what she wanted? Was that what thrilled her? Roughness? Toughness? She felt her parted lips lift in a slight smile, a teasing, tempting smile.

'You little witch!'

His strong hands came down upon her, jerking her upwards, pulling her to her feet. She stook passively, allowing him to shake her, grip the firmness of her upper arms. It was no surprise to feel the cloth of her bodice being torn from her breasts, to feel the sudden coolness of the air on the upper swells of those pale mounds. They were quite bare above the upper limit of her corset; bare and uplifted. They felt swollen and the nipples burned fiercely.

With the supple ends of his fingers he slapped the pale,

pouting hillocks. The blows were not hard enough to hurt, but they were swift and sharp causing an immediate flushing of the ivory flesh.

The finger slapping of her breasts came as no surprise to Mirabelle and she found herself welcoming the light blows.

'You need a man who can tame you,' he said, pulling her to him, so close that he could feel the heat of the flesh which he had so recently slapped.

She nodded shyly. This was why she had rejected all the young men chosen for her by her father. She realised that now.

'Take off your skirt,' he said. The command was given softly, almost lovingly, but firmly.

Obediently, she slipped the button at the waist and let the tailored garment slide to the deck. The shedding of each garment, she noticed, increased her sense of vulnerability.

'Petticoats,' he urged bluntly.

The frilled, starched cotton garments slid from the neatness of her waist and over the fullness of her hips. She saw his gaze drop to the darkness of the curls between her thighs, peeping so coyly from the opening of her drawers.

'Those, too,' he said, meaning the cotton garment which covered her from waist to knee.

What was he planning to do? she wondered. Would he slap her buttocks gently, as he had her breasts? Would he play at taming her?

Slowly, she tugged at the bow of satin ribbon which held her drawers at her waist and felt them slither over the resilience of her corset. She heard him sigh and she looked up, looking into the lust she could see in the eye which was open. Very aware of the lushness and darkness of the curls against the creamy skin of her thighs, she cupped her hands at that place.

'Stop that!' The command was as sharp as a lash. 'You were willing enough to allow the stoker to be intimate with you. It is no time now to pretend modesty or innocence.'

Mirabelle opened out her hands, her palms facing him. It was a gesture of complete submissiveness although her legs were still clenched tightly together.

'Good,' praised the Captain. 'Keep your hands open and by your sides.'

She knew that his gaze was firmly fixed on her dark bush and she knew that it shone slickly with Ernest's love dew. She shuffled her feet, wanting to hide the fact from him. She felt that he might be offended by the sight.

'Open your thighs,' was his next command. 'Just a little. I want to feel your treasures.'

Stains of scarlet appeared on her ivory cheeks and she lowered her eyes, humiliated by what he wanted. Why couldn't he punish her as she deserved to be punished instead of this slow torture?

'Look at me and do as I say,' he said crisply. He sat down in a high-backed chair, crossing his long legs and linking his fingers in a relaxed manner.

Slowly, Mirabelle lifted her spoiled coiffure, feeling her heavy hair fall about her smooth shoulders. This last increased her vulnerability; the vulnerability which was growing as every second passed. She looked at him steadily; saw him gesture with a nod of his head at the jet triangle below the pale strip of her belly. An increased awareness of the tight confinement of her corset was yet another facet of her increasing defencelessness in his presence.

She opened her thighs, feeling the stickiness of juices, her own and Ernest's, slick as the pale skin parted.

'More,' he urged softly. 'Make sure that your young labia are open. Fully open.'

Her cheeks flushed at the intimate word, but she did as he asked, feeling her clitty emerge from its little hood, stiff and erect. She felt ready for him and she glanced at him, a smile curving her lips and an invitation in her deep blue eyes.

He shook his head and frowned in disapproval. 'This is exactly what I dislike in you, Mirabelle.'

An involuntary gasp sighed through her moist, parted lips at the sound of her name from him. It sounded sweet, caring, loving.

'Your forwardness.' He clicked his tongue critically. 'You are bold and far too insolent for your own good. Perhaps it is an American trait, but if you are to succeed in your quest in England you must change.'

How dare he? thought Mirabelle. How dare he criticise her character or her country? The blue eyes blazed as did her cheeks.

'Walk to me,' he said softly. 'Stand here.' He pointed to a spot in front of his chair. 'Close to me.'

As if in a dream, Mirabelle walked slowly towards him, taking tiny steps in her little black button boots. Her breasts were thrust high and proud and the black triangle of curls swayed prettily before her.

'Good,' he breathed. 'Very good. You seem to be learning already.'

The compliment pleased her. It made her pussy thrill, feel full and swollen, flushed and inflamed.

'Let me feel the softness of your treasure,' he said softly. He looked up at her, testing her reaction.

Her pussy ached to be felt, opened, spread, but she hesitated. He seemed so stern, despite the flashes of tenderness which she heard in his voice. This taming was quite different from the roughness of Joshua and Ernest. The alternate loving and severity meant that she never knew exactly when he would be pleased or angry.

'I shan't hurt you.'

She took another step and he sighed. She saw him spread his own thighs and adjust his cock before lifting his fingers to open and part her labia.

'So hot,' he murmured and Mirabelle felt the warm plumpness spread with a finger and thumb. 'So scarlet and flushed.'

Something made her tilt her pelvis, to give him a clearer

view, she supposed, but she would not, could not, look down herself.

'Pretty,' he sighed, and she felt a gentle fingertip stroke the arch of her clitty downwards. Swiftly, the caress changed direction, drawing the little hood back from the sensitive tip. Mirabelle moaned, a soft sigh like a breeze on a still September day whispering through the trees.

'Not yet!' he rapped suddenly and, in a flash, he pulled her over his spread knees, her breasts squashed tight against one thigh while her open thighs were spread upon the other. 'Do you know what I shall do now?'

'Of course, I know!' said Mirabelle sharply. They were the first words she had spoken for many minutes, she realised. Silence, she understood, was part of what he required of her.

She felt his big hand caress her buttocks, feeling the shape and smoothness, gently pressing them open, a finger sliding up the heated tight valley. She wriggled.

'What do you deserve?' he asked, his large hand encompassing the twin hillocks.

'A spank,' she said without hesitation. Was this what she wanted all along, she wondered. Spanking, punishment and a subsequent purging of her sins?

'Correct!' A palm, wide and long, beat down upon her vulnerable flesh, making the full hillocks shudder with the force of the blow.

The place smarted, a glow emanated from it but this was over-ridden by the wonderful feeling which followed in her pussy. It seemed only right, thought Mirabelle, that she should open her thighs further and pout her bottom upwards.

'Good! Obedience at last!' Several more blows followed until she felt that her bottom was on fire, but she knew that the spanking was done in such a way as to leave no welts, only the inflammation.

Passively, she lay across his lap, feeling his ever-increasing thickness press into the uncorsetted place of her lower belly. She was breathing fast, she knew, and she also knew that the smacking had greatly increased the longing in her pussy. She could feel the swelling of the plump labia and the urgent jerking of her clitty.

'What will you do when you no longer have me, Mirabelle?' he said, bending to whisper the question in the jet softness of her tumbled hair.

'I don't know,' she said, feeling the pressure of his hardness pressing more vigorously into her belly as he bent over her.

'Will you continue searching? Untamed and unloved?'

That was true, she silently agreed. If she could not have Joshua or someone like him, she would remain unloved.

His big hands grasped the hanging fullness of her breasts, pinching and nipping until tears came to the periwinkle-blue eyes.

Later that day, at an inn on the southern border of the county of Cheshire, a cloaked gentleman wearing a wide-brimmed hat stepped over the low threshold.

'You have a room ready for her?' he asked. His voice was low and a little strained, perhaps disguised. He measured his words as though English was not his native tongue.

'Very nice room,' the host of the inn assured him. 'Everything a lady could wish!' He tapped the side of his nose and winked conspiratorially. 'If you get my meaning, young sir?'

The tall stranger gave him a studied glare from under the large hat. There was something about the cold look which made a shudder ripple down the portly landlord's spine. If anyone were to ask him, this young fella was up to no good and the sooner he left his hostelry the better!

'You be staying long, sir?' he asked hopefully. He pulled a frothing pint in a pewter mug and set it before the stranger.

Wide lips dipped into the foam, but were, immediately twisted into a grimace. 'Warm!' he complained. 'Your ale's warm.' He took another sip. 'Almost hot, man!'

The landlord looked bemused. 'Well, sir,' he said, shrugging apologetically, "tis summer, ain't it?'

'The beer!' The stranger spat into a copper scuttle near the inglenook fireplace. A globule of spittle hit the scuttle fair and square and made the bucket ping noisily.

'Well, sir, will you?' The landlord leaned on the scrubbed bar in a confidential manner.

'Will I what?' The cloaked man took another tentative sip of the frothy liquid.

'Be staying long?'

The mystery man rested a booted foot upon a brass rail, placed for the convenience of customers, around the rough-hewn bar.

'Depends,' he said enigmatically.

The landlord frowned. 'On what, young sir?' he said carefully. He had a feeling it would be wise not to cross this man. He gulped nervously before speaking again, 'If I might be so bold as to ask.'

'On whether you can keep your beer in a drinkable condition!' he retorted sharply. 'My work gives me a terrible thirst!' Although he supplied this information with a smile the landlord felt the same sense of apprehension as when he looked into the cold green eyes.

He spun neatly on his heel, his cloak swirling around him, striding out into the sunshine. The rural air had a tang to it; damp earth, fallen leaves, the heartier smell of horses. It was different. Quite unlike anything he had experienced before.

The sun was high in the sky. It was almost time. Across the fields he could see a haze and it could cause problems. Then he smiled grimly. If the mist came down it would at least obscure them.

'My horse!' he ordered.

An ostler led a fine chestnut mare already saddled, patting the mount's sleek neck. 'Think this'll suit you foine, mister,' he said politely, touching a forelock with a bent finger.

The man frowned, taking the mare's reins, smoothing its flanks and each strong leg in turn, then he nodded, satisfied.

'It'll do,' he said and swung easily into the saddle.

# Chapter 6

Gently, the Captain turned her to face him. The deep blue eyes were wide, she knew, as she stared up at him; the soft lips were parted.

With a finger tip he smoothed stray curls from her forehead and smiled. 'How do you feel, Mirabelle?'

Words came to her mind, some of them angry, some resentful, some telling of her sadness, but she remained silent. Most of all her feelings were centred on her pussy. It was soft and open between her thighs and she could feel her own liquid joining Ernest's in a warm trickle over her burning buttock cheeks, soothing them.

His smile broadened and his hand strayed to her mound, lying there still, and cupping the plumpness. The firm flesh, covered so prettily with glossy, tight, jet black curls, twitched under his light touch. There was nothing she could do to stop the involuntary spasm.

His eyes smiled knowingly. 'Good, Mirabelle. My treatment is working.'

Her mind was in a torment. She didn't like the humiliation to which she was being subjected; the smacking and the pain, but she knew it was this which was having such a profound effect on her pussy.

'Open your thighs wider, Mirabelle,' he said.

Powerless to prevent herself, she obeyed him and looked up at him proudly. Her labia were fully open now, she knew. Each was a fat lip, swollen with increasing longing, inflamed beneath the tiny curls.

One of his fingers and a thumb eased into the heated valley and pressed the slick inner lips together, slipping them over the erect bud of her clitty until she thought she would scream, so great was her desire.

'Have I teased you enough?' he asked, one hand grazing across the taut mounds of her breasts, across the nubs of her swollen nipples as the other stroked her cleft.

Her breathing was ragged, her thighs opened to the limit. She nodded. 'I am tamed,' she said briefly, thinking this admission would end the beautiful torment.

He laughed, throwing back his handsome head. 'No, Mirabelle,' he said. 'I think not. I think there will be many incidents before you are tamed.'

A shock thrilled through her as he slipped two fingers into her receptive passage. Her soft mouth circled in a perfect 'O' and her breath sighed from her in ecstasy.

'But for now,' he said, extracting the fingers slowly and cradling her gently in his arms, 'I am satisfied that you are ready.'

Closing her heavy lids and wincing a little as his serge uniform sleeve abraded her reddened, castigated bottom, Mirabelle rested her head on her shoulder and slipped her arms about his thick neck.

Breath whispered in his chest beneath her ear. The breathing was quick, ragged, eager as he strode across the stateroom to lay her upon her bed. She wanted him naked and was pleased when she saw him tear swiftly at his jacket, trousers and shirt. Her dimpled fists rose to her mouth as she watched him take off the last garment; slip the button holding his under drawers about his slim hips.

His cock was as she imagined it, spearing strongly from his groin, pinnacled by a smooth, naked globe, already glossy with the dew of his longing. He approached her without haste and knelt, almost in homage, between her splayed thighs. Stretching his hands behind him, caressed her slim ankles, still tightly confined in her black button boots. The caresses continued along the length of her silk-clad calves to the band of milk-white thighs coyly exposed above the welt of her stockings.

Still he tortured her, thought Mirabelle. This waiting for the relief which only a strong man could give her, was this part of the taming, too? she asked herself.

The eyes, the blue colour deepened by the yearning she felt in her innermost depths, focused upon his cock. It was big and eminently sturdy. The colour was dark, almost purple at the pinnacle but fading to a brownish-red at the base. Veins, dark under the satin skin, trailed the thick stem, throbbing as she watched.

'Tell me what you want,' he said, his voice a hoarse rasp, coming from low in his throat.

A mew, a sound quite unlike Mirabelle; the confident, haughty Miss who was so much a mistress of herself, sighed from between her soft lips.

'Speak to me, my darling,' he taunted, circling the thick girth spearing from his groin with light fingers. 'Tell me softly what you most desire.'

'You,' she managed, the single syllable barely audible.

Chuckling, he sat back on his heels, drawing the magnificence of his cock away from her. 'What part of me?' His fingers moved quicker up and down the girth.

Frantically, she reached out, afraid that the moment would end all too soon.

'Your cock,' she croaked. 'Please! Your cock!'

He leaned closer, but not so close that she could touch him, and her fingers clawed hungrily at the air. 'What do you want of it? This cock of mine?'

'You know!' She flung her body from side to side as though she was restrained by invisible ropes and was powerless to move. Her corsetted body arched from the bed, her dark mound at the peak of the arch and her cunney open and so vulnerable, but for what?

The smiling mouth opened and chuckled again. He sat

back upon his heels, but she could see the fullness of his ballsack full and turgid beneath his stiff mast. 'Of course I know, my darling, but it would please me so much if you would tell me plainly what you most desire.'

Mirabelle's head ached with that desire. Never had anyone tormented her in this manner. Never had she welcomed the torment. Joshua's face shimmered in her mind's eye. Perhaps she would find, somewhere, a man who would satisfy her fully. She drew breath deeply, lay still, ready to say what she knew he wanted to hear.

'Hold me in your arms,' she murmured, watching his face.

He frowned, warningly.

'And fuck me,' she added. 'Take me deep and long.'

'Oh, Mirabelle!' he sighed. 'How beautiful!'

Slowly, he covered her body. She could feel the warm, satiny stiffness against her groin, resting there, a slick of liquid dampening the soft skin. He kissed her, his lips velvety upon hers, the tip of his tongue darting into her mouth.

Yes, she thought, she could still feel the heat of the spanking and when he lay upon her, it increased and spread to her cunney.

The silky roundness of his globe nudged between her labia, drawing a long sigh from her. She tensed, ready for the thrust which she knew would come quite soon, but he paused, again tormenting her. The polished wetness of his thick knob edged with terrible slowness between her slick inner lips. This caused tension upon her clitty, pulling at the sensitive little bud. She moaned and drew up her legs.

'Beautiful,' he whispered, nuzzling in the dark tresses which were tumbled about the elegance of her neck.

The bending of her knees had softened the delicate tissues of her cunney, making them pliable. It seemed only natural to let her bent legs fall outwards, opening her up still more.

She was rewarded by the sudden thrusting of his mast until it lay, fully steeped in the warm juices. It butted, gently, at the limit of her womb, making her throw back her head. The arching of her neck offered her throat to his petting lips and he showered the unblemished ivory skin with tiny kisses.

Her cunney flesh cossetted his length, pampering it until it drew a groan from him, but still he would not be hurried. With shapely legs wrapped around his invading body she drew him closer, tempting him to thrust hard and fast into her.

'Oh, Mirabelle!' he sighed into the spread blackness of her hair against the white linen pillow. 'You are still untamed! How can any man resist you?'

She felt him throb inside her. Felt him begin to slide, very rapidly, back and forth in her depths. She moved with him, tormented for so long for this moment.

It was a spillage, a long drawn spillage when he succumbed to her pampering. Mirabelle, too, could not hold back the glorious sensations which swept over her, again and again.

Her cheeks were damp with tears, she noticed, when he calmed, lying still and relaxed, at peace at last.

'Hold up there!'

The voice was hoarse and muffled, but threatening enough to scare Aunt Hatty out of her wits. She heard it over the throb of the motor car engine and it came eerily out of the Liverpool mist.

'You want me to drive on, missus?' asked the driver of the vehicle which she'd hired at the dockside. He slowed only a little and she could hear the thunder of horse hooves close behind them.

Aunt Hatty May huddled down in the seat, feeling very lost and alone. It was too bad of Mirabelle to disappear after breakfast. She had no idea where she had gone. She bit her lace-mittened fist, trying to think.

'Well, missus?' The driver sounded bad-tempered. 'What's it to be? Drive on or stop?'

Hatty saw him look round nervously at the thundering hooves which flashed up and down beside the vehicle.

'Them hooves are getting a bit too close for comfort to my way of thinking.'

Peering through the full black veil which was part of her elegant motoring hat and was tied securely about her neck, Hatty May bit her lips again. She needed Mirabelle. She couldn't handle such difficult situations on her own.

'Yes!' she said, in a voice which squeaked with fear.

'Yes what?' The driver peered round at her, frowning through his goggles. 'Drive on or stop?'

The hooves drummed in Hatty's ears. The open top car seemed so vulnerable jogging along so close to the big chestnut horse.

Aunt Hatty gnawed at her fist through the veil. 'Drive on!' she said. She was shaking from head to toe beneath the long driving coat. 'No!' she said, taking another nervous look at the rider.

The vehicle swerved to a stop. 'Make up your mind, missus!'

The car slowed and, finally, stopped.

This was awful, she thought, huddling deeper in the seat. She had no idea that highwaymen were still a threat to travellers in England. She was sure that Amelia Jane, Mirabelle's mother, would never have suggested this adventure if she had been aware of it.

A revolver was pointing at the very place where she had tied her veil. Her mittened hands went to the place in a futile, defensive gesture. The masked man peered down at her, trying to see under her veil. Hatty drew back, terrified.

'Come with me,' he said.

A black scarf hid the lower half of his face and his hat was pulled down low over his eyes.

'What will you do if I don't?' asked Hatty May with a

defiance which sounded much more courageous than she felt.

'Shoot!' he said with a softness which was, in itself, threatening.

'Oooh!' Hatty felt light-headed as though she would swoon at any moment. Drat Mirabelle, she thought, anger becoming a great panacea for faintness. She had felt so muddled when the ship docked and things were in such a to-do on the dockside, in such chaos, it was a wonder that anyone found anyone or their luggage! When the driver suggested that he should take her south, she was only too pleased.

'He ain't a proper highwayman, missus,' said the driver, looking up, belligerently, at the masked figure.

'Isn't he?' Hatty looked up, following the driver's eyes with her own. Perhaps the situation was not as dangerous as she had first feared.

'Nah! Got rid o' them in old Dick Turpin's day!' He grinned up at the mounted figure who sat so still and silent on the big chestnut. He thrust his face upwards, belligerence and defiance even more apparent. 'We 'ung 'im!'

Hatty heaved a sigh of relief and sat straighter in the leather seat as she, too, defied the cloaked figure. 'Hear that?' she said, her voice suddenly strong and brave. 'You could be hung!'

The figure laughed softly. It was a sound which made Hatty quake with fear. A light mist swirled about them, blotting out the pale sunshine. He tucked the revolver into his belt and held out a hand.

'Git up behind me!'

Hatty shrank deeper into her seat, huddling into her high-collared coat, wishing the ground would swallow her up.

'I said git up behind me!' This time the command was rapped out more sharply.

The grey eyes behind the veil fluttered nervously. She seemed to have no choice but to obey. There was another thing. For all that she was Mirabelle's chaperone, she was young and widowed and far from home. She had to admit there was a certain thrill about being held up by a highwayman!

Bending down from the big horse, he held open the automobile's door and beckoned to her. Trembling, she stood and stepped down on to the rough road.

'Don't you worry, missus,' the driver said, patting her arm in a consoling manner. 'I'll have the police on him. You see if I don't!'

As if in a dream Hatty allowed herself to be swung up on to the big horse behind the highwayman. 'No, don't!' she said softly, wondering whether she should place her arms around the big cloaked figure.

'Don't, missus?' questioned the driver, standing up behind the wheel of his vehicle. 'Did I 'ear you right? You'll encourage the blighters! We'll 'ave 'undreds of 'em galloping about again, thieving and molesting.'

The big chestnut whinnied, pawing at the air over the little car, making the driver cringe away from the creature. The highwayman laughed hugely as he dug his heels into the horse's flanks and they galloped off down the narrow road. Hatty May clung to his cloak for dear life.

Captain King kissed the back of Mirabelle's hand, gazing deep into her blue eyes.

'It's farewell,' he said and she heard a catch in his deep voice.

Dressed and elegantly coiffured, feeling her confident self, she smiled up at him, her gaze bold and assured. 'Yes,' she murmured. 'It's been a most memorable voyage!' Her fingers tingled at the touch of his hand. 'Most memorable!' The last two words were almost a whisper, a sigh of regret.

Looping her arm through his, he led her out on deck, into the mêlée of docking once more. 'And regrettably my last with this splendid vessel.'

Mirabelle looked up at him, her eyes wide with surprise. 'Your last?'

'I, too, am being put off,' he supplied calmly.

'But why?' She was shocked. Captain King seemed so much in command of everyone about him. With lowered eyes she was reminded by her glowing buttocks how very much he was in command of her own frail body.

He patted the hand which lay upon his arm. 'The Chairman of the Line . . .' he said vaguely.

'A reprimand!' she cried, interrupting him. 'But he couldn't possibly know about . . . anything!' She lowered her eyes modestly.

He sighed and shrugged enigmatically, still patting her hand consolingly as they walked along the deck. They had a moment to gaze into each other's eyes.

'Ah, Captain!' Lord Carshalton was hurrying along the deck towards them. Captain King looked somewhat put out and made to walk swiftly in the other direction, but Mirabelle assured him that his lordship was a dear friend.

'But I have things to do before I leave the ship,' he told her agitatedly.

'No longer Captain, is it?' continued Lord Carshalton angrily, standing foresquare in front of them.

'Yes,' agreed Mirabelle, looking up into Mr King's handsome features with an expression of sincere sympathy in her blue eyes. 'All a misunderstanding. I shall write to the Chairman and explain.'

Mr King became more agitated, his eyes darting hither and thither looking for escape.

'Bad business, eh?' Lord Carshalton shook his head worriedly.

'Nothing happened!' exclaimed Mirabelle. 'The dear Captain didn't have time to show Aunt Hatty the Golden Rivet.'

'Golden Rivet?' His lordship looked puzzled, his eyes darting from Mirabelle to the Captain and back again. 'I'm talking about the iceberg!' He pointed at the Captain's swiftly retreating rear. 'The blighter nearly had us all in the drink!'

Mirabelle paled and was thoroughly shocked. Her hand flew to her pale lips in a gesture of dismay.

'Hundreds of lives could have been lost,' continued Lord Carshalton. 'Hundreds. You don't survive in these waters for long, you know!' He held her shaking shoulders, admiring her elegant outfit, smiling into her eyes as though nothing was at all amiss.

If only he knew, thought Mirabelle. And what exactly was the Captain doing, she wondered, when the ship was sailing, inexorably, towards the deadly iceberg? She shuddered in both fear and anger. No doubt, she thought, taming some other poor creature! To his lordship's surprise she stamped a little boot most forcefully upon the deck.

'Quite agree!' she said. 'Shocking thing to happen when we were all peacefully asleep in our bunks, relying on the Captain to steer us safely through the perilous seas.'

Mirabelle smiled at him, dragging her mind from what had happened that morning. Every moment was delightful but Captain King, she felt, failed in his own duties, just as she was failing in hers.

'Have you seen Aunt Hatty?' she said. Someone must have seen her chaperone in the last hour or two.

'What?' Lord Carshalton was gazing with interest, at the bustle on the dockside.

Mirabelle joined him. 'I've lost Aunt Hatty.' She felt very guilty at the loss of her relative. She had, perhaps, spent too much time saying her farewells to Ernest and the Captain.

'Saw her before breakfast,' said his lordship. 'Looking for you if I remember correctly.'

'Oh, dear! I'm dreadfully worried!' Mirabelle leaned much further over the rail than was safe and wrung her hands in severe agitation. 'We were supposed to set off together.'

'My dear girl! My dear, dear girl!' exclaimed Lord Carshalton, throwing a hand about her shaking shoulders. 'Don't take on so! She'll turn up, you know. Things usually do!'

Mirabelle's head, so deeply bent in anguish, snapped up and she glared at his lordship. 'How dare you? My aunt is not a "thing"!'

Somewhat subdued, he relaxed his grip, which was the most awful shame since his fingers were on the very points of stroking the sideswell of a delightful breast. 'Oh, quite!' he agreed.

Mirabelle turned to him, her sudden anger dispelled by her deep concern. 'What am I to do?' she murmured, her blue eyes wide and seeking advice from an older and wiser man.

'Can't see why you're taking on so,' said Lord Carshalton, sounding bemused.

'Can't see why I'm taking on so?' Mirabelle echoed crossly. 'If you lost your aunt, wouldn't you take on?'

His lordship patted her arm, looking up and down the deck. Mirabelle's voice when she was cross tended to become loud and shrill. The patting, he hoped, would calm her and he brought his fingers closer to the taut fullness of her tempting bosom.

'Well, no, actually!' he said with a rueful grin. 'Frightful harridan, my aunt!'

'Well, mine is a dear! Gets things wrong most of the time, but a dear for all that.'

'Quite!' agreed Lord Carshalton, taking the most agreeable way out of the question of aunts. 'But really no need to be in such a taking,' he patted her arm again, leaning closer to the slender but voluptuous figure. 'Realising that the aunt was, shall we say, not quite tickety-boo in the upper works, took the liberty of giving her directions to the Hall.'

This was a great relief to Mirabelle and she showed her gratitude in a sweetly intimate kiss at the very earliest opportunity.

# Chapter 7

The summer mist swallowed the big chestnut with its two riders.

Hatty May clung frantically to the broad back of her abductor. Her mind was filled with questions. Who was he? Why had he taken her? Was she to be held to ransom?

She shuddered, not with fear, but with a thrill of anticipation. 'Who are you?' she managed, her voice shaky with the steady jolting upon the horse. Her words were blown away by the slipstream of their passage along the country road and he was silent.

Drawers damp at the apex of her thighs, she wriggled upon the horse's broad, warm back. She was, at one and the same time, afraid of her fate, but thrilled at the excitement the man engendered.

The mystery man was tall and broad and, no doubt, handsome beneath the mask. What could he want with her? She closed her eyes against the green misty landscape of England, remembering her marriage.

'Samuel!' she whispered mutely. How she missed him, her husband of such a short time. 'Samuel!' she whispered again, louder this time.

The horseman turned his head. 'Samuel?' he questioned. Despite his mask and the low brim of his hat, Hatty knew he was frowning, puzzled.

The sound of his voice brought her out of her reverie. 'Who are you?' she asked again. 'Why are you taking me?' The jolting of the fast gallop made her buttocks ache and she wondered when it would end. The mystery thrilled her to her core. It was like Samuel's games. She smiled behind her veil at the memory.

'Not far now,' the stranger said tersely.

Once long ago, so it seemed to the young widow, Samuel had ridden into a thickly wooded area and stripped her of her clothes. It was raining that day, she remembered, a steady fine rain which drifted through the trees soaking her long fair hair and wetting her pale skin.

'Stand straight,' Samuel ordered.

He was fully clothed against the chill of the rain. A broad-brimmed hat and a long weather coat covered him from head to toe. He held a hank of silken rope in one hand and a paddle in the other.

'Look ahead,' he ordered. 'Don't watch me.'

His tone wasn't cruel, Hatty remembered. It was soft, caressing, as the voice of a lover should be. She saw his dark eyes flicker over her shining body, lingering for a moment upon her pink, erect nipples which had tautened in the chill of the drifting rain. His gaze drifted lazily to the honey-gold triangle which was her pussy. He watched the fine rain gather to form heavy drops which eventually trickled down the pale firmness of her thighs.

'Do you want me to do it?' he said, lifting his eyes to look into her grey ones.

A dew of rain had gathered on Hatty's lashes and it fell upon her breasts as she looked up pleadingly. 'You know I do!' she said plaintively. 'More than anything!' Her full lips trembled as though tears were about to fall and join the rain on her tip-tilted breasts.

'You don't mind the pain?' he asked. He slipped the hank of rope further up his arm and slapped the broad paddle on his flattened palm.

Slowly, she shook her head, feeling the movement of her hair, made heavy by the rain.

She could bear the pain, she thought, for the beauty of

the sensations which Samuel created afterwards. Her silky skin rippled at the thought of what he would do afterwards. Love dew was warm as it seeped from her cunney, mixing with the chilling rain. Even that, the fine, drifting curtains of rain, were part of the beauty of that day.

'If you're sure,' Samuel murmured.

Hatty turned of her own accord, knowing what he wanted of her. She faced a big tree, so big that her shapely arms could not encompass its girth. Stretching up, her fingertips just touched the lower branches. The movement lifted her breasts and pressed them against the rough bark of the tree, abrading the tender skin.

Her husband stood behind her. She could feel his caped coat pressing against her back; could hear his breathing, fast and ragged as he wrapped the silken rope, first around one wrist and then the other. It was long, the rope, and he allowed the loose end to trail down the length of her back. He pressed it into the deep cleft of her bottom, pressing it tight. The rest he used to tie her ankles, spreading them wide, her toes just resting upon the thick root boles of the old tree.

This was what she enjoyed: the helplessness of his tethering. She was vulnerable to his whim; submissive. A soft footfall on the leaf-strewn ground told her that he had stepped away.

Sometimes he teased her; running into the depths of the woods and leaving her for a while. It was during such times that her clitty plagued her mercilessly.

She could feel it growing, becoming hard and erect, peeping out of its tiny hood. Had her hands been free she would have appeased its need, but tied to the tree, she could do nothing.

The tying was so tight that she could not tilt her pelvis to rub the plump cunney lips against the rough bark or press them open. 'Open,' she sighed. How delicious that would have been!

'Come back!' she would sigh to the empty air, but the only sound was the whisper of a breeze through leaf-heavy branches and the splatter of rain drops upon her skin.

Seepage, warm and silky, began slowly within the place between her spread thighs. The place seemed swollen, together with the folds within it. Heat burned the tender places and exquisite sensations made her head swim.

The tethering placed a tension not only upon her wrists and ankles, but also on her breasts, stretching the fullness and making the nipples tender as they brushed the rough bark. This, in turn, added to the sensations between her splayed thighs.

'Now, my darling,' she heard above the rain. He was there in the forest, hiding, watching, taunting her. 'Not long now.' His voice was closer, but from a different direction. 'And you shall have your heart's desire.' Closer still.

Her buttocks, the fine, high, haughty buttocks, twitched involuntarily. The silken rope in the cleft rubbed the tender place, made more tender by the relentless rain.

'I can see that you're ready for me.'

She tried to turn her head in the direction of the voice, but the tethering prevented it. The long blonde hair swung this way and that, a wet shimmering hank of gold. She felt it stroke the upper limits of her buttocks, tantalising the sensitive skin.

The paddle slapped the wet, quivering flesh. She could not help but murmur in surprise for he'd crept up on her from out of the woods.

Maybe the rain on her wet skin made it more sensitive, but certainly the next and subsequent slaps of the big paddle had a profound effect upon her flesh. Heat made the skin glow so hotly that she was certain, had she been able to view her rear, wraiths of steam would be rising from the place. Her breasts, too, shuddered at every blow, shaking them against the bark.

Very soon, he released her, allowed her to lean against the tree. Her cheeks were wet, both with rain and tears. Opening her eyes, she saw him and her sobs became a quick drawn gasp.

'Is this what you want, my darling?' he whispered.

He was naked and the rain streamed down his handsome body, gathering at the dark bush from which speared his penis. It was strong and hard and eminently manly. It was beautiful, she realised, and made more beautiful by what she had suffered.

'Yes!' she sighed, holding out her pale arms, to gather him to her.

Her legs were straddled, ready for him. She knew her plump labia were open. It only remained for him to spear her with the wonderful thickness. Trembling, she arched her mound towards him, offering herself.

His excitement was great, matching hers. With no effort, they coupled in that alien environment, ecstatic in each other's arms. His thickness filled her, throbbing against the warm cushion of her passage.

All too soon it was over and he took her back, still naked, riding behind him in the drenching rain, her bottom pained but adding beautifully to the memory of their loving.

'We're here.'

The voice was strange, not Samuel's.

'Wake up!'

Had she been asleep? Under her petticoats the soft cotton of her drawers felt warm and slippery. She was lifted down from the horse. She smiled up, expecting to see Samuel's face, but the features were masked by black silk. She shuddered.

It was the stranger. The abductor.

'So Aunt Hatty has not arrived?' asked Mirabelle worriedly.

Lady Carshalton smiled at Mirabelle sympathetically. 'I'm sorry, my dear,' she said sincerely. 'Not a sign and my husband gave me a detailed description, I am sure I should have recognised such a delightful lady.'

The party at Carshalton Hall was in full spate. All the English rich and famous were there and it promised to be the party of the Season. Such a pity that Mirabelle could not enjoy it to the full; could not fulfill Mama's instruction to find a clutch of husbands for the Washington Estate.

Mirabelle adjusted her *décolletage*, pulling it to a position upon her smooth shoulders of which she knew Diddy, her maid in Atlanta, would thoroughly disapprove. She tried to concentrate on her appointed task but she was so worried about Aunt Hatty.

'Ah, thank you, Amos,' said Lady Carshalton to a handsome footman who offered a silver salver holding several frosted champagne glasses.

It did not escape Mirabelle that a most intimate look passed between the liveried footman and the elegant Lady Carshalton.

'A little diversion!' whispered her ladyship, behind her fan. Lady Carshalton's cheeks were flushed and her eyes were bright as they followed the footman across the room.

Mirabelle licked her lips, contemplating what the fine figure of a man would feel like beside her in a bed of . . .

'We rode to the folly at the far end of the estate,' revealed Lady Carshalton dreamily, her voice a hushed whisper as she related the history of the diversion with Amos. 'I could not resist him! He took me roughly upon a marble bench in the folly.'

Mirabelle gazed at her hostess. She looked too distant, too aristocratic, to do anything so outrageous as to entertain a liveried servant in such an intimate manner. Under her splendid gown, Mirabelle went through an agony of frustration.

Amos naked, lying over her on the ice-cold marble of the folly, thrusting into her roughly. Her own diversion with Captain King had set up the most perilous of sensations.

Joshua, her first love, had been the appetiser and Ernest, too. What of him? She must forget them. Concentrate on Mama's instructions.

'Could you introduce me to one or other of the titled gentlemen?' asked Mirabelle, gritting her teeth in anguish, but determined to please Mama.

'Oh, my dear!' said Lady Carshalton. 'How dreadfully boorish of me! To prattle on in such a fashion about my . . .' She dipped behind her fan before continuing. 'Diversions, when you have such pressing matters upon your own sweet mind.' She looked around the room. 'There is the King, of course,' she said, closing her fan and pointing to the bearded King Edward deep in conversation with his mistress, Mrs Keppel.

'Such a dear man!' exclaimed Lady Carshalton. 'Such fun, but married to dear Queen Alexandra.' She pointed across the room to a handsome lady who did not seem at all put out by the presence of a mistress.

Lady Carshalton frowned, her eyes darting about the glittering gathering. 'Sir Everard Mountjoy,' she murmured almost to herself. She patted Mirabelle's arm and shook her head. 'I don't think he is at all right for you.' She used a delicate finger to lift kiss curls from Mirabelle's ear. 'Has some strange tastes in sexual diversion, so I hear, but unmarried.' Her ladyship looked at Mirabelle questioningly.

Adjusting her *décolletage* she was about to march briskly up to the knight, but before she could do so, a jolly voice interrupted the intimate tête-à-tête of the two ladies.

'Introduce me!' demanded the newcomer.

'Oh, Lord Reginald!' exclaimed Lady Carshalton. 'What a fright you gave me appearing at my shoulder!'

Mirabelle gave a secretive smile, wondering whether her ladyship was put in a fright in case the newcomer had overheard their intimate revelations.

'Dash it all!' Lord Reginald straightened his white tie and

groomed his moustache. 'Didn't mean to do such a thing, but this raven-haired filly looked so . . .' His dark eyes glinted at the ivory mounds peeping so fully over the plunge of Mirabelle's neckline. 'So positively . . .' Again words failed him as she turned the lustrous blue eyes upon him. 'I have never seen . . .'

Lady Carshalton, ever the gracious hostess, came to the stuttering lord's rescue. 'This is Miss Mirabelle Washington, newly arrived from America.'

'Can't tell you how delighted!' exclaimed Lord Reginald taking the hand which Mirabelle offered as she dipped a deep curtsy.

'Lord Reginald Rover is a dear friend of my husband,' explained her ladyship.

Mirabelle graced the gentleman with a sweet smile, although her heart was heavy and his lordship left her pussy as cold as ice. Why, oh, why did she disobey her father and dismiss the handsome young men as of no account in her life?

'Planning to stay in London?' asked Lord Reginald, leading her through a vast doorway and into the hot house environment of the conservatory.

'I haven't decided where to stay,' she replied, eyeing his lordship's mature visage. She could almost have been looking at her father. Her gaze strayed into the ballroom, perhaps searching for Amos or other stimulating company.

'Could give you a jolly time in London!' Lord Reginald was patting her leg, rather too far above her knee for her peace of mind.

Gently and with a sweet smile, Mirabelle removed his hand. 'I've lost my chaperone,' she said, explaining her modesty.

'Careless, that!' said Lord Reginald, becoming bolder and edging along the love seat to be in a position to enfold Mirabelle in his arms. 'Losing one's chaperone.'

'So you understand I cannot . . .' She fluttered her fan meaningfully.

'Oh, quite!' agreed Lord Reginald, but failed to remove his arm from the silky smoothness of Mirabelle's shoulders. 'Absolutely! Wouldn't compromise you!'

What would it be like, she asked herself, sitting very stiffly in the little love seat. What would it be like to be compromised by this gentleman? Until this moment she had known only the caresses of employees. Was she being unfair in dismissing the aristocracy as being of no account in her love life?

She sighed deeply. Life was such a trial since Papa took everything so much to heart!

'Aaah!' she heard beside her. A soft finger trailed across the ivory hillocks of her breasts. 'Forgive me, my dear!' pleaded Lord Reginald. 'Such a charming sight was created to be caressed!'

Perhaps he was right, she thought. Perhaps she was dismissing him too soon, just as she had dismissed her beaux in Atlanta. Another sigh caused her bosom to heave once more.

'Such sadness in a beautiful young lady!' exclaimed Lord Reginald. 'What is affecting you so?'

With dewy blue eyes, Mirabelle gazed at his lordship and a visible shudder seemed to overtake him. Looking down in an attitude of modesty she noticed how very patently she was affecting him.

'Is there somewhere—?' she said in a sweet low voice.

'Yes!' he interrupted hurriedly. 'What do you require, my dear? I am yours to command!'

Anxious to pursue the investigation of the nobility she took his hand and hurried him outside upon the gracious terrace. 'Do you know a folly on the estate?' she asked, looking up into his dark eyes with her own feverish blue ones.

'There are several, my dear, or so I'm led to believe,' he informed her, sweeping her close to him.

Mirabelle was immediately aware how deeply Lord

Reginald felt about her. His cock was stiff and pressing through the several layers of her skirts and petticoats.

'Oh, drat!' she exclaimed, biting her full lower lip. 'Do you know where the nearest one is situated?'

Lord Reginald chuckled merrily. 'I wasn't aware that I could have such an effect on young ladies these days!'

Mirabelle, her lovely face lifted to his in the summer moonlight, pouted her rosebud lips. 'Well, you can!' she assured him. 'Now are you going to take me to this folly or not?'

'Absolutely!'

Taking her by the hand he fairly ran with her to a rough path which branched from the main drive. Beyond the brightness and music of the party they were suddenly plunged into darkness for they had entered a small copse of old, and overhanging, yew trees.

'Can we go to one of the other follies?' said Mirabelle nervously. 'It's so dark!'

A strong arm swept around her tiny waist, drawing her to him. 'Don't be afraid,' he soothed. 'I especially want you to see this one!'

Mirabelle shuddered as her bare shoulders were brushed by overhanging branches. 'Why?' she asked in a voice which trembled.

'It has an interesting history,' he said, unable to disguise a chuckle. 'Very interesting.'

Barely able to keep up with him, Mirabelle's little feet stumbled as he hurried hastily through the trees.

'Dear friends of mine used this folly as a diversion,' he explained breathlessly, stopping for a moment to calm himself and to hold her close. Mirabelle felt his hands smooth over the pouting slope of her lower back until they reached the splendid swells of her bottom. 'Dear friends!' he reminisced happily.

'A lady and gentleman?' queried Mirabelle, her blue eyes as innocent as an angel's as they gazed up at him. Forgetting her own diversions with her strange assortment of lovers she allowed herself to enjoy his slow caress, swaying her shapely body back and forth against him.

'No!' denied his lordship vehemently. 'More! Much more!'

The slow caresses stopped abruptly and they were hurrying through the trees with Mirabelle puzzling as to the meaning of the cryptic explanation.

'Here we are!'

Mirabelle peered through the darkness. There was a round temple, Grecian style, she supposed, sitting on the peak of a grassy knoll, starkly white in the pale moonlight.

'It's pretty,' she remarked.

'Dash it! It's more than pretty once we get inside! It inspired my three friends no end!' exclaimed Lord Reginald excitedly.

It took a few moments for Mirabelle's eyes to become accustomed to the gloom, but when they did she could only gasp. There were several large stone figures arranged in a ring. They were male and exceedingly large.

'Ooooh!' she exclaimed. 'Lord Reginald . . .' She looked around her, her eyes widening, thinking that they were deceiving her. His lordship was nowhere to be seen. She was, apparently, alone in the little folly.

'Lord Reginald?' She tried to keep the panic from her voice and found herself stroking the coldness of one of the statues, as if to receive comfort from it.

'That's it, m'dear!' she heard. 'Stroke as much as you like! As intimately as you like and for as long as you like!'

'Lord Reginald?' she whispered, surprise and fear of this strange place taking away her voice.

'No need to be afraid!' assured his lordship. 'That's me you are stroking so tenderly.'

Mirabelle pulled back her fingers as though the muscular stone thorax was as hot as the fires of hell.

'No, no, no!' Lord Reginald sounded impatient. 'Stroke

and stroke lower. I'm in the statue, don't you see? It's a game, a little diversion.'

Dimpled fingers twitching nervously she replaced them at the waist of the big statue. The stone was as cold and as unresilient as ever. 'I don't understand!' she murmured.

Lord Reginald sighed. 'Down!' he ordered. 'Sink to your knees before the statue and close those gloriously pretty little rosebud lips around the cock and you will see!'

Kiss a statue, thought Mirabelle, puzzled beyond measure, but she did as she was bid. Her elegant gown had suffered during the impatient dash through the overhanging trees. Her breasts were exposed by a tear at the low neckline. She felt them brush, not cold stone, but warm flesh as she sank to the marble floor.

'Oooh!' she exclaimed once more, wondering what part of the statue's anatomy could possibly have brushed the soft cushion of her breast.

'Aaah!' echoed Lord Reginald quite plainly.

It could only be one thing, she decided. Lips parted and softly moist, she pecked at the end of an exceedingly erect and turgid, although marble-white, penis. It was warm and beautifully smooth. She tasted the salt of male sap and licked her lips hungrily.

'Aaah!' came the sigh of pleasure again.

'But how?' she said, feeling her own pleasure in the nakedness of her breasts. The taste caused her young nipples to spring to instant erection and her hands caressed the pliant and tender pillows, increasing her pleasure.

'When you were so busy gazing round at my companions,' Lord Reginald explained, 'I applied a little enhancement to my own marble!' He was breathless, she noticed, and his terse voice was a measure of his impatience. 'Now, please, dearest Mirabelle . . .'

Wide blue eyes perused the long and throbbing organ which protruded from the statue's hollow shell. It blended quite elegantly with the muscular torso and it was so hard to believe that it was not marble like the rest.

'If you don't do something to relieve my passion,' continued Lord Reginald, 'I shall be stuck here for the duration!'

Softening her lips once more Mirabelle impaled herself upon Lord Reginald's cock, allowing it to touch the very limit of her palate. The sigh of pleasure issuing from the statue was prolonged and one of ecstasy.

Mirabelle felt the excitement of forbidden pursuits just as she felt with Joshua, Ernest and the Captain. She realised that, with her strict upbringing, she required a sense of naughtiness to enjoy sexual diversions.

Her tongue caressed the throbbing length within the soft moistness of her mouth with more vigour. Yes, she assured herself, she could enjoy the cocks of the nobility . . .

The throbbing increased and she pampered the length vigorously, feeling the silk of the globe in the welcoming moistness of her gullet. Creamily, the issue foamed upon her tongue and she swallowed it with great enjoyment.

All it needed, she told herself, was a little imagination!

# Chapter 8

Gathering her into his arms, Hatty's abductor held her snugly. She quivered against him. Her breasts seemed suddenly over full and painfully tight within her peachy skin. The nipples, she felt, were as hard as cherry stones and tender against the light covering of her softly frilled bodice. She felt him brush against these tender places and she felt a sudden seepage of warmth moisten the soft cotton of her drawers.

The two, captor and captive, stood close in the cobbled yard of the inn. Unmoving and silent, they held each other for a moment which seemed an age.

Beneath the veil Hatty's face was pale. She was apprehensive, still wondering why he had taken her. What did he want from her? It was at times like this that she needed Mirabelle. Darn the girl! Where could she have gone on the *Gloriana*?

She looked up, peering through the veil, questioning the motives behind her abduction. She had little money. What did he expect from her? She shuddered again, remembering her daydream. Of Samuel and his gentle torment.

The clasp of his hands upon her arms loosened. 'Shall we go inside?' he asked. The question was posed tenderly, as though they were on intimate terms. It was another puzzle and she frowned behind the dark veil. Did he think he knew her?

'We're expected,' he continued. His hand led her firmly at one elbow. The touch was casual, but eminently sensual.

'Expected?' Hatty's voice repeated the word tremulously. He had planned everything, she realised. Meticulous, she labelled him, as she peered at him through her veil. It frightened her, this careful planning. She was suddenly anxious to escape his disturbing presence. She wrenched from his grasp, unsteady on the uneven cobbles.

'Where do you think you're going, you little fool?' he snapped sharply. He stood in the middle of the courtyard, tall and somehow menacing in his billowing cape and wide-brimmed hat.

Hatty trembled from head to foot, stumbling backwards with small uneven steps. 'I . . . don't . . . know!' she admitted in a small quavering voice. Why was she so nervous, she asked herself. As yet, he hadn't threatened her, but she should be angry with him. What right had he to bring her to this place? Where was she? Tears filled her grey eyes. 'I don't know,' she repeated, her voice breaking into a sob.

'Exactly!' he said triumphantly. 'You have no idea where you are, so there is nowhere for you to go.' His voice was quiet and assured, knowing that he had the ascendancy. 'So why don't you do as you're told and behave.' He stood, arms folded, taking on an arrogance.

This made her uncertain mood veer to anger. 'Just who the hell are you?' she spat, her gloved hands suddenly at the deep cinch of her waist in an attitude of defiance.

Looking down at her he clicked his tongue and shook his head in mock disgust. A dry, cynical chuckle preceded a reprimand. 'Is that any way for a lady to talk?'

Her pulse began to pound erratically. His attitude, the annoying arrogance coupled with his evasive manner, made her react angrily. She strode briskly back across the cobbles to challenge him. 'I'll talk any way I want to!' She glared up at him from behind her veil. 'And you haven't answered my question. Who are you?'

His green eyes glinted at her sardonically over the mask.

'You'll find out soon enough!' he told her. He snaked a muscular arm about the tininess of her waist, pulling her to him.

She could feel his manhood, hard and hot, through her skirts and she felt herself melt against it. The world was suddenly filled with him. A protest rose in a throat suddenly too dry for speech. A terrible weakness suffused her limbs and a great moistness washed between the folds of her pussy. She closed her eyes, giving herself up to him, but suddenly, he gave that infuriating chuckle and released his tight hold about her waist.

'We're expected,' he said again, leading her into the inn.

A portly gentleman, the landlord, greeted them with a smiling face and twinkling eyes. His eyes swept approvingly over Hatty, but she lowered her head, not wanting to meet his gaze.

'Your room is ready for you,' he said, turning his attention to the tall man at Hatty's side. 'Chambermaid has been fussing up there for an hour or more.' He leaned on the bar, trying to peer through Hatty's veil. 'Pretty little thing . . .' He eyed her intimately, allowing his eyes to linger especially on the swell of her hips and buttocks which were so fashionably full. 'Aye, splendid figure of a woman!'

Hatty darted a reproving look at her abductor. As much as she liked compliments, she didn't like being appraised like a prize cow!

'I think there's been some mistake!' she cried, making a dash for the open door.

'No, you don't!' The highwayman was too quick for her. He grasped her small hand as she darted past him, gripping it cruelly and she was pulled back close to him, held in his arms.

He held her so tightly that her body was bowed, pressing the yielding softness of her pussy into his hardness. For a brief moment, Hatty May felt herself melting into him again. He seemed to have a magnetic effect upon her.

'No mistake!' he countered. 'No mistake at all!'

The landlord chuckled, resting his hands upon the white apron stretched so tautly over his belly. 'Lover's tiff?' he asked, his dark eyes darting from one to the other.

Hatty May saw green eyes glinting at her through the darkness of her veil. His hand flew up as if to tear the big hat from her head, reveal her face to his flashing eyes. The swift movement caused her to cringe away, stiffening and tugging at his hand. He sighed behind the mask and Hatty relaxed as she saw the green eyes soften.

'Go upstairs,' he said, releasing her and thrusting her away at one and the same time. 'And wait for me.' He turned to the landlord, pointing to the huge barrel of ale.

'What right have you to tell me . . .' Hatty stamped her foot crossly. 'I'm not a child and I shan't be treated like one!'

'Oh, my word!' interjected the landlord, looking at the scene over his broad shoulder.

'Wait for me!' There was both fire and ice in the repeat of his command and something which made a thrill ripple from the button of her clitty. The folds of her cunney felt soft and moist and her breasts swelled gloriously.

Part of her wanted to disobey him, but the sensual core of her melted at the sound of his command.

'Sassy little madam!'

The words followed her up the flight of narrow, uneven stairs which led to the upper floor of the inn. Deliberately, she found herself swaying her buttocks and hips as she imagined him watching her progress.

The maid, a fresh-cheeked girl, waited for her by an open door, beckoning her into a low-ceilinged room.

Hatty May gasped with delight as she entered, unfastening her veil and throwing her hat upon a large four-poster bed.

'Anything wrong, Miss?' asked the girl, looking nervous as she heard the gasp.

'Everything's just fine!' Hatty threw herself upon the

bed, allowing the duck-down mattress to enfold her. Would he lie beside her on the vast space? Would he force her to accept his manhood? She hugged herself, shivering with anticipation. It had been so long since Samuel held her on just such a bed as this.

'You'll want water to wash after the journey,' said the girl, as Hatty began to unpin her long blonde curls, shaking them free, letting the tresses fall heavily over her shoulders.

Hatty nodded, taking a deep breath as she tried to relax. She smiled at the girl as she scrambled down from the big bed.

The maid gave a little bobbing curtsy. 'It's on the range,' she said softly. 'I'll be back in a trice!'

The door closed behind the pretty girl's firm, but voluptuous figure. Thoughtfully, Hatty slipped her travelling coat from her slender shoulders, letting it fall to the floor in careless abandon.

The man, the highwayman, seemed to think that he knew her, but he was a stranger, she was sure.

Scarcely a minute had passed, it seemed to Hatty, when the door opened and she looked up expectantly. Expecting what? she wondered. Him? It was the pretty maid bearing a great porcelain jug of hot water.

'Here we are,' said the girl brightly, setting the jug on a marble washstand. 'The gentleman said I was to tend you.'

'Tend me?' Hatty repeated shivering.

She could see the girl in the dressing mirror and Hatty noticed that she was staring, quite blatantly, at her breasts, the slenderness of her waist and the swell of her hips.

'Yes, Miss.' The maid licked her lips, smiling almost lasciviously. This was no young innocent as Hatty had first supposed. The look made her belly soften beneath the confinement of her corsets.

Deliciously attractive and perhaps, thought Hatty, the same age as Mirabelle. She had the same glorious bloom of youth on her cheeks and the same expectant glimmer in her wide eyes.

The firm young breasts were free of restriction under her white cotton blouse. The nipples were dark and large under the thin cloth. A black skirt fell heavily from a clearly defined waist and swung attractively over the generous curves of her hips.

'My name's Rose,' she said leaning over Hatty's trembling shoulders to begin slipping open the tiny buttons of her frilled blouse.

Her fingers were cool and gentle on Hatty's hot flesh. They brushed across nipples which immediately sprang to hard erection. Both blouse and under-bodice were quickly removed to bare her pale mounds.

Rose gazed into the mirror, looking into Hatty's eyes, seeking approval. In a moment they were standing close together with the maid taking each bud in turn between her lips. Sharp little teeth grated lightly, making tiny shocks of pleasure spark through Hatty's body.

'Not hurting, Miss?' asked the maid.

'Oh, no!' gasped Hatty breathlessly.

'Ain't you never been kissed by a woman before, Miss?' Hatty felt her nipples, still damp from Rose's kisses, circled by light fingertips.

Hatty shook her head, her cheeks reddening in an infuriating manner, embarrassed at her own innocence. For all that dear Samuel was an inventive lover, he had never introduced her to another woman in an intimate manner.

'The gentleman downstairs—'

'What about him?' Hatty rapped out, her grey eyes wide.

The girl slipped a button at Hatty's waist, letting her skirt fall heavily over her hips. 'He said you were an innocent!'

'How dare he?' Hatty was suddenly angry that he should make such an assumption about a married lady, and a widow at that!

'He wanted me to prepare you.' Rose's voice was suddenly appealingly low and husky.

'Prepare me?' Hatty felt Rose's nimble fingers at her

petticoat waistband. Again there was this assumption of innocence, she felt, frowning. Her belly softened as the fingers stroked across the slight swell and she knew that her drawers were quite saturated with warm, moist evidence of this strange afternoon.

'Prepare me for what?' she asked.

The question was ignored.

'A lovely little figure you have, Miss,' murmured Rose. 'So shapely and neat, but perhaps rather tightly confined by those stays.'

The dampened drawers were quickly discarded and Rose admired the curves conjured by the corsets with lightly dancing fingers. These strayed quickly to the plump softness of her mound with the light frosting of blonde curls.

Hatty May swayed against the girl, moaning softly. 'That's nice,' she murmured.

The plump pad was gently tantalised by Rose's fingers. 'I know, miss,' she agreed. She cupped the trembling softness, making Hatty May wriggle joyously.

'Don't you feel better for these caresses?' purred Rose, standing back to admire her charge.

Hatty watched the maid pour water from the jug into a porcelain bowl. This simple action, executed by Rose, took on a delicious sensuality. She felt her little belly suck inwards, soft and pliant, and her pussy mound pout eagerly from the lower margin of her corset. A soft piece of flannel was dipped in water, wrung out and rubbed with the finest of soaps.

'If your ladyship would be so kind as to lie upon the bed with her legs outstretched,' suggested Rose.

In a daze, Hatty climbed upon the high bed, quite aware that she was giving Rose the plainest of views of her pale buttocks. She knelt in this position for a long time, it seemed; bottom high and thighs open. Flirting, she thought. She was flirting with the chambermaid!

'Very pretty, Miss!' remarked Rose. The warm, soapy

flannel was wiped lightly over the pale hillocks. The flannel was silkily smooth with lather and it caressed the trembling mounts deliciously.

Unable to prevent herself, Hatty parted her thighs and tilted her pelvis to give Rose a plain view of her plump and swollen cunney.

'Oh, I can see it!' the girl cried delightedly. 'A dear pink nest!'

The piece of flannel was wiped, so gently that the touch was feather light, down the moist length of Hatty May's cunney. Each fold was given the same gentle treatment. It was so beautiful that it was torment. She found herself pressing firmly upon the touch of the flannel, eager for satisfaction.

'Lie flat for me, my dear,' begged Rose. 'Flat upon your back with legs wide open.'

Trembling, Hatty May did as she was bid, looking up at Rose with pleading, wide grey eyes. The girl was kneeling between her open legs, her bodice open and her heavy, but beautifully shaped, breasts quite bare.

The flannel was set aside and a plump index finger touched the very peak of the little button which was Hatty's eager clitty. The touch made her whole body jerk at the power of the sensation which shot through her.

'Gentle stimulation,' murmured Rose. 'You are a lady of especial sensitivity.' Immediately, she bent between Hatty May's accommodating thighs and a tongue, moist and light in its touch, lapped the urgent peak of the clitty.

Rosebud lips, parted moistly, whispered a moan. Since dear Samuel had been taken from her Hatty had been starved of intimacy. Involuntarily, she arched from the bed, offering her cunney to the soft gentleness of the questing mouth.

The tongue was agile, softly abrading every part of the jutting clitty. The peak, which protruded so tautly from the tiny hood, was given special attention as was the sensitive under part. No woman, especially a young lusty one like Hatty May, could take such tender caresses for too long without reaching a climax.

'It is upon me!' cried Hatty May. 'My spend!'

'Yes, my dear!' answered Rose. 'I feel it! I see it! Your love sap trickles over my fingers. Your entrance grips them so sweetly.'

'My need was great,' murmured Hatty. 'I have been alone for so long.'

'So I believe, my dear,' answered Rose.

Puzzled at this, Hatty opened her mouth to speak. What could Rose know of her? she wondered. Questions remained unasked as the girl claimed her lips.

'Let me please you, Rose,' murmured Hatty. 'How shall I do it?'

Rose swayed heavy breasts over Hatty's. 'Would you . . . ?' she began hesitantly.

'Anything, Rose,' promised Hatty. 'Anything at all.'

Their nipples caressed, one causing the other to become erect. 'But you are so innocent of the ways of the world.' Rose brushed kisses across closed eyelids, making Hatty shudder deliciously.

'Teach me!' pleaded Hatty.

Rose took a deep breath. 'Would it be too much to ask of your ladyship for her to allow me to straddle my thighs about her lovely face?'

Hatty May gave a cry of delight. She was about to say that Rose was as inventive as her dear husband, but something warned her against such boldness. 'Nothing would please me more!' she replied and she held out her arms.

Rose's lips were warm and sweet on hers as she struggled to free herself from the simple garments which remained on her body. Their tongues fenced and Hatty was surprised at the delicious taste of her own musk in the other's mouth.

Soon, Hatty May found her mouth buried in the softness of the musky pleasure of Rose's cunney. With questing fingers she spread the plump lips to delve more deeply with tongue and teeth.

'That's right, my beauty,' whispered Rose huskily. 'Spread me wide to feel every fold and pleat.' The girl grazed herself back and forth upon Hatty May's lips and tongue.

'Feels so good!' moaned Rose. 'You touch my clitty so lightly. Just the tip is lapped by your lovely tongue.' Rose bent over Hatty May's body and reciprocated the action, lapping gently but, at the same time, spreading the plump pussy lips to their limit.

The girl stopped, her body stiffening against Hatty's soft mouth. 'Young sir!' she exclaimed, but immediately afterwards there was a long sigh of pleasure with the pliant flesh fluttering against Hatty's lips.

Hatty, her view of the room occluded by Rose's body, felt herself flush. The highwayman had entered the room and could see every part of her intimate folds.

'What's this?' He spoke with a low, terse tone.

'Only doing as you ordered, sir,' excused Rose. She sounded put out and breathless from her spend. 'Preparing her for you since she is so unfamiliar of worldly ways.'

Hatty May froze as her cunney lips were pinched tightly together and the soaked blonde curls were smoothed.

'Yes,' murmured the highwayman, 'I realise that you are carrying out my orders, but . . .' The damp blonde pussy curls were tweaked so roughly that Hatty was obliged to squeal in pain. 'The question is . . .' The plump lips were caressed gently and the inflamed sensitive clitty was kissed lightly. A thick male finger was slipped into the inviting entrance. 'Who is this woman?' Rose was pulled from Hatty's body and the green eyes glared in amused bewilderment into Hatty's grey ones.

# Chapter 9

'Out of the question, old boy!' said Lord Carshalton. He was quite adamant as he glanced nervously across the room at Mirabelle who was only partially concealed by a large parlour palm.

His mouth watered at the glimpse of a naked milk-white globe tipped with the pertest of erect nipples. His tongue slipped between his lips, fairly itching to lap at the little dear.

'But her ladyship seemed quite taken with the filly!' said Lord Reginald. 'Not as if there was animosity between them.'

His cock twitched at the thought of his playful frolic with Mirabelle among the yew trees. It fairly throbbed as he focused on that same revealed breast.

He gave Mirabelle an encouraging wave. 'Getting along famously earlier.'

He had to admit that the yew trees had done no end of damage to her gown. She looked every inch a street waif. As she danced between the conservatory foliage he caught a transient view of a gloriously rounded buttock. He gasped at the beauty of it sloping down to a perfectly shaped thigh.

Tristham Carshalton forced himself to glance away from the deliciously tantalising peeps of female flesh. 'Never around when one needs them!' he muttered crossly.

'Servants?' asked Lord Reginald helpfully.

'Wives!' came the reply. 'Dash orf on some household duty at a whim! Consequently, not around to answer questions.'

A dainty ankle clad in the neatest of button boots beckoned Lord Reginald from behind the parlour palm. Nothing made his standard rise aloft like a well-turned ankle. He sighed and made a mental note to speak to his tailor about the tightness of his evening trousers about the crotch.

'Hm,' he agreed, wondering whether the mention of Lady Carshalton disappearing into the cellars with Amos would spoil the conviviality of the evening. I mean to say, he thought to himself with a frown, was she engaged in other than household duties?

Mirabelle waved again, leaning boldly to the side of the lush foliage and displaying far more of her bounteous loveliness than was acceptable in English polite society. Perhaps, thought Lord Carshalton, they were more liberal in America.

'Get back!' mouthed Lord Reginald, gesturing that Mirabelle should spirit herself away into the depths of the conservatory jungle.

'A gown, Tristham,' he said turning to Lord Carshalton and dabbing his glowing forehead with a large pocket handkerchief. 'That is all I require. Merely for the duration of the Ball. I'm sure your good lady would be only too pleased if she has – er – completed her household duties.'

'If it was entirely up to me, old boy,' said Lord Carshalton, 'I'd say "yes" like a shot!' From the corner of his eye he saw his friend, Mr George Lloyd disappear into the jungle-like foliage.

'Haven't I heard you say, on more than one occasion, that her ladyship has, in her wardrobe, sufficient gowns to fill Bond Street?' Lord Reginald appealed to his friend's generosity.

'And Regent Street!' agreed his lordship.

'Then one would not be missed, would it?'

Lord Carshalton shook his head. 'Catalogues them scrupulously, old chap. She would miss a single button!'

His worries, he had to admit, were not entirely focused upon buttons. The American filly made one's balls draw up and cock rise. He feared that his self control was not up to restraining his lust. Caught too many times at infidelity, he had no wish to try Lady Carshalton's tolerance at this particular time.

Lord Reginald was put out. He had been hoping to spend the rest of the evening, not to say the weekend, in the company of the delightful Miss Mirabelle. Now, because of a spoiled gown and a hostess who disappeared when she was most needed, his plan was foiled.

Downheartedly, he approached the conservatory. Such was his distraction that he failed to notice a shapely limb being tossed willy-nilly in the air, followed by the pert hillocks of delicious buttocks only partially covered by a silk gown. Neither was he aware of raised voices issuing from the dense foliage.

'Sir! I am a Southern Belle!' came the cry.

'Who likes to dally with a bit of rough in the valleys, I believe!'

'If my dear Daddy was here he would flay you alive!'

A piece of silk, not unlike that which formed what was left of Mirabelle's ballgown, fluttered down from the topmost branch of an Amazonian redwood sapling.

'But you're all alone,' chuckled a well-known Welsh voice, 'and almost naked, isn't it?'

The sound of a playful slap echoed about the conservatory followed by the tearing of fine cloth. 'My boys from the valleys would enjoy you no end! Just what you're looking for, I believe, and certainly what they're looking for!'

'How dare you, sir?'

This, at last, brought Lord Reginald from his reverie. He dashed through the undergrowth on a mission of rescue.

'Lloyd! You blackguard!' cried the hero. 'What are you up to?'

A luxuriant white moustache was stroked lasciviously as it bobbed up from Mirabelle's pale thighs. 'Up to my eyes in the most glorious pussy flesh ever to grace these islands!' said George Lloyd.

Mirabelle, looking dreamily satisfied, lay back languidly upon a small sofa. She smiled up at Lord Reginald assuring him that nothing was amiss.

'Damned good mind to give you a punch on the nose, sirrah!' said Lord Reginald, glaring at Mirabelle.

George Lloyd looked bemused. 'Indeed to goodness!' he exclaimed. 'Why would that be?' His tongue stroked along the love dew glossed moustache, savouring the delicacy of the musk.

With a possessive hand upon Mirabelle's shoulder, Lord Reginald made his announcement. 'This is the girl I mean to marry!'

'Here we are!' said Lord Reginald happily.

Mirabelle peeped cautiously over the softness of a travelling rug. She was still not at all sure that she had done the right thing in agreeing to the suggestion that she should accompany him to London.

'It's lovely,' she said with a distinct lack of enthusiasm.

'Number Six, Peacham Place,' said Lord Reginald. 'My town house.'

Almost naked beneath a travelling rug which chafed her sensitive little teats to the extent that they sprang to instant erection, making her wriggle at the delicious sensation, Mirabelle smiled wanly.

'My darling girl!' sighed the lovestruck peer. 'Say you like it!'

Dimpled fingers eased out of the folds of the travelling rug. They edged towards the fullness within Lord Reginald's trousers. Periwinkle-blue eyes widened ingenuously. 'I adore it!' she murmured softly.

'Ah!' sighed the peer. 'I meant . . .'

Whatever he meant paled into insignificance as the softest of rosebud lips closed around his moist globe.

Her departure from Carshalton Hall had been ignominious with Lord Reginald throwing punches at Mr Lloyd and Mr Lloyd promising that a valley-full of miners would descend on Peacham Place within the week. And she was still extremely concerned about Aunt Hatty May. Where was she and how would she ever find her now?

Wet, cosseting tongue lapping the very base of a splendidly throbbing shaft, Mirabelle pushed unhappy thoughts to the rear of her mind.

'See how it spears up for you, my little turtle dove!' sighed Lord Reginald.

'Hm,' agreed Mirabelle, tracing the length of a pulsing vein to the very pinnacle of the stiff organ. But it does not spear so nicely as Joshua's and Ernest's, she added to herself.

Shivering a little in the dewy dawn of an English summer morning, Mirabelle drew the rug around her. Her soft fingers warmed themselves upon the organ's urgent heat and delved down to the glorious ardour of the turgid ballsack.

'My staff . . .' said Lord Reginald breathlessly.

'Feels beautiful in my hand,' said Mirabelle bobbing up momentarily. The lovely creature was smoothing her satiny palms up and down his length.

'And what ingenious hands they are, my love!' He felt that his vitals were being drawn, inexorably, through his pole. He could think of nothing else but the glory of the sensations being created by the delicious American.

'Oooh!' A ladylike exclamation of dismay issued from Mirabelle's lips.

Lord Reginald's languid eyes were tugged reluctantly to the carriage window. Three pairs of eager eyes gazed, unblinkingly, in at them.

'My staff . . .' grunted Lord Reginald.

'Pulses beautifully!' said Mirabelle, returning her attention to the flesh pole which she massaged so rhythmically.

'I must—!' gasped Lord Reginald.

'Go ahead!' encouraged Mirabelle excitedly. 'Be my guest!'

A high fountain of pearly spend gushed from Lord Reginald's pulsing stem. With a sly smile into the three pairs of unblinking eyes Mirabelle closed her soft lips about the source of the gusher.

'My staff—' he began his lordship once more.

Mirabelle cradled the wilting length. 'Must rest for the moment,' she said, stretching up to plant the softness of kisses upon his parted lips.

The carriage door opened and she was confronted by three bowing figures. 'Oooh!' she said again.

'My staff have lined up to greet you, my dear.'

Mirabelle felt her face flush and she pulled the rug about her. 'I thought . . .' she began glancing at Lord Reginald's trousers. She had thought that by 'staff' he referred to the appendage which was now safely tucked away.

'My loyal staff have turned out to greet the future Lady Rover,' he said with a flourish.

Mirabelle paled. The future looked vague and shadowy. 'I'm not sure . . .' she began, taking Lord Reginald's proffered hand as he helped her down from the carriage. She was not sure that she was ready to be a Lady!

In her mind's eye she saw visions of Joshua, Ernest and even Captain King. If she married Lord Reginald she would miss the joys of the plebian cock. But there was Mama to consider. She smiled winningly at his lordship. Wasn't this exactly what Mama required?

'My Mama is a most beautiful lady,' she said, hoping to encourage him to consider Amelia Jane for the position of Lady Rover.

'I'm sure she is, my dear,' he said vaguely, slipping his hand into the folds of the travelling rug.

His hand encountered the naked fullness of a breast, bereft of gown and bodice. The sensitivity of a nipple was suddenly awakened from its languor to taut erection, probing eagerly between his lordship's tweaking fingers. Mirabelle leaned against him, encouraging his caresses. Perhaps, in time, she would grow to enjoy the soft hands of the aristocracy as opposed to the callouses of the workers.

'Ah, Henry!' boomed Lord Reginald. 'And you Pelham and, of course, Broderick—'

The sudden trumpeting in her shell-like ear startled Mirabelle no end. As a consequence, she stumbled, let go of the travelling rug and was hurtled at full stretch into the elegant entrance hall of Peacham Place.

Her naked breasts encountered the chill of the graceful floor. Her arms and legs were splayed as she slid across the black and white Italian tiles. Her heated pussy, bared by the convenience slit in her drawers, was deliciously cooled by contact with the floor and she sighed, almost blissfully.

'Help Miss Mirabelle Washington to her feet,' ordered Lord Reginald calmly, as though naked ladies careened through the portals of his London residence every day.

Henry Peak gaped lustfully at the beautiful lady spreadeagled upon the floor. Their eyes met and smiled conspiratorially. Levering herself by her hands, she allowed him sight of the splendid mounds of her breasts, peeping over the upper limits of her corsets. With a sly arch of her back she pouted her buttocks, posing the creamy valley revealed by the slit in her drawers.

'My word!' gasped Pelham, the footman.

'How splendid!' crooned Broderick, the butler.

'Cor!' growled Henry appreciatively.

Lord Reginald, busy perusing the pile of letters which had accumulated in his brief absence, left the task of setting Mirabelle upon her feet to his staff.

'Servants aren't what they used to be in the Old Queen's day,' he observed apologetically.

'How do you do, Henry?' she said, stretching up a pale, shapely arm with dainty fingers ready to greet.

The periwinkle blue eyes shifted to Pelham and Broderick. They were all so handsome and rugged that they made her belly soften quite beautifully.

Henry, a young fellow of eighteen, held out his own hand and shook the dainty fingers. 'Very nicely, thanks, Miss,' he assured her. 'Very nicely indeed.'

The greeting exposed the perfection of Mirabelle's breasts as she gazed up at him. The hand which held hers, she noticed, was large and calloused. It was impossible to prevent the flowage of warm love sap bathing her sex lips which the touch of this manly hand engendered.

'Shall I help you up, Miss?' asked Henry, allowing an index finger to twirl around her palm playfully and suggestively.

'Allow me!' said Pelham, smoothing his waistcoat about his muscular chest as he crouched beside her.

'No! No! I insist!' Broderick jumped forward to smooth dark curls from Mirabelle's ivory forehead. 'As master of the servant's hall I feel it is my duty . . .'

Mirabelle gazed up at them. They all sported comely and encouraging bulges between trunk-like thighs. The pretty Miss could not restrain her pink tongue which probed so eagerly between her rosebud lips.

She could taste them now. They would be all freshly dewed with the delicate salt of male sap. 'Hm!' she sighed, quite involuntarily.

'Are you hurt, my lady?' murmured Pelham solicitously.

'Help her up, why don't you?' bellowed Lord Reginald, still much preoccupied with his correspondence. 'I said so, didn't I?'

A great deal of scuffling between the three servants took place. Broderick pushed Pelham aside while the latter swung a punch at Henry. Henry ducked nimbly and the punch landed squarely upon Broderick's nose.

The handsome young Henry tossed a surreptitious glance at his superiors and scooped Mirabelle into his arms. 'Taking madam to the guest suite!' he said quickly, almost running across the polished tiles.

'Most grateful, Henry,' replied Lord Reginald.

Laying her head upon the boot boy's broad shoulder, Mirabelle sighed as she felt the roughened skin of his hand graze over the silky plumpness of her bottom. She shuddered pleasurably as she felt a finger part the deep valley between the graceful hillocks.

'I'll leave you in Henry's capable hands, my dear,' said Lord Reginald abstractedly, disappearing into his study.

'Hmm,' murmured Mirabelle, nuzzling into the welcoming warmth of Henry's neck, prior to caressing the skin with her lips. 'I'm sure he's very capable!'

On strong legs which tended to shake with passion, Henry made his way across the hall.

'Where are you taking me?' murmured Mirabelle, looking up with those glorious blue eyes.

Unable to resist the urge to caress the glorious sideswell of a breast and the underswell of the perfect buttocks, Henry returned her gaze. 'The guest suite, Miss, unless you would rather be accommodated in Lord—'

'No! No!' exclaimed Mirabelle, with a shudder. 'For the time being . . .' She left the words hanging in the air as she was laid gently upon a large and luxurious bed.

The door burst open.

'Now, then, young Henry!' Pelham, his eye looking somewhat the worse for wear, having made contact with Broderick's vengeful fist.

'Oooh!' exclaimed Mirabelle with an excited chuckle.

'Trust you're mindful of your elders and betters!' Broderick, his nose flushed and swollen, appeared at Pelham's shoulder.

Henry looked down at Mirabelle tenderly, his eyes heavy and languid, his lips parted and moist. The large bulge between his thighs seemed, if anything, to be larger. It throbbed noticeably, making the dark cloth of his Peacham Place livery pulse.

'I reckon—' Henry began breathlessly.

'Yes?' sighed Mirabelle, holding out her pale naked arms in an inviting manner.

'Aaah!' he groaned, bending his knees as he adjusted his large and throbbing shoe horn. 'I reckon I'd better go and tend the boots!' he managed.

'That's it, young-fella-me-lad!' crowed Broderick. 'Showing some respect now!'

Mirabelle gave a tiny pathetic sob.

'Something's upset you!' cried Pelham, running to the bedside.

Broderick looked murderous as he took an elegant stride towards her. 'Was it our employer?'

Jet curls shook in wild profusion upon the satin sheets. The ivory breasts shuddered in unison as she negated the question.

'What then?' asked the bemused Henry, returning to the bedside.

'It was Hertfordshire,' explained Mirabelle, cupping her perfect breasts and holding them out to them and stroking the silky hillocks.

The blue eyes were at their most beckoning. The rosebud lips were parted, slick and glossy from the action of her tongue tip.

'Hertfordshire?' The three frowned, puzzled. They were not aware that that respectable county was renowned for tearing ladies gowns from their backs.

'Yew trees,' explained Mirabelle. Her dimpled hands flew to the slit in her drawers. 'With overhanging branches!' Fingers taking the place of twigs she tore the delicate cloth of her under garments and bared the lushness of her jet curled pussy. Her thighs flew apart to display the pinkness of her sex lips.

With a sigh, she closed the eyes which these rampant young fellows could drown in. She was playing for sympathy and she succeeded beautifully.

Swallowing hard, the three men slid across the expanse of satin sheets, closing in upon the lovely maiden in distress.

'And then there was a member,' she continued, 'who kept me prisoner in the conservatory.'

'A member, Miss?' questioned Broderick hoarsely. His own member was imprisoned quite painfully so he was entirely sympathetic to the lady's predicament.

'A Member of Parliament,' she explained. 'He threatened to descend on London and Lord Reginald with co—' Mirabelle burrowed into the cool softness of the pillows once more and the last word was muffled.

Henry, who, despite his youth, was always willing to help a lady in distress, sat next to her, stroking the shuddering shoulders. 'With his co-horts, Miss?' he said helpfully.

'His co—' she attempted again, but Henry's large, capable fingers had drifted down to the elegant erectness of a nipple and quite distracted her from her tale.

'Conscripts, Miss?' said Pelham helpfully.

Mirabelle's glorious face rose from the depths of the satin. 'Coal-miners!' she managed.

'Coal-miners, Miss?' Broderick was already digging into the blackness of Mirabelle's seam. His question was posed absently as the hospitable girl opened her thighs to allow them the secret treasures of her mine.

'Oh, Broderick,' she sighed. 'How very wonderful your fingers feel as they open my passage!'

Bending over the prone loveliness Pelham took the full, ripe cherry of a nipple between his teeth and grated gently while the other was tweaked tenderly by his fingers.

'Oh Miss!' hissed Broderick, abrading his irritated horn against the inner cloth of his trousers. 'Could I perhaps—?'

The large bed was bouncing as an echo of lusty movement by all parties. In her passion Mirabelle tore her drawers from the splendours of her full buttocks and shapely hips while Broderick straddled her, struggling to release his rampant horn.

'Could I perhaps—?' he began again.

'Anything, Broderick, anything!' promised Mirabelle.

'Bury my pick in your shaft!' Broderick managed at last. The long discussion on coal mining had inspired him.

His fingers pressed open the pink folds which nestled within the coal-black lips. 'What a beautiful diamond I see glinting at me in the depths!' he exclaimed.

'My clitty,' she sighed modestly. 'It is rock hard with wanting at the touch of your fingers! Polish it as you would my silver,' she begged.

Broderick glossed a firm thumb over the nubbin in question. 'How it gleams!' he exclaimed. 'How it longs for my spit and polish!'

Lithe hips arching eagerly from the bed, Mirabelle offered herself to the rampant servants. How, she wondered, would she ever bear the boredom of aristocratic lovers when those of the working variety were so inventive and attentive.

True to his word, Broderick delicately drooled a pearl of saliva on to his fingers and, with a loving look at Mirabelle, proceeded to polish the urgent little nubbin which twitched with eagerness beneath his expert buffing.

'Oooh!' sighed Mirabelle, which Broderick rightly took as the signal that more vigorous thrusting was required.

Baring his rigid pick, the amorous young swain plunged deep into Mirabelle's workings. 'This is wonderful!' he cried. 'Never have I had the pleasure of plunging into such willing depths!'

Mirabelle swung her legs over Broderick's shoulders to encourage yet deeper penetration. Her young, well-trained, passage pampered his length, massaging him until his pleasure could not be contained.

Finding Mirabelle's rosebud lips so parted and willing,

Henry softly grazed the silkiness of his swollen globe about the open orifice.

'Hm!' encouraged Mirabelle. 'Push and I shall swallow your wonderful length.'

It took no second bidding for the eager young boot boy to prise his thickness between the soft lips. Pelham, having taken his fill of the pliant breasts, looked for his own entrance to this glorious body.

'Aaah!' he said as inspiration struck. With a little effort on the part of his lithe body, he slithered between Broderick's pumping length and positioned himself at the rear rose of the lovely girl. The little bud fairly pulsed invitingly as he put the moist globe of his length at this tight place. No sooner, however, was he poised to enter than a great cry rang out from Broderick.

'My spend!' he cried.

'Joins mine!' added Pelham, spouting great gushes of pearly issue over the glorious ivory hillocks of that pretty bottom.

Henry, too, felt soft pecks of glorious lips upon his considerable scrotum before that knowing tongue wrapped itself around the throbbing length of his manhood. She traced the length of each tortured, pulsing vein until she reached the glossy skin of the silky globe. Trembling from head to foot with delight Henry was forced to relinquish the considerable contents of his ballsack into a mouth which fairly gloried in the release.

Mirabelle had, once again, found her true loves in the ranks of the lower orders. The calloused fingers and lengthy cocks giving her splendid satisfaction. Oh, dear, she thought, Mama would not be pleased!

# Chapter 10

'I was waylaid!' wailed Aunt Hatty May.

Mirabelle's chaperone flapped her lace handkerchief about her pale features and her splendid bosom heaved as she recounted her adventures.

The strange thing was, thought Mirabelle, her aunt did not look at all distressed by this dreadful turn of events. In fact, she looked quite elated.

Aunt Hatty May glowed. Her honey-blonde curls had a lustre which sent sparkles of gold dancing about the drawing room. Her lips seemed fuller; her cheeks had an attractive bloom. The grey eyes were deeper and wider, with a glint of mischief which Mirabelle had not noticed before.

Mirabelle frowned. 'And who,' she asked 'waylaid you?' She looked askance at the change in her aunt. The very air in Mirabelle's Peacham Place apartment was redolent with mystery and something indefinable; something, thought Mirabelle, decidedly sensual.

'A highwayman!' imparted Aunt Hatty. She cast a sideways glance at her niece to discern the effect of this revelation.

Mirabelle could not hold back a little gasp of dismay, nor could she contain a certain thrill which settled below a suddenly softened belly, but then she laughed uncertainly.

'Surely,' she said, 'you mean a tramp!'

The honey-gold curls shook vigorously and Aunt Hatty's breathing became more agitated. Her bosom, that wonderfully uplifted heroically feminine breast, rose up and down in a most fetching manner.

'He was not a tramp!' she denied. 'He had a horse.'

'A highwayman?' Mirabelle's voice was husky with disbelief. 'Are you sure?'

'Of course, I'm sure!' Aunt Hatty sounded quite unlike the fluffy dithery lady to whom Mirabelle was accustomed.

Sure of herself, Hatty sat very straight in her chair, with her fullsome hips and buttocks jutting rearwards. She glared at Mirabelle, daring her to defy her opinion.

'But, my dear Aunt,' said Mirabelle in an English accent which had taken days to acquire, 'there are no highwaymen in this modern age!'

She sat stiffly on the edge of the sofa for her corsetière had assured her that young ladies in society wore their rear stays extremely rigid to give a good straight appearance and to add prominence to the buttocks.

'I have to disagree, Mirabelle, honey,' said Aunt Hatty, patting her niece's hand reassuringly. 'Has to be at least one because I've seen him with my very own eyes!'

The rosy bloom on Aunt Hatty's cheeks became deeper. The soft lips parted and curved upwards in a most inviting fashion. The grey eyes rose, expectantly, almost as though there was a third person in the room.

'He held up my vehicle at gun point!'

A pleasureable thrill rippled through Mirabelle's nether regions. Surely such things only happened in romantic novels, she thought. She was envious that Aunt Hatty was on the receiving end of the experience.

'At gun point!' Mirabelle was suitably horrified.

'I could have been murdered for all you cared!' Aunt Hatty dabbed at her eyes with her handkerchief.

'But you weren't!' reminded Mirabelle. 'What did he want from you?'

Aunt Hatty flushed, but said nothing.

'Well?' prompted Mirabelle.

The lace was chewed pensively and Aunt Hatty smoothed

her rumpled skirts modestly. 'I thought he wanted money,' she imparted.

'But he didn't?'

Aunt Hatty shook her golden curls. 'Not at all! When I offered him my reticule he laughed behind his mask and pushed it from him.'

Puzzled, Mirabelle frowned. 'What did he want if not money?'

'He wanted a woman!' Aunt Hatty whispered the information in a voice full of dark portents.

Mirabelle shuddered pleasurably. She felt her limbs quake, itching to be opened by some roughneck calling himself a highwayman. She felt phantom fingers spreading the folds which guarded the swiftly moistening entrance.

'Any woman?' she managed in a voice which was barely audible.

Aunt Hatty lowered her pretty blonde head and knotted the handkerchief which was swiftly falling to lacy shreds.

'There was a maid,' she said evasively, 'who relieved me of my clothes at an inn.'

Mirabelle gasped at the romantic image which was conjured in her mind. She saw herself splayed upon a huge old-fashioned bed, being tended by a willing maid. Her shapely limbs were open. The jet mound was full and pouting. Her tender sex lips were swollen with longing with her bud sharply erect.

A sigh escaped the soft scarlet lips. 'What did he look like?' she asked with a tongue which could barely do her bidding for the dryness of excitement.

Could the mystery man be Joshua, she thought. Followed her across the Atlantic to marry her for love? But it was impossible. Her mother had stressed the importance of riches and a title.

As she waited for Aunt Hatty's answer, Mirabelle felt hot seepage dampen her drawers. She knew that her jet bush would be thoroughly wetted by her fantasies. Her little nubbin would jut hard and high from the softness of its surrounding folds.

'I didn't see him fully,' admitted Aunt Hatty.

'But he held you up at gun point!' exclaimed Mirabelle, the heavy languor which had come upon her so swiftly and enjoyably dissipating like a mist in morning sunshine. 'You saw him!'

'He wore a mask!' exclaimed Aunt Hatty, demonstrating the shape of the mask about her own nose with what was left of her handkerchief.

'A mask!' Mirabelle was ecstatic and threw her clasped hand to her own heaving bosom.

She felt her nipples spring to swift erection and chafe upon the tautness of her white blouse. Her black lashes fluttered upon the paleness of her ivory cheeks and her rosebud mouth parted to release the very tip of a pink tongue. 'He must be such a rogue!' she murmured.

'And a large hat pulled down over his eyes,' added Hatty May.

Something about the tone of her aunt's voice made Mirabelle look up expectantly. 'The colour of those eyes?' she asked in a hoarse whisper.

Aunt Hatty frowned, thinking hard. 'Grey, I think,' she said hesitantly. 'Like mine.'

Mirabelle looked downcast. Her well-rounded shoulders slumped in a most dejected manner and her bosom was no longer upthrust in that delightfully pouting and expectant manner.

'Or were they?' Aunt Hatty asked herself, frowning with a forefinger resting thoughtfully upon her dimpled chin. 'Perhaps—'

'Oh, please, Aunt Hatty!' exclaimed Mirabelle excitedly. 'Do try and remember!'

'Perhaps they were . . .' Aunt Hatty smiled indulgently at her niece. 'Hazel! Yes, I'm sure they were!'

Still Mirabelle looked dreadfully disappointed.

'Or green!' decided Aunt Hatty May.

Blue eyes shining with excitement, Mirabelle took her aunt by the shoulders, shaking her gently. 'Were they? Were they really green?'

Aunt Hatty smiled again. 'At the inn I didn't notice his eyes!' she said meaningfully.

Imagining the rogue of the road leaning over her threateningly, Mirabelle wanted to lift her arms above her head in sweet abandon. Perhaps he would wish to bind her wrists to the head of the bed and her ankles to the foot. She would be helpless; at his mercy and she would not know the identity of her plunderer.

'What bliss!' she murmured to herself.

'He mistook me for someone else,' volunteered Aunt Hatty.

Mirabelle, still at the mercy of her imagination, did not reply. She could see green eyes laughing down at her over a mask. Feeling the weight of a very male body, she allowed herself to sink deeply into the bed on which she lay. There was no harm in welcoming him into her body. He belonged there, she told herself.

She felt the silkiness of his swollen globe open her fully. A murmur of greeting soft upon her lips followed swiftly by a murmur of surprise.

Even his laughter was passionate. The sound came from deep inside him, making his flesh ripple against hers, heightening the sensation of his cock thrusting into her.

'Did you hear me, honey?' persisted Aunt Hatty.

Mirabelle looked dazed as her attention was diverted from her imagination. 'Hm?' she questioned vaguely.

'He thought I was someone else,' repeated Aunt Hatty May.

'I don't understand,' whispered Mirabelle, feeling strangely out of tune with time and space.

'It was my hat, you see,' Hatty looked down at the shreds of lace.

The blue-black curls shook in mystification. 'Your hat?'

'It sported a full veil,' Aunt Hatty went on to explain, 'since such a one is considered *de rigueur* for driving.'

Mirabelle nodded. 'So until you were entirely naked he had no idea of your appearance?'

'Exactly!' exclaimed Aunt Hatty triumphantly. 'He seemed most put out when he saw me splayed upon the bed revealing my all.'

Mirabelle wriggled uncomfortably upon the sofa. She felt the thick coarseness of her pussy hair graze upon the plump lips. A hair or two tickled the soft moistness of her cunney folds and tantalised the tenderness of her erect clitty.

Something was niggling at Mirabelle's consciousness. What was the most important difference between herself and Aunt Hatty May? Their colouring, of course, which was apparent upon their skin, the lushness of their head hair and, of course, the nests at the top of their thighs!

Mirabelle found herself breathing rapidly. Her mouth was desperately dry and her soft little pink tongue flickered swiftly from one corner to the other.

It could be Joshua, she thought. He could have sailed with them in steerage quarters, or maybe even stowed away! Her fists were clasped to her heaving breasts once more. How very romantic, she sighed.

'When he discovered his mistake,' said Mirabelle with a soft understanding smile, 'he no longer required you?'

Aunt Hatty May was most put out. Her pink and white china doll face paled and then flushed, almost immediately, to scarlet. Mirabelle could see the angry thrust of her erect nipples against her gown and her sweet mouth became a tight line.

'Now that, young lady,' she hissed, 'is where you are quite mistaken!' She jumped up from the little sofa and rang for a servant. 'If anything, it made him more passionate than ever!'

Grey eyes hardened to granite slits Aunt Hatty glared

down at Mirabelle. 'You, in case it has escaped your notice, are not the only beautiful woman in London!'

Without waiting for the appearance of a servant Aunt Hatty flounced, in high dudgeon, from the room.

'It wasn't my intention...' said Mirabelle. She rose from her seat and walked gracefully to the window. Across the street she saw a tall man, a hat pulled low over his eyes, his arms folded, simply waiting.

'Joshua!' The name sprang to her lips and she rushed to the main door, flinging it open and crying the name across the street, but he was gone.

He needed a woman.

The tall man walked quickly through this smart area of town. It had been foolish to tarry so long when he was so conspicuous in his shabby clothes.

A lamplighter was wending his way along the street known as Peacham Place and the tall man grabbed his sleeve.

'Is there an inn close by?' he asked, shaking the frail man somewhat roughly.

The lamplighter pulled away, his lined face a mask of fear. 'You'll be wanting something cheap, sir?' he asked with a tremor in his voice.

'Aye, cheap enough!'

'Best not stay here then.' The lamplighter looked furtively over his shoulder. 'Strangers aren't welcome hereabouts.'

The tall man was directed to a dockland bar in Wapping and he cursed the lamplighter for sending him so far.

'A room!' he ordered bluntly. 'And a woman.' The inn was full and noisy. 'A clean pretty one,' he added.

A tankard of warm ale was set before him, but this time he drank it down. The day had been a thirsty one and, within moments, he felt a tug at his cloak. He looked down and saw the prettiest little milk-chocolate-coloured girl he'd seen in years.

The man gave the girl's body a raking gaze. She had high, exotic cheek bones in a delicate face. Tiny, curling tendrils escaped to her dark forehead and a great silken mass of black hair curved over her bare shoulders.

Her smile was tentative as she looked up at him. 'They told me you wanted me,' she said in a low voice.

'They?' he questioned. The girl reminded him of Mirabelle. Darker, of course, much darker than the delicate ivory of his love's smooth skin, but there was a similarity. Something about the way she held her firm breasts high and pert and the way she held her hands upon the rounded curves of her hips.

'The people who own this place,' she explained.

There was a pensive shimmer in the shadow of her eyes, a tremor in her voice. Her full breasts heaved nervously.

He frowned. 'How old are you?' he asked, whispering harshly into her ear and grabbing the softness of her bare upper arm. He wouldn't be responsible for corrupting an innocent.

A defiant glare made her soft face look harder, the features more defined. 'Eighteen, sir,' she said firmly.

'You sure?' Mirabelle was eighteen when he took her. He wanted to free his mind of the obsession with the Southern belle's glorious body.

The girl laughed, leaning her head back and tossing the glorious mane of hair. "Course, I'm sure!'

The hesitation left him. With a low grunt he threw his arm about her waist and half-carried, half-dragged her up the rough stairs, barely hearing the ribald comments of the other customers. They were a rough crowd.

His need was great and the journey across the Atlantic had been long with the end of it full of plans and disappointments.

Looking vulnerable, she stood before him. 'Will you be gentle with me, sir?' she said gazing up at him with dark and limpid eyes.

The large, slouch hat was thrown upon the narrow, untidy bed. The dark, swirling cape was tossed upon a hook behind the door.

'Gentle?' he questioned, his rugged face marred by an angry scowl. In a place like this he'd found a girl who pleaded for gentleness!

Bending her head she tried to hide the tears which filled her dark eyes, but they spilled on to the plain cotton blouse. With a slow, measured step he approached her and took her chin in his hand.

'A virgin?' he asked. He traced a finger down the milk-chocolate cheek and wiped away a stray tear.

A nod was her answer. He felt her shudder against him as she looked at him directly, taking his measure. The soft dark lips were parted invitingly and he could see the soft breasts become firmer, pressing tightly against the thin cloth of her blouse.

'Are you sure you want this?' he asked, remembering Mirabelle. He rubbed the thickness in his breeches.

'I don't understand, sir,' she answered. The glowing dark skin of her forehead was creased in a frown of puzzlement.

He cupped each breast, quite naked under the blouse, and thumbed the stiffening nubs which hardened at his touch. 'Do you want me to take you? Fuck you?' he asked.

The answer was immediate, unhesitating. 'Oh, yes, sir! You must! They're all laughing at me because I'm still a virgin!'

He sighed. It was like Mirabelle all over again. He felt his cock rise to full stretch. The girl felt it too. The tears were replaced by a shy smile. Hands locked against her spine, he pressed her to him and his tongue explored the recesses of her mouth.

He felt her small rough hand slip into one of his and she pulled him to the bed. 'Hey!' he said with a chuckle. 'Allow me!' Easily, he lifted her into his arms and laid her tenderly upon the rumpled rags which were the bed covers.

Wearing only two garments she was quickly naked for him and she lay, waiting upon the narrow bed, for him to lie beside her. 'A virgin,' he murmured, as he tugged at his clothing. 'Why must I be beset with virgins?'

He grinned at her as he said it, impatient to hold the pert, dark breasts, to feel the slenderness of the waist and the swell of the hips as he held her. His eyes drifted down to the apex of her thighs where there was a thick mat of tight curls guarding the unsullied entrance.

'Damn it, girl!' he sighed as he lay upon her. 'You remind me of someone!'

His cock was painfully turgid, stretching the fine skin to the limit. His globe was already moist with the spread of pre-issue from the tiny pore. If he was to enter her now he would tear her apart, he warned himself.

His dark tousled head bent to take the hardness of a nubbin between his lips. A whispered sigh breathed from her lips as his tongue lapped eagerly around the hardness. The breast flesh was pliant, moving with his delving fingers. She began to writhe against his mouth.

'Easy!' he soothed, his head rising from the silk-smooth body. 'Patience!'

'I want you to fuck me!' she said shyly. 'I gotta pain, I want it so bad!'

Mirabelle, he thought. Apart from the colour, this girl could be Mirabelle. She'd wanted it just as bad and it all went wrong.

Slithering between the length of the sweet body, he lay between her thighs, spreading them wide. With his thumbs he opened the plump labia.

'You gonna kiss me there, on my cunney?' she asked, sighing deeply as she spoke.

'It'll prepare you,' he said kindly.

The girl stroked his thick hair. 'I know,' she said, wisely. 'My sister told me. It'll make nice feelings come and make me want you more; make me want you to open me up.'

A thumb balled the hot little tip which jutted so eagerly from the dark folds of the cunney between his fingers. She sighed and he felt her body rise from the bed as she offered herself willingly.

The clitty hardened, pouted from the folds. Her sigh became more urgent. He could feel her breathing quicken and could smell her musk strengthen. With the tip of his tongue he flicked at the still closed entrance.

'Oh, yes!' she murmured, and he felt the grip upon his head become tighter.

The scent of her was heady and he felt the stream of it quicken upon his tongue. Creamy and hot from the depths of her body, he sucked upon it greedily.

'Won't you fuck me now?' she murmured, tugging at his head. It was a plea which he could not deny and, besides, his need was growing as quickly as hers.

'Aye,' he agreed, sliding easily up her warm body. He could taste her love dew on his lips and tongue and it inflamed him. As he touched his length he could feel it throbbing, its globe moist and slick.

Closing his eyes, he could see Mirabelle beneath him, as willing as the girl.

Remember to make the thrust slow, he warned himself. He pressed forward, the smooth ball of his globe easing the tightness of her entrance. He could feel it giving, stretching. She was ready for him; seemed to pull him in with her need. He could feel her bathing him in her juices.

'Mirabelle!' he murmured unknowingly as he thrust slowly and easily into the girl. He could feel his body slick with sweat as it was in Atlanta. Time reversed for him.

With great strength of will he held back his orgasm, just as he had with Mirabelle, but the girl was tight. She gripped him and, at last, he had to let go the flood which he held in his balls.

'Yes!' she screamed. 'That was good. Very good.'

He lay still, cradling her in his arms, dreaming of

Mirabelle. There had to be a way of staying close to her, watching over her and making sure no harm came to her.

The girl moved against him and his cock twitched against his leg. She giggled, taking its thickness in her rough little hands.

'Does it feel nice when I hold it?' she asked shyly.

'It's good.'

'What would you like me to do?' The question was asked more boldly and she wriggled, snakelike, down his muscular body, looking up at him with those lustrous dark eyes.

Watching the black lashes flutter over those wonderful orbs was like looking into Mirabelle's eyes. 'With your tongue,' he said hoarsely. 'Caress it with your tongue.'

The soft moistness of the girl's tongue petted his length obediently. Curled in the cradle of his open legs, she looked so pathetically humble, so small and submissive and yet she was in command of herself as she engulfed his thickness. She enjoyed pleasing him.

He lay back, his eyes half-closed, thrusting his loins in tune with the rhythm of her petting. Her small hands held the heaviness of his scrotum, rolling the balls together in the sac.

Watching her, he was, more than ever, reminded of Mirabelle. At this thought he felt his body tense, ready to fall into the void of ecstasy.

Afterwards, the small figure clung to him, not wanting him to leave. 'Will you come again?' she asked sadly. She seemed to know that he would not.

'Maybe,' he said, not looking at her as he dressed. The image of Mirabelle tortured him. Taking the girl hadn't eased it. His need was worse. He stumbled from the room, throwing the cape about his shoulders and jamming the hat on his head.

The bar was noisier and more crowded than ever. 'Dash it all!' he heard. 'One of you fine fellows would enjoy a trip to the country, I'll be bound.'

The pompous voice belonged to a smart, although not young, gentleman who was holding up a photograph of a young lady.

'And this is the prize!' He beamed, sweating in the heat of the crowded room. 'To be gaoler to this young beauty and to play the games of the infamous Hell Fire Club!'

A roar of laughter rose up. 'And what's the pay?' said a hefty docker.

The gentleman offering work looked put out. 'All found,' he said, lifting his tankard to his lips. 'But surely a belly-full of food and a few nights with this young beauty is pay enough!'

'I'll take my chances earning three shillings a day!' laughed the docker.

Edging closer the man gasped as he saw that the beauty was Mirabelle. His hands balled into massive fists. His jaw clenched, but he stayed his anger.

It would do no good to break this man in two as was his first thought. 'I'll be your servant, sir,' he said, 'for a decent meal and a roof over my head.'

'Ah, at last!' said Sir Everard Mountjoy. 'A man of sense! You won't regret coming to my seat, young sir! And if you can ride a horse, so much the better.' He grinned, looking Joshua up and down. 'I might even pay you a shilling or two!'

# Chapter 11

Mirabelle peeped over her copy of the London *Times* and viewed Aunt Hatty May with some degree of dismay. Over the weeks they had resided at Peacham Place she seemed to have blossomed; was a full-blown rose.

'Aunt Hatty,' began Mirabelle cautiously.

'Yes, my precious?' said the chaperone, beaming rosily over her second bowl of porridge oats, laced with treacle and cream fresh from the churn that very morning.

A frown creased Mirabelle's ivory cheeks. She hardly knew how to phrase the problem. Poor Aunt Hatty had been so miserable in her brief period of mourning; so thin and gaunt, but now . . .

'How are your new corsets?' said Mirabelle, the words tumbling from her sweet mouth.

Helping herself to kedgeree, kippers and a fillet of smoked haddock at the sideboard, Aunt Hatty May turned with a grimace on her now plump, rosy cheeks.

'Far too tight!' Aunt Hatty looked meaningfully down at her bosom which positively ballooned over the upper rim of her corset and blossomed under her dainty bodice, sending the nipples fairly bounding through her frilled blouse.

She sat down rather heavily at the breakfast table and tucked into the mound of fish dishes. 'These English surely do know how to eat!' she said happily.

Mirabelle frowned again. 'The reason your corsets are tight is because you are eating too much!'

Her aunt's pink cheeks, stuffed to brimming with tasty

fish, glowed happily. 'Broderick thinks I look charming,' she said, swallowing the flavoursome mouthful.

'So I've noticed!'

That very morning, Broderick bounded into her aunt's apartment to deliver morning tea. His livery trousers were bursting at the seams as his ardour made itself known. Mirabelle, up early and about to greet her aunt, was all but bowled over by the butler in his haste to see his love.

'Your breasts, my dear,' Mirabelle heard, listening at the door, 'have a sheen on them like the earling morning dew. They are like full-blown roses.'

'Oh, Broderick!' cooed her aunt. 'You say the dearest things.'

'May I ease your night garment from them? he asked huskily.

'Oh, yes!' sighed her aunt, pleadingly.

Mirabelle peaked through the keyhole and was not at all surprised to see Broderick burrowing between the twin pink mountains of her aunt's breasts. He placed soft kisses along the valley before transferring his lips to each splendidly pert nipple.

'And may I lift the sweet folds of your nightgown to kiss the fair curls which nestle so prettily between your wonderful thighs?'

Mirabelle heard Broderick sigh heavily as her aunt trilled with delight.

'Let me snuggle down on the pillows,' said Aunt Hatty May, 'and part my thighs for you to ease your task.'

Through the keyhole Mirabelle was aghast to see just how large the creamy limbs had become, but Broderick seemed to wallow in the pale flesh, diving between what used to be such slender and shapely legs.

'I love a woman with flesh upon her bones,' murmured Broderick as he popped up, licking his lips of the evidence of Aunt Hatty May's delight at his attentions. 'I shall instruct cook to make all your favourite dishes.'

'Would you really, Broderick?' cooed her aunt, her dimpled little fingers opening the plumpness of her nether lips to reveal a very swollen and erect clitty.

'Roast beef?' suggested Broderick.

'I love roast beef!' sighed Aunt Hatty. 'And roast lamb and pork.' Her fingers fairly flew over the shiny little bud, making it glow scarlet in its moist bed.

'I believe you enjoy a favourite of King Edward's,' continued Broderick, slipping a finger of his own in the pulsing passage framed by the creamy thighs. 'Oysters!'

'Oooh!' fluttered Aunt Hatty May. 'I dearly love oysters. Oh, yes!'

A sound behind her startled Mirabelle. Her upended buttocks as she bent to the keyhole felt suddenly vulnerable. She whirled round, flattening her pert bottom against the door.

A grinning Lord Reginald confronted her, his hand poised in a position which could only have been so for pinching.

'Something wrong, my dear?' he asked quickly putting the guilty digits to his own rear.

Mirabelle smiled. 'Nothing,' she said. 'About to go down to breakfast.'

Lord Reginald cast an eager eye at the keyhole, for he was not averse to playing the Peeping Tom himself, as readers of previous sagas will know.

'That's it, my dear!' he said magnanimously. 'You trot along. My present cook is quite the best I've had.'

'Too good for Aunt Hatty's well-being!' murmured Mirabelle over her shoulder as she walked slowly down the sweeping staircase. She saw Lord Reginald stoop slowly to place his eye at the keyhole.

Aunt Hatty May finished her breakfast with a large dishful of strawberries, sprinkled with sparkling sugar and thick Devonshire cream, especially sent up from those southern parts only the previous day.

Mirabelle rustled her newspaper crossly.

'That Broderick!' said Aunt Hatty with a girlish giggle before placing a large sugared strawberry in her mouth. 'Such an innovative man! He brought me strawberries with my morning tea because he knew they are a favourite of mine.'

Mirabelle eyed her aunt's ballooning figure. 'Is there anything which is not a favourite?' she said sharply.

'And you will never guess what he did with them!' said Aunt Hatty, ignoring her niece's abruptness.

An eyebrow, dark and beautifully etched upon the ivory skin, was raised. 'Wouldn't I?' asked Mirabelle.

'Such a sensual man!' Another strawberry, liberally laced with thick buttery cream was popped into the dainty rose-bud mouth.

Mirabelle had a sudden vision of Lord Reginald bending at her aunt's door and remembered the eyes bulging in his handsome face. A smile wreathed her pretty face.

'He spooned strawberries into your cunney!' said Mirabelle.

'How did you know?' said Aunt Hatty, quite aghast.

'And then he hooked them out with his tongue,' continued Mirabelle, stifling a giggle, remembering the lustful expression upon his lordship's face.

Aunt Hatty May spooned the last strawberry and the last scraping of cream from the dish and popped both into her mouth. 'I do believe you have taken a course in mind reading!'

'And having hooked the strawberry from your cunney with his tongue,' continued Mirabelle, 'he kissed it into your mouth!' She rose from the table, slapping down her napkin and smoothing her own slender waist and the delicate swell of her hips. 'Aunt Hatty,' she declared, 'you must curb your appetites.'

'But Broderick likes me plump and—'

'Mama requires us to find titled gentlemen, not butlers!'

snapped Mirabelle, exiting to the small room adjoining the dining room which she used as a study.

During her perusal of The London *Times* she had espied an advertisement which she intended to answer on behalf of Aunt Hatty May.

On good quality parchment she penned a note to the address in the advertisement which was placed to fill the requirements of 'ladies of unusual appetites'. Reading over her reply Mirabelle felt satisfied that she was helping Aunt Hatty overcome her sudden tendency to over-eat. Pelham was instructed to deliver the note to the address in Mayfair that very morning.

'But, Miss Mirabelle—' protested Pelham.

'Immediately, if you please, Pelham!' said Mirabelle sharply.

'But this place . . .' He tapped the address on the envelope. 'It's not what you think!'

Mirabelle shooed him on his way. 'Don't be silly!' she chided. 'What could it be but an establishment to prevent over-eating?'

Pelham shrugged, seeing that Mirabelle would not be swayed from her opinion. 'I am sure the ladies who run the establishment will call upon you directly, Miss Mirabelle.'

'Splendid!' said Mirabelle. 'Tell them that it is urgent and I shall expect them for afternoon tea tomorrow.'

The very next day, at precisely four o'clock, Lady Prunella Cabot and Lady Bertilla Sayer, presented themselves in Mirabelle's drawing room where tea was to be served.

'I should not have thought that a lady of your beauty, Miss Washington, would have need of our services,' said Lady Prunella, darting a look at her companion, who nodded fervently.

Mirabelle gave a little laugh, tossing her glimmering jet curls and arching her splendid breasts. 'It's my aunt I wish you to see!' she trilled. 'She is ballooning over her corsets!'

'I see!' said Lady Bertilla. 'And it is because of this that she is not getting enough!'

Mirabelle's laugh became a frown. 'She's getting too much!' she exclaimed. 'Of everything!'

It was Lady Prunella's turn to frown. 'Our establishment was set up—'

'To help ladies to fit into their corsets!' interrupted Mirabelle. 'Aunt Hatty is bursting at the seams and Broderick, the butler, will not leave her alone but Mama requires titled gentlemen—'

'Then we can help you!' said Lady Bertilla. 'We specialise in pleasing titled gentlemen!'

Lady Prunella and Lady Bertilla, ahead of their time, ran a bordello which pleased gentlemen downstairs and ladies upstairs.

'I don't understand,' said Mirabelle, looking from one to the other of the two ladies. 'I thought you curbed appetites!'

A tea trolley, loaded with cucumber sandwiches and various sweetmeats, was wheeled in by Pelham, who was promptly fondled in a most intimate manner by Lady Bertilla.

Mirabelle spied this intimacy with her blue eyes wide and her lashes fluttering upon her ivory cheeks.

'Indian or China, my lady?' he asked unperturbed.

'Oh, you know how I like it!' said Bertilla, stroking the growing bulge in his livery.

Meanwhile, Mirabelle, casting an occasional glance at Pelham, tried to concentrate upon what Lady Prunella was recounting.

'Would you believe that there's a highwayman galloping about the streets of London?' said her ladyship.

Mirabelle, one eye upon Lady Bertilla who was slipping her hand, not at all surreptitiously, into Pelham's trousers, sat up very straight. 'He's still in London?'

'You know of him?' asked Lady Prunella, helping herself to a dish of peeled prawns.

'Not I!' denied Mirabelle. 'But my aunt was waylaid by

him on her journey from Liverpool. A huge fellow, by all accounts.'

Lady Bertilla slowly drifted her gloved fingers up and down Pelham's cock. 'One has to keep one's hand in in our line of business,' she explained. Pelham groaned pleasurably. 'Wouldn't be a bit surprised if the blighter isn't one of our clients having a lark. After all, highwaymen are quite out of fashion with all these motor vehicles, trams and velocipedes cluttering the roads.'

'Indian or China, my lady?' said Pelham, being dismissed by Lady Bertilla and moving on to Lady Prunella.

Mirabelle watched again, this time with growing interest as Lady Prunella took her Indian tea with lemon and kissed the tip of Pelham's thickness. She felt a stirring in the very depths of her loins and a buoyancy in her mind. It was difficult to keep her suddenly heavy eyes open. Her breasts felt full and tender, the nipples grazing against the confinement of her bodice. Within her fine cotton drawers, between her milk-white thighs, she felt a warm swelling dampness.

'Wonder what the blighter thinks he can get up to in London,' said Lady Prunella between tastes at the ooze of love sap from Pelham's globe.

Looking up at Pelham, Mirabelle had a sudden vision of Joshua and her hidden nub of flesh jerked intolerably. A warm trickle of creamy issue bathed her cunney folds.

'Handsome fellow?' asked Lady Bertilla. A tremendous urge to lick her lips came over Mirabelle. She could taste the creamy salt of Pelham's juices. Unable to overcome the urge she roved the tongue tip around the softness of her mouth.

'My aunt described him as handsome,' she reported. And, if it was Joshua, he was a god among men. The thought set up a thrill in her confined nether regions.

How long would it be before Pelham would reach her? she wondered, her cup tinkling nervously in her saucer. Her limbs trembled, her heart fluttered in her breast and the room felt suddenly very warm.

'Was there any time when the man was naked?' asked Lady Bertilla.

'Indian or China, Miss?' Pelham bent solicitously over Mirabelle, his splendid urn arching from his livery.

'Naked?' echoed Mirabelle, trying quite desperately to keep the tremor from her voice.

Pelham's spout brushed the smooth length of her neck, feeling wonderfully silky and warm upon her skin.

'Yes, there was,' said Mirabelle, reaching out her hand and holding the throbbing thickness. It felt so warm, so vital, so splendidly ready. Pelham tried to stifle a groan. By closing her eyes she felt that she was holding Joshua.

'Feel free to practise upon Pelham,' invited Lady Prunella. 'He is quite used to it.'

Mirabelle's hand fairly flashed up and down the offered length. The thickness she held caused her cunney flutter in an echo of the enjoyment which she experienced on her first morning at Peacham Place. The throbbing magnificence could have been Joshua's or Ernest's as she felt a sudden jerk in Pelham. His spend took him by surprise, spilling copiously over a plate of cream pastries.

'She was taken, blindfolded, to some place,' said Mirabelle, her voice lowered in a tone of confidentiality, 'in the depths of the country, she thinks.'

'Will there be anything else, Miss?' asked Pelham, his voice sounding quite weary and a little weak.

Waving a dismissive hand, Mirabelle ushered him out. 'That man has no staying power,' she said to his departing back. 'I long for a man with staying power.'

Lady Prunella and Lady Bertilla exchanged knowing looks. 'Perhaps we can be of assistance in that area,' suggested Lady Pru, 'but do tell us what clue made your aunt believe that she was in the depths of the country?'

'She heard the lowing of cows and the clip-clop of horses' hooves upon cobbles,' explained Mirabelle. 'Do you know where it could be?' she asked eagerly, leaning forward upon her chair.

Both ladies shook their heads and looked at her, sympathy in their eyes. 'Could be any one of a number of country estates near London,' said Lady Pru. 'Can't you give us any other clues?'

Mirabelle frowned, looking down at her hands in her lap and then she looked up brightly. 'That's it!' she exclaimed. 'She did have the opportunity to feel the highwayman's cock and she tells me that she is quite sure that it is a lordly one.'

'Why does she think that?' asked Lady Bertilla, intrigued.

'Because,' said Mirabelle, looking from one to the other of the ladies, triumph in her eyes, 'it was so large. At least,' she added, since this was not Mirabelle's opinion, 'that is what she surmises.'

'I shall write out a list of candidates,' said Lady Pru, anxious herself to know the identity of the mysterious highwayman, 'who have large appendages and country estates.'

'In our line of work,' added Lady Bertilla, 'we have experience of society gentlemen and often have the opportunity of visiting their estates.'

'And feeling their cocks,' Lady Pru couldn't resist confirming.

Mirabelle clasped her hands in delight to have found such good friends. 'They will be titled?' she queried, becoming more serious once more.

'Of course!' said both ladies in chorus.

'Wouldn't it be wonderful if we could find the highwayman and a husband for both Aunt Hatty and Mirabelle?' trilled Lady Prunella.

'Do they still hang them?' asked Lady Bertilla. 'Can't have the blighters dashing about the countryside frightening ladies out of their corsets, can we, dear?' She squeezed Mirabelle's thigh in a most sensuous manner, looking at her through half-closed dark eyes.

Mirabelle returned the look in a similar manner and shook her head, agreeing that the highwaymen had to be stopped in their tracks.

Lady Pru took a pencil from her reticule and a notebook fixed neatly in a gold case. She licked the pencil thoughtfully and then looked up sharply.

'Are you two paying attention?' she snapped.

Lady Bertilla had drawn Mirabelle down upon the sofa and was trailing a gloved finger across the twin mounds of the American's creamy breasts.

'Carry on,' said Bertilla. 'If we have anything to add we shall do so.'

'Hmph!' huffed Lady Pru doubtfully. 'Leaving me to carry out the difficult parts as always.' She licked her pencil once more. 'Charles Chertsey is a very likely candidate as the highwayman,' she said thoughtfully. 'A dear boy, but dreadfully wild. Always has been.'

Mirabelle could not resist Lady Bertilla's caresses. The soft fingers were as light as butterfly wings and yet there was an air of efficiency about the touches which fascinated her, made her wonder what would happen next.

'Is he a lord?' asked Mirabelle huskily, struggling up for air from the depths of Bertilla's embrace. Her skin tingled deliciously where the fingers grazed and she shuddered as the delicate digits pressed beneath her skirts to her thighs, pressing them open.

'Is he a lord?' repeated Lady Pru with a light laugh. 'My dear, the Chertseys came over with the Conquest and they are dreadfully arrogant. Wouldn't put it past young Charles to act a highwayman for sheer devilment!'

Devilment, thought Mirabelle. Could Joshua be acting the highwayman and being so elusive to taunt her?

The satin ribbons which held her drawers about her waist were suddenly unfastened and Mirabelle, not at all taken aback by these unusual ladies, could only lie, weak and prone with passion, allowing the delights to continue.

'Oooh!' mewed Mirabelle, not expecting Bertilla to retain her gloves when she actually invaded her depths. It felt strange! The gloves were a fine chamois, feeling like velvet as one finger slicked into her passage, lying there, quite still and warm for a brief moment.

'Sir Everard Mountjoy!' exclaimed Pru, scribbling with her pencil.

'Ever Hard?' questioned Mirabelle, jerking back and forth upon the chamois clad finger. 'That's a name?'

Pru nodded. 'A pleasant fellow, but perhaps rather old for such games as we are discussing.' The pencil was licked once more. 'Far too old to go galloping off into the night and asking people to stand and deliver.'

A shudder ran through Mirabelle's body. The softly clad finger slid wetly up and down her opening, making her deliver a copious flow upon the perpetrator. The erect little clitty jerked eagerly against the moistened chamois glove.

'I— I— I do beg your pardon, ladies!' apologised Mirabelle. If her Mama knew that she was coming in the drawing room she would swoon.

'Not at all,' said Lady Pru airily. 'We take these things in our stride.'

'Absolutely!' said Bertilla, rubbing the little jerking nubbin all the harder. 'Come and be blowed, we always say!'

'The list!' said Mirabelle trying to compose herself, wriggling back into her drawers and smoothing her skirts, but still looking hungrily at Lady Bertilla's dark carmine lips. She was, indeed, an exotic-looking lady.

'Vitus Wyndham,' said Lady Pru, with an affectionate smile.

'Is he a lord?' asked Mirabelle, reaching for Lady Bertilla's hand.

'A viscount,' replied Lady Pru. 'A handsome chap only recently married to a Miss Poppy Field.'

Mirabelle pursed her lovely little rosebud lips, brushing

aside a kiss from Lady Bertilla for the moment as she made her response. 'Could he be the highwayman?' It was certain that he was no good as a marriage prospect.

Lady Pru tapped her teeth with the pencil, making Mirabelle cringe. 'I did hear that his father left him rather short in the purse because he disapproved of his choice of a marriage partner.' She placed an 'H' for 'highwayman' by the viscount's name.

After another moment's thought, she announced: 'Buster!'

'An American!' exclaimed Mirabelle joyfully.

'Good lord, no!' denied Lady Bertilla throwing her lovely arms around Mirabelle once more. 'Whatever made you think so?'

'With a name like Buster,' said Mirabelle with a sigh as her breasts were laid naked from her frilly blouse, 'he must be.'

Lady Pru laughed uproariously. 'I see the problem! The spelling! No, my dear,' she said to Mirabelle who had given her breasts to the tender ministrations of Lady Bertilla. 'It's the Marquess of Buttcester, although it is pronounced Buster.'

'How odd!' remarked Mirabelle.

Lady Bertilla was now mounted upon Mirabelle's breasts, softly brushing her dark cunney curls back and forth, first across one upstanding nubbin and then across another.

'He's a great chap with the horses!' proclaimed Lady Pru.

'A good mount!' added Bertilla.

'We should get along extremely well!' exclaimed Mirabelle somewhat breathless. 'Any more?'

'I believe the Earl of Westchester, that's Bertilla's pater, is still searching for a second wife,' said Pru pencilling him in.

Mirabelle was astounded. The person who was attempting to delicately intrude her titty into her cunney, was an earl's daughter. Mirabelle felt greatly honoured and fell to female lovemaking with more gusto.

'And the most eligible of them all is the Duke of Shelmere,

unmarried and fabulously rich.' Lady Pru lay down her pencil and stretched.

'What do you think?' she asked.

'Hm!' mumbled Mirabelle, from the joyous depths of Bertilla's cunney. Would Mama mind, she wondered, if she brought home to Georgia, a lady instead of a lord?

# Chapter 12

Mirabelle felt blood coursing through her veins like an awakened river.

As the young baronet came into the room time seemed to stand still. A quick involuntary appraisal of his features told her that this could be the man Mama would welcome as a son-in-law.

'Lord Charles Chertsey, my dear lady,' he said with a slight bow. 'My friends did not exaggerate the tales of your beauty.'

Mirabelle dipped her head and looked at him through lowered lashes, a sweet smile playing about the rosebud of her mouth.

'Thank you,' she said softly, looking up at him as he took her small hand in his.

His grip was strong, Mirabelle noticed, and she winced as her fingers were crushed in his. He did not release his hold until he succeeded in placing her close by his side on the sofa.

Mirabelle could feel her soft curves being moulded to his hard, lean, young body and she could feel the whisper of his breath against her neck above the lace of her high collar. Could it be, by marrying him, she could please both Mama and herself?

'I understand your family conquested Britain in 1066,' she said conversationally, gazing up into his dark features.

'Not entirely on our own,' he said modestly.

His profile was sharp and confident, arrogant. He had a

generous mouth, noticed Mirabelle, and a clean-cut aquiline nose. Yes, he looked like a conqueror, she decided.

'Do you live in a castle?' she asked brightly, for she had seen pictures of Norman castles in the small library of Peacham Place.

'It fell down,' he said with a rueful smile, touching the silken blue-black coils in which her hair was dressed.

Mirabelle's sweet hands twisted together in her lap. This wasn't a good start, she thought, nervously. Her sharp little teeth began to gnaw at her lower lip.

'No money to re-build, I suppose,' she said, ready to ask him to go, even before Broderick brought in the champagne she had ordered.

Lord Charles let out a triumphant laugh. 'Good grief, no!' he said, as his laugh faded to a throaty chuckle at the sweet naivety of this lovely American. 'The Chertseys have oodles in their coffers.'

Mirabelle's blue eyes flew eagerly to the young man's lap, searching for oodles which might be bursting from his particular coffer. Her hand itched, aching to feel the monster, but propriety, in view of the briefness of the meeting, stayed her dimpled digits.

His hand stroked the stray curls which spilled down the pale ivory of her neck. The touch spoke volumes and her blue eyes met the fiery darkness of his own without flinching.

'Mean, perhaps?' she suggested tentatively. She had to admit that he had the most sensuous of touches and his fingers on her neck sent quivers coursing to the very core of her cunney.

Lady Prunella and Lady Bertilla had been comprehensive in their notes about each of the gentlemen on their list. Lord Chertsey was deemed as 'rough in his love-making and mean in the pocket'.

'Not at all!' denied the young man, throwing her flat upon the sofa, a frown marring his handsome features and his arms holding hers roughly above her head. 'Who told you that? Whoever it was, is a liar of the first order!'

Mirabelle's sprigged organza skirts were suddenly pushed roughly up the silk clad thighs. She sighed. How such rough treatment reminded her of dear Joshua, not to mention the exciting stoker on the voyage across the Atlantic.

'Oh, please!' murmured Mirabelle.

'Dash it all!' exclaimed Lord Charles. 'Beg pardon, madam! Got quite carried away with myself!'

He set her upright upon the sofa, rather as he would a life-size doll. He smoothed her skirt down over the shapely legs and sat sedately beside her, staring into space.

'No!' cried Mirabelle. 'Don't stop!' She was aghast that he should think that she was averse to his caresses.

'You mean . . .' He looked down at his lap. Mirabelle followed his eyes and spied a bulge in his morning suiting.

She nodded, bowing her head in her sweet, modest manner.

'You mean . . .' he repeated hesitantly. 'It's all right to do the thing?'

Mirabelle nodded again. If 'doing the thing' would please Mama, then she would go to any lengths to do so.

Lord Charles fell upon her once more, flounced organza being thrown hither and thither until Mirabelle was naked apart from drawers and corsets. Two strong hands grasped the glorious mounds of her breasts, making her wince only slightly as the sweet nipples were taken, one after the other, into his generous mouth.

A flush spread through the shapely contours of Mirabelle's body. The heat flowed downwards to the moist valley of her cunney.

'Oooh!' she groaned, arching her gracious hips from the sofa.

'Dash it all! Wonderfully willing filly, aren't you, Miss Washington?' Lord Charles crowed. 'Like a willing woman! Can't abide the blushing violets who won't have a chap near their nethers!'

With that pretty speech, the conquering hero tore Mirabelle's drawers asunder. The roughness spurred her on. How like dear Joshua he was!

'Please, Lord Charles . . .' she murmured.

'Confound it!' he declared, about to open his immaculate trousers. 'Haven't upset you again, have I?'

'Quite the opposite!' exclaimed Mirabelle. 'I find your manly methods very exciting!'

'Splendid!' crowed the baronet, opening another button.

'I rather like to . . .' Mirabelle's excitement at Lord Charles Chertsey's roughness made her stutter and stumble upon her words.

'Yes, my dear?' urged Lord Charles, one hand upon a perfect breast mound while the other popped another button. 'How can I please you?'

'By allowing me to suck upon your cock!' Mirabelle managed.

'Dash it all!'

This exclamation made Mirabelle blush, thinking that she had shocked the baronet. For all his roughness perhaps he did not like bedroom language in the drawing room.

The young lord's handsome visage reddened. His chest puffed out quite enormously under his starched shirt front, but most of all, his hand upon his fly trembled alarmingly.

'Dash it all!' He seemed to be stuck for words. His dark eyes seemed about to pop from his skull. His mouth opened and closed. For all that he still looked aristocratically handsome, he was beginning to look like a fish out of water.

'Is it an action you find objectionable?' asked Mirabelle, wishing she could melt into the floor.

'Not at all, my dear!' he managed. 'Like it enormously! But didn't think you were the type to do it, don't you know?'

Mirabelle pushed his trembling hands away from his bulge as she smiled up at him. 'It is a favourite occupation,' she assured him, popping open the remaining buttons.

'Is it really? That's wonderful!'

Feeling the tremor of excitement run through his strong limbs, Mirabelle steadied him by holding the hard hips and sliding his skilfully tailored trousers down to release the probing object which jutted from his groin.

'Ah!' he sighed as he felt his freedom.

'Oh!' murmured Mirabelle, somewhat disappointed. The freed length was thick and turgid, it was true. The globe was splendidly smooth, large and glossy. It rose up from a jet-curled bush similar to her own, but the length! Oh dear, she thought, what a sad disappointment when she had been expecting an aristocratic pike-staff similar to Joshua's. Aristocratic this may have been, but it was stubby and squat.

Mirabelle sighed and licked her lips. She had promised, after all, and she was not a girl to go back on her promises.

'Something wrong, my dear?' said the baronet, digging his strong fingers into the depths of her curls.

'Champagne, Miss Mirabelle!' announced Broderick entering the drawing room.

'Ah!' sighed Mirabelle, closing her lovely milk-white thighs for the sake of propriety in front of the servants. 'Excellent!'

Broderick stood quite still, holding a silver salver on which sat an ice bucket containing an excellent vintage and two glasses.

'Where shall I place the Bollinger?' asked Broderick, his eyes flickering from Lord Chertsey's revealed and decrementing weapon and Mirabelle's puffy mounds.

'Dash it all!' snarled the baronet. 'Don't it occur to you to knock, my man?'

With another glance at the busy young people, Broderick placed the Bollinger upon a side table and silently withdrew.

'Would you like a glass?' asked Mirabelle.

Lord Charles looked much downcast. He sat upon the sofa, looking dolefully into his lap where the decremented flesh had withdrawn even further between his thighs.

'Tell you what!' exclaimed Mirabelle, trying to cheer him up.

He looked into her shining blue eyes expectantly.

'Why don't we open the champagne and bathe your cock in bubbles and I'll lick it off!' Mirabelle knelt over him, brushing the splendour of her breasts across his lips. The nipples hardened at each touch of his mouth and Mirabelle murmured pleasurably.

'Can't do any harm, I suppose,' said Lord Chertsey without total enthusiasm. He reached for the bottle and icy droplets from the frosted bottle made Mirabelle coo as they cooled the heated flesh of her thrusting breasts.

Lord Charles eased the cork from the bottle and apathetically watched the bubbles effervesce from the bottle, looking at Mirabelle inquiringly.

'Now we pour,' she explained, taking the bottle from him and upending the ice cold liquid. This had an immediate reaction.

'Aaagh!' cried Lord Charles and his lithe hips rose from the sofa. The stubby pike-staff rose with them and Mirabelle homed in upon the fizzing bubbles. Her little tongue lapping into the jet bush at his groin and caressing the proud ballsack. The soft lips took each in turn between them before she turned her attention upon the thick little shaft.

'Wonderful!' he sighed, relaxing after the initial shock, giving an appreciative wriggle of the lithe hips. Mirabelle felt the short, but strong, little shaft throb expectantly between her lips. 'You have the most stimulating of touches,' he murmured, thrusting the freshly upright lance between her lips.

Mirabelle's cunney, much neglected in recent weeks by large gentlemen, yearned silently to be invaded by such a one. Aunt Hatty May had been pleasantly plundered by the highwayman and Mirabelle wriggled enviously, freeing one hand from the root of the cock between her lips to partially relieve the yearning.

'Oh, please!' said the baronet, seeing the direction her little fingers had taken. 'Allow me!'

Mirabelle allowed a little mew of delight to escape around the thickness which so fully filled the space in her mouth. She felt a finger graze silkily over the hard pip of her nubbin and she could not help urging the friction to become swifter until it was flashing faster and faster.

In turn Mirabelle poured another helping of Bollinger over the turgid balls and lapped hungrily at the bursting bubbles. That done, her tongue urged into the pulsing hole at the peak of the baronet's weapon, sucking upon the sweetness of the champagne and the saltiness of the oozing issue.

'My dear lady!' cried Lord Charles. 'I cannot hold back!'

'Hm! Hm!' murmured Mirabelle urgently, for she was swiftly approaching the summit of delight. The baronet's thick, strong finger delved deep into the moist heat of her cunney and she squeezed it gratefully. This last proved to be too much for both of them and spurts of spunk filled Mirabelle's lovely mouth. Her own issue was a dew upon the silky whiteness of her thighs.

'You have conquered me, Lord Charles,' she whispered, shuddering with pleasure.

He smiled smugly. 'In that case, my dear, dear girl, would you do me the honour . . .?'

Mirabelle shook her head. 'I must find my true love!' she said adamantly.

'Lost, is he?' Lord Chertsey nodded understandingly, almost as though he was relieved of a burden.

'I am bored!' exclaimed Mirabelle next morning. The exclamation was accompanied by a dramatic sigh. 'London does not hold the promise for which I had hoped.' She tossed away her romantic novel and rose gracefully to her feet.

'Now, honey,' exclaimed Aunt Hatty May, looking up from her tatting, 'how can you be bored when only yesterday you entertained the most delightful young lord?'

'They have such itty-bitty guns!' cried Mirabelle. 'And no staying power! I might as well have stayed in Atlanta!' Our young heroine was quite distraught.

'Stumpy!' she said crossly, bringing her finger and thumb together to emphasise her point. 'Stumpy and no stayingpower!' She flew to her aunt, throwing her arms about her shoulders. 'What have I done, Aunt Hatty? Everything has gone wrong!'

'There! There!' soothed Hatty. 'You're being a little impatient, that's all. Lady Prunella has only introduced you to one of the gentlemen . . .'

'Who was stumpy!'

Aunt Hatty sighed. 'But at least he was a lord.'

Mirabelle, a picture of tragedy, stood to lay her lovely curls upon her arms which she folded upon the mantel. 'What am I to do? Mama will be so disappointed if I do not find a titled gentleman.'

The plumpness of her pussy mound seemed to lessen as she contemplated her failure. The pouting lips became less full; her clitty was no longer erect. Mirabelle shuddered. An old maid, she thought miserably; an abandoned old maid. Joshua. How she longed for a Joshua!

Aunt Hatty tatted thoughtfully. 'Your Mama will be more than disappointed, honey,' she murmured. 'The future of the Washington Plantation depends upon your success.'

'Oh, Aunt Hatty . . . I can't!'

Joshua's fine maleness rose in her mind's eye. It was thick and splendidly erect and the thought of it penetrating her caused a sudden seepage to renew between her pussy folds.

'You must!' said Aunt Hatty firmly. 'A heavy burden upon such young shoulders, I know, but one which must be borne with fortitude.'

Mirabelle's rosebud lips were dangerously close to a petulant pout when her blue eyes brightened. 'The highwayman!'

Aunt Hatty looked uncomfortable and her hands trembled as she tatted.

'He was handsome and tall . . .'

'Don't you go getting any ideas about that man,' said Aunt Hatty, pointing the lace shuttle at Mirabelle in a threatening manner. 'Your Mama says we gotta get rich men, not some no account highwayman.'

'Sir Everard Mountjoy is without, my ladies,' announced Broderick who stood at the open drawing room door, looking especially grand.

'Is without what?' snapped Mirabelle. 'If he's true to form with the rest of the men in this one-horse town . . .'

'Mirabelle!' cried Aunt Hatty, aghast at her niece's rudeness. 'Show him in, Broderick.' She could not resist giving him a warm smile and a promising wink. The butler caused a flutter of anticipation in her drawers which could hopefully be brought to fruition before too long.

Sir Everard blustered in, all ruddy-faced and bursting with bonhomie.

'By jove, awfully nice to be here again!' he said, taking Mirbelle's hand in his to kiss the soft sensitive centre of her palm.

The kiss caused a sensation which made her breasts swell deliciously and her pussy regain its young vigour. Mirabelle smiled, fluttering her dark lashes upon her ivory cheeks.

'Sir Mountjoy!' she greeted.

Although not in the first flush of youth the squire sported attractively muscular thighs.

'Everard,' he corrected quickly.

'Oooh!' murmured Mirabelle, her earlier unhappiness quite forgotten. 'Are you really?'

Her heart pounded alarmingly with excitement. Was this truly the man she sought? Ever hard and willing?

A slight frown creased the squire's forehead, but this was soon dispelled by the touch of Mirabelle's dimpled hands delving between the thighs which she found so attractive.

'Oh, gosh!' he exclaimed as the sweet fingers found their mark and his trusty lance thrust upwards.

'How I have searched for you!' sighed Mirabelle, slipping her agile digits between his buttons.

'I say!' He beamed happily and his cheeks took on an even ruddier glow. 'Lady Pru mentioned that you were searching for something or other.' He settled himself more comfortably upon the sofa to enjoy the intimate attentions of this lovely girl. 'Didn't realise it was me! Would've been round to Peacham Place sooner . . .'

'How I wish you had!' interrupted Mirabelle, glorying in sliding her hands up and down the splendid length. Her dainty fingers slid over the slippery globe, pausing only to investigate the pulsing eyelet with the very tip of a digit.

'When it releases its lovely fountain . . .' she crooned, her marvellous breasts surging upwards to the boundaries of her deeply cut gown.

Sir Everard burrowed into this inviting valley, finding that the kisses which he placed upon the revealed flesh increased the surges of sensation.

'Damned good brandy this!' murmured Lord Carshalton, partaking of a lunchtime snifter. 'Damned good!' He took a sip and smacked his lips appreciatively.

'Hm,' agreed Lord Reginald Rover, but his agreement was vague and lacked enthusiasm.

'Seem a bit downcast today, old boy,' remarked Carshalton, leaning forward in the deep club chair.

'Jolly well am!' Lord Reginald looked up from his own brandy glass.

'Problems besetting you?' Lord Carshalton took another sip of brandy, savouring the smooth fire as the liquid trickled over his palate.

'Dashed well are!' Lord Reginald gazed into the golden liquid as if looking for answers in the depths. 'Coming from all sides, don't you know? Can't cope with the blighters.'

'Ah! Bothersome trivia getting you down, eh? Happened since the gel moved into Peacham Place, I'll warrant!'

'Dashed right!' agreed Reginald. 'Absolutely! Taken over the place and the servants are becoming unmanageable!' He shook his head, swirled his brandy and looked around the gentleman's club, hoping that no-one had heard the latter admission.

'Unmanageable?'

'Totally!' Lord Reginald looked more downcast than ever. 'My cellar is practically dry, old boy!'

'You mean . . .'

'Broderick and Pelham have purloined every drop of Chablis, champagne and brandy in the place!'

'Sack the blighters!' exclaimed Lord Carshalton without hesitation.

Lord Reginald helped himself to another generous helping of White's Extra Special Napoleon Brandy placed upon the silver salver beside him. 'But then I have to go through the whole ghastly business of interviewing and . . .'

Patting his friends's knee consolingly, Lord Carshalton shook his head. 'Got the very fellows! Turned up at the Hall only the other day and Lady Carshalton took 'em on, although damned if we needed another two. Got hundreds of the blighters running about the place. But she's too softhearted, always has been.'

'Would you really . . . ?'

'Absolutely delighted,' said Lord Carshalton magnanimously. 'So you sack Brodders and company forthwith. Now, regarding Mirabelle . . .'

'I yearn for her!' said Lord Reginald, looking desolate.

Lord Carshalton looked aghast. 'Do you really, old boy? Fallen in love? Dangerous that.' He shook his head, a worried frown upon his ruddy face. 'Curb it, if I were you,' he advised.

'Would you?'

'Hm, go for the chaperone. Safer.' He held the brandy balloon up to the light, seemingly admiring the rich colour. 'Older, plumper. Be more grateful, d'ye see?'

Reginald nodded reluctantly, knowing his friend was right. 'Mirabelle's got this bee in her bonnet about huge cocks. Can't compete, d'ye see?'

Lord Carshalton kept his own knowledge of Mirabelle's likes and dislikes to himself.

'Wants a title desperately,' imparted Reginald. 'Happened to read a letter to her mama just this morning. Thinks that young Henry, our boot boy, is a descendant of the Duke of Wellington!'

Lord Carshalton sat bolt upright in his chair. His face was a mask of disbelief.

'Boots, you see?' said Reginald, trying to explain the possible connection.

'Ridiculous!'

'Quite!' agreed Reginald. 'The mama must be quite gone in the upper works if she believes that nonsense.'

'Well, as I said before,' advised Lord Carshalton, 'go for the chaperone and don't you concern yourself with Brodders and Pelham. We'll see them off the premises of Peacham Place and perhaps everything else will slot into place.'

# Chapter 13

Aunt Hatty, beautifully marmoreal buttocks upended as she peeped through the keyhole of the drawing room door, gasped with joy at the sight of her dear niece in the arms of Sir Everard.

Her breasts heaved in sympathy. Mirabelle, her eyes closed and her legs splayed to the utmost, was giving her all to the squire.

'Amelia Jane!' she murmured to her absent sister. 'I feel that we have finally struck lucky. He is elderly, rich, endlessly passionate and titled.' She sighed joyfully and could not help giving a little twitch of her glorious haunches as she spied the scene in the drawing room.

'Oooh!' she murmured, feeling a wash of sensation about her pussy folds which could not be ignored. 'Perhaps dear Broderick is free and could give poor little me some gentle relief.'

With this stimulating thought in mind she bustled happily through the hall of Peacham Place intent on her manly goal. It caused some surprise, therefore, when she was whisked swiftly and roughly, petticoats flying over her head into the sanctum of Lord Reginald's study. Her blonde curls bobbed in shock and her grey eyes stared into his lordship's eager face.

'Marry me!' he begged, taking his dear friend's advice and striking while the iron, and Hatty, were hot.

'But I am deeply in love with Broderick!' she sighed, lowering her eyes modestly.

Lord Reginald caressed the generous sweep of her *derrière*, and, finding it a stimulating sensation, continued by putting a large hand to her waist. The tantalising curves were too delicious to resist and he pulled her close.

'Broderick has gone!' he told her, whispering the information hot against her ear.

Aunt Hatty May's eyes flew open, flashing grey fire. 'Gone?' she echoed.

He nodded, smiling triumphantly.

Shrugging, her blonde curls held high and the splendid mounds of her breasts fairly bursting from her bodice, she tossed back her head. 'No matter!' she exclaimed defiantly. 'I also love Pelham.'

Lord Reginald sighed and shook his head. 'Gone!' he said succinctly.

Eyes starting from her pretty face and sweet lips parted as she gasped for air, she shook her head in disbelief. 'They can't both be gone!'

'Forget them!' he begged.

'Why?' she cried. 'I don't understand. Was it because of me?' A triumphant smile lit her pink and white cheeks. 'You are envious!'

'Henry, the boot boy, is the only one of my male staff I have retained,' he admitted. 'A fine young fellow!' he remarked persuasively. 'Any good for your purpose?' He had a mischievous twinkle in his eye and he cocked his head at her as he pulled her to his portly frame once more.

'Let go of me!' cried Hatty May, beating his broad chest with clenched little fists. 'Why did you do this to me? I was so happy with my little *ménage à trois*.'

Lord Reginald's hands slipped up her arms, bringing her closer, letting her feel the strength and heat of his passion. 'Marry me, Hatty. I shall make you very happy, I promise.' He kissed her on her dainty little nose. 'And you will be Lady Rover,' he added, throwing in his final Ace.

Hatty May's cherubic little face brightened considerably

at this. 'I shall, shan't I?' she said, preening in the circle of his arms.

'It's time I married, you see,' he explained, 'and produced a son or two.'

Eagerly, Hatty opened her bodice and Lord Reginald dived into the fullness thus revealed. He fingered the tiny pips which hardened so willingly under his digits. After looking forward to Broderick's caresses, she felt the need for relief.

'Shall I help you replace them?' she said sweetly.

Lord Reginald was already opening his morning suit trousers and, almost immediately, a splendid thickness sprang towards her.

'Who, my dear?' he asked dreamily, slicking his thickness with an expert finger and thumb.

'Broderick and Pelham!' she reminded him, edging to the corner of the desk behind her.

'Done, my dear, done!' he said huskily. With his free hand he lifted her skirts and a look of delight spread across his face as he felt the nakedness thus revealed.

'You are quick and efficient,' complimented Hatty May, replacing his hand with her own upon his cock.

'I hope you'll always think so,' he sighed, thrusting his loins until they brushed hers. The sigh was prolonged as her fair curls became enmeshed with his dark ones.

'Oh, I'm sure I shall,' assured Hatty May, sinking to the softness of the rich Persian carpet and looking up at him as she licked her pretty lips.

'Wonderful!' sighed Lord Reginald. Everything was turning out just as Lord Carshalton promised and Reginald gave himself up to the marvellous sensations issuing from sweet Hatty's fingers.

Behind the drawing room door Sir Everard was grappling sensuously with Mirabelle's milk-white thighs.

'I'll take you to my country seat!' he panted.

She stroked the silky turgidity of Sir Everard's hugeness. 'Is it in the middle of a field?' she asked innocently.

'What say?' he asked absently.

She imagined a rough hewn bench, perhaps beneath an ancient oak dappled by ever changing light. 'Your country seat?' she asked. 'Is it in a field?' Her huge blue eyes stared at him ingenuously.

Sir Everard let out a great bellow of laughter. 'How marvellously sweet you American gels are!'

As if to feel that sweetness his hand strayed to the inviting slit in her drawers. She felt it tremble in its impatience as it palpated the plump flesh of her cunney.

'One's country seat is not a seat as such,' he explained as he regained his breath. His broad body enfolded her slender form.

Mirabelle allowed a frown to crease the smoothness of her forehead. She was puzzled. A seat was something one sat upon. How could it be anything else? She wriggled her buttocks to confirm her theory.

'It isn't?' she gasped, glorying under his touch and transferring her sway to his wonderful length.

'It's my estate,' he told her hoarsely. 'Acres of it. In East Anglia.' He was becoming so excited that he could barely convey his background. 'Family goes back to Hereward the Wake, don't you know?'

Mirabelle spread the smoothness of her thighs and urged Sir Everard to mount her with joy.

'Dashed accommodating,' he panted, doing so. 'Interesting place,' he added, inserting his lance into the cushiony socket.

Mirabelle fluttered her thick eyelashes, flattered by his comment. 'Thank you, sir!' she murmured, gyrating the sweet nest for his pleasure.

Sir Everard looked down at her, frowning slightly, the thick, but well-drawn, eyebrows meeting upon his high forehead. 'Eh?' he asked, followed by: 'Ah! No! Crossed purposes here!' He gave an extra-deep plunge.

'Are we?' murmured Mirabelle, feeling her clitty being grated rather pleasantly.

'Yes,' panted Sir Everard. 'I was talking about my country place and you, mistakenly, thought I referred to your sweet little . . .'.

Mirabelle stiffened, clenching Sir Everard's length with her skilled muscles in some measure of anger.

'Ah!' groaned the knight. 'Wonderful! My spend overtakes me.'

Mirabelle, too, despite her fury felt the warm pleasure of her climax obliterating all other thought.

Coming to the real world Sir Everard kissed Mirabelle softly upon her lips. 'Coming?' he murmured tenderly.

'I have!' she said sharply, looking at the knight's rapidly shrinking cock. It didn't appear to have the ability to remain ever hard. Disappointment came down upon her like a dark cloak.

'Eh?' Sir Everard again looked puzzled, but quickly realised that they were again at crossed purposes. 'No!' he said with a jolly laugh. 'I mean will you join me at my country place? Needs a woman's touch.'

Smoothing her lovely gown and tossing the dramatic fall of jet black hair, she pondered upon the nuances of the English language which caused misunderstandings across the Atlantic.

'I'd adore to join you,' she said, giving him one of her sweetest smiles, 'but Aunt Hatty May must come too. She is, after all, my chaperone.'

Sir Everard looked slightly put out, but was polite enough to keep his thoughts to himself. 'Of course,' he agreed. 'Quite.'

Taking his large and capable hand in hers which, it must be remarked, had a wonderful effect upon the shrinking of his lance, Mirabelle looked directly into his eyes. 'Shall we go today?' she asked breathily.

'The devil we shall!' exclaimed Sir Everard, his voice full of enthusiasm and an extra helping of bonhomie.

The suspicion of a frown only slightly marred Mirabelle's beauty. 'I must make arrangements,' she said. 'Does that mean we shall go or shall not?'

'Of course we shall go!' cried Sir Everard as though leading the hounds to his hunt. 'Tally-ho!'

Mirabelle saw Sir Everard off from Peacham Place herself since the servants were nowhere to be seen.

'Aunt Hatty May!' she cried, immediately hurrying through the gracious hall. 'We're going to sit on a country seat!'

Looking considerably dishevelled Aunt Hatty May appeared from the study, closely followed by Lord Reginald.

'It might be the very one to which you were taken!' said Mirabelle excitedly. 'The one to which you were taken blindfold.'

Aunt Hatty patted her curls and re-arranged her bodice. Her eyes shone and her pretty lips were swollen from recent attentions. The splendid bosom fairly brimmed from her gown and Mirabelle noticed a certain stagger in her aunt's gait.

'Do you think so?' Hatty May managed, but her mind, and perhaps her heart, seemed far away.

'It's a possibility,' said Mirabelle, her enthusiasm waning, and as it waned she began to note her aunt's changed demeanour. 'What has Broderick been about?' she said quite sternly.

'He's been about my wine, my dear!' said Lord Reginald, appearing at Aunt Hatty's shoulder. 'That's what he's been about. The blighter!'

Aunt Hatty, pulling herself tautly together, attempted to look prim. 'My fiancé . . .'

'Your what?' Mirabelle's periwinkle-blue eyes looked wide and startled. 'Broderick?' Surely her silly aunt had not completely lost her senses.

'Oh, my darling Mirabelle!' exclaimed Aunt Hatty. 'As if I should do anything so silly!'

As if you wouldn't, thought Mirabelle grimly.

Taking Lord Reginald's arm in a possessive fashion, Aunt Hatty May drew him forward. 'This is my fiancé!' she said proudly, looking up at him with adoring eyes.

Lord Reginald smiled and looked a little sheepish, patting Aunt Hatty's dimpled fingers, unable to reach anything more intimate except her sweet face which he stroked immediately.

'My fiancé,' said Aunt Hatty, continuing her tale of Broderick, 'was forced to send the butler and footman on their way but he has fortunately procured two other gentlemen who are more trustworthy.'

Lord Reginald looked down at Aunt Hatty with greater adoration. 'Rather!' he exclaimed. 'Splendid chaps! Disciplined and of military bearing.'

Mirabelle was pleased. Mama, she thought to herself, would have swooned if Aunt Hatty May took vows with a butler or a footman.

'Do you think one of the new gentlemen could take our trunks to the carriage?' she said excitedly.

Aunt Hatty May turned to her new love. 'You will come, Reggie?' she pleaded. 'Where are we going, Mirabelle?' she added turning to her niece.

'Sir Everard Mountjoy's country seat,' supplied Mirabelle, hardly able to contain her excitement.

Lord Reginald turned a deep puce and huffed mightily. 'That blackguard!' he blustered. 'Man's a roué! Absolutely! Couldn't describe him as anything else!'

The two ladies stared at him aghast. 'Why do you say that?' Mirabelle felt obliged to ask.

The puce faded only slightly to an unhealthy flush. 'Chap's family well-known as founder members of the Hell Fire Club. Shocking behaviour all the way round.'

Hatty May's eyes were bright and feverish. Her bosom

rose and fell mightily. Her splendid buttocks seemed to pout to greater swells.

'What is it?' asked Mirabelle, looking at her aunt's fevered face. 'I've never heard of it.'

'I have!' said Aunt Hatty May huskily. 'My dear late husband was familiar with the goings on.'

Lord Reginald flung himself at his loved one's feet. 'Don't go, my dear!' His arms circled Hatty's buttocks while she looked beyond him, with delight in her grey eyes at some inner vision.

'Manacles!' she murmured.

'Dreadful goings on!' groaned Lord Reginald, clutching at the rustling taffeta of Aunt Hatty's gown.

'Whips!' exclaimed Aunt Hatty, beating at his lordship's hands as he clutched.

'I don't understand!' gasped Mirabelle, bemused.

'The man has a torture chamber at his country place!' groaned Lord Reginald. 'Enjoys the fringe of polite society, one might say. You won't go, will you, my precious?' he said rising to his feet.

With fervid eyes and lips parted in a most lustful manner Aunt Hatty May circled his neck with loving arms. 'Oh, I know you will miss me dreadfully, my love!' she said in a low voice. 'But don't you see? I must! It is my duty to my niece as her chaperone.' She kissed him lovingly on the very tip of his aristocratic nose.

With a patient sigh, Lord Reginald agreed that this was true. 'But please do not be tempted to join in Sir Everard's little games.'

Crossing her fingers behind her back Aunt Hatty May promised. Mirabelle remained puzzled as to the nature of Sir Everard's games, but then she was young, dear reader, and innocent in the ways of the world.

The two ladies dashed to prepare for their visit to the country. Several trunks were required to take the vast number of changes of gowns needed for a few days in the country in those splendid days of King Edward's reign.

'Instruct the footman to collect our trunks, Amy,' said Mirabelle, satisfied that she had forgotten nothing.

'Yes, Miss,' said Amy with a pretty curtsey. 'He's nice, Miss,' the girl added, turning on her heel to leave the room.

Mirabelle frowned. 'Who?' she asked sharply.

'The new footman, Miss,' Amy supplied. 'Not like that Pelham. Almost a gentleman, you might say.'

Sharply etched dark eyebrows raised, Mirabelle looked forward to meeting the new addition to the household. Pulling on a glove she opened the door as it was knocked upon.

'Miss Mirabelle!' exclaimed a voice.

Had she not been such a strong young lady she could have swooned at the new footman's feet. As it was her gloved hands flew to her perfect lips in astonishment. She could not believe her eyes.

# Chapter 14

'You!' cried Mirabelle, feeling her smooth ivory skin pale to transparency. The temptation to swoon was great, but she steeled herself to keep her wits about her.

'Yes, Miss Mirabelle,' he said. The grin he gave her was engaging. His strong features seemed to light up from within at the sight of her. 'Strange how things turn out, isn't it?' They stared at each other for some moments. 'I sent a note,' he said at last.

There was a heart-rending tenderness in his gaze as he looked her over seductively, his eyes raking the slender voluptuousness of her figure and taking in the graceful lines of her classical travelling suit.

'You did?' she murmured, surprise making her voice a high whisper.

Mirabelle felt dumbstruck by the sight of him, dressed now in footman's livery, waiting to do her bidding. His steady gaze bore into her in silent expectation.

'You've never been far from my thoughts,' he said at last.

Mirabelle nodded slowly. She felt unable to do more. Her throat felt constricted; her mouth dry; her tongue too swollen to do her bidding. She knew how he felt. For that short time, not so very long ago, they were bonded together by the intimacy of their lovemaking and since then life slipped by.

'I didn't receive it,' she told him truthfully at last.

He shrugged and shook his head, telling her that it didn't matter. 'But I had a feeling that we should meet again,' he continued.

There was a tingling in the pit of her stomach as she fought an overwhelming need to be close to him. Despite that, she knew that he disturbed her in every way. She lowered her eyes, trying desperately to shut him out of her sight and out of her mind.

'Mirabelle, honey!' cried Aunt Hatty May, fairly flying down the sweeping staircase. 'My trunks are ready!'

The shining jet curls beneath a most splendid cartwheel of a hat shimmered in the morning sunshine as Mirabelle tried to pull her wits together.

'Do you hear me, honey?' Aunt Hatty stood, tense with excitement, at the door of Mirabelle's apartment.

'The trunks,' she said hoarsely to the hovering footman. 'The carriage has been brought to the front of the house.'

In her ears, her voice sounded strange and hollow and her eyes refused to focus upon his handsome features, sweeping beyond him to Hatty's bouncing figure.

Mirabelle knew that she wanted only to feel the strength of his arms around her but now she was obliged to leave Peacham Place for the country. Reaching out she touched his arm, her body stiffening as his strength was transmitted to the very core of her body. Her cunney was unbearably swollen, the plump lips chafing against the soft cotton of her drawers. The love dew was copious, saturating the fine cloth as she took a step to leave her apartment.

'Be gone long?' he whispered hoarsely, lifting one of the trunks easily.

Mirabelle licked her lips. 'A few days,' she answered, trying to smile. 'No longer.'

Aunt Hatty May clutched at the sleeve of her gown, trying to hurry her. 'I can't wait to play with those lovely little toys of Sir Everard!' She took only a glance at the new footman, dismissing him as nothing more than a menial, although they all three knew that this had not always been the case.

'You're betrothed, Aunt Hatty!' reminded Mirabelle sharply.

The bobbing blonde curls were tossed disdainfully and the pert little nose was held high in the air. 'Oh, pooh!' exclaimed Hatty. 'A little fun with toys doesn't mean I don't love Reginald! I'll love him all the more when we return to town.'

Mirabelle cast a disbelieving sideways glance at her aunt as she watched the footman take the several pieces of luggage to the carriage. A curious swooping tug was violent behind the tightness of her corset. As she eyed the man heaving the considerable weight of each trunk to the top of the carriage she saw the exciting ripple of his muscles under his shirt. She wanted him to clasp the strength of those arms around her so that she could feel the contours of his lean, hard body.

'All done, Miss Mirabelle,' he said smiling down at her.

Now that the time had come to leave Peacham Place, if only for a short time, she would have given anything to stay. She wanted to feel his breath hot against her cheek; wanted to feel the warmth and strength of his very masculine arms; she wanted to bury her hands in his thick hair.

Aunt Hatty May was already in the carriage, her face eager and her grey eyes glittering with excitement.

Mirabelle smiled at her over her shoulder. 'Have you made your farewells to Lord Reginald?' Her eyes darted back to the footman who was watching her sadly.

'He says he doesn't care for farewells,' said Aunt Hatty impatiently, 'but it's not that at all. He's pure and tooting jealous! That's what he is! Jealous that my body will be a plaything of another man.'

'A plaything!' The footman was taken aback. 'Miss Mirabelle, may I ask what this place is to which you are repairing?'

Mirabelle reprimanded him with a tap of her closed fan upon his forearm. 'No, you may not, Captain King!'

A glowering figure stared down at the little group by the carriage. 'Come now, King!' chivied the butler. 'We have other tasks apart from seeing the ladies off to the country.'

With a final backward glance the Peacham Place footman, formerly Captain King of one of the greatest liners in the world, hurried to do the bidding of Ernest, former stoker.

The latter grinned at Miss Mirabelle. It was a knowing grin and was accompanied by an inviting touch of the genitals, which Mirabelle could see were thick and heavy in the trousers.

Patches of pink stained her creamy cheeks and she was forced to lower her eyes, which felt gritty and hot about the fine lids.

'I don't believe we are ever going to get to Sir Mountjoy's country seat! exclaimed Aunt Hatty May.

'Everard,' corrected Mirabelle absently, at last climbing into the waiting carriage.

'But will he be?' said Aunt Hatty May anxiously. 'We may have kept him waiting so long that the feeling may have left him!'

Mirabelle gave the order to the coachman. 'Mountjoy Manor,' she said, wondering what awaited them in the flatlands of East Anglia.

The house was set in extensive grounds. Warm red brick was set in ancient timbers in typical Tudor style. Old yew trees dipped their branches to form dappled caves at the rear of the house.

'It's real quaint, Mirabelle, honey,' said Aunt Hatty as they were handed from their carriage on the wide gravelled drive.

Mirabelle hardly said a word during the journey from London, thinking about the note she had not received.

Sniffing the air, Hatty May frowned.

'What's wrong?' Mirabelle asked the question softly, as though she cared little for the answer.

'The smell!' exclaimed Aunt Hatty. 'The gravel, the cobbles. They're all familiar.'

Mirabelle gasped. 'The highwayman?'

At that moment Sir Everard came bounding up to them, full of his usual bonhomie. 'Ladies!' he exclaimed. 'So good of you to grace my humble little country cottage with your presence.'

'Not at all!' simpered Aunt Hatty, her eyes glittering with pent-up excitement. 'Delighted and it's far from humble.'

She threw her arm through his, leading them into the house, almost running into the polished entrance hall.

'The dungeons,' she said excitedly. 'You must show us the dungeons.'

Sir Everard Mountjoy tossed an eager look over his broad shoulder at Mirabelle. She, in turn, was staring at a groom leading the carriage and horses away from the imposing frontage. The set of his shoulders was familiar. It was more than familiar. She knew him and knew him well.

'That man!' she cried, looking after the retreating figure and, immediately, turning to her host who was taking great delight in caressing the splendid curves of her aunt's buttocks.

'Eh?' asked Sir Everard, too busy with the investigation of Hatty's voluptuous fullness to bother himself with other matters. 'So you enjoy the taste of a flagellum, my dear?' he whispered hoarsely into Hatty's ear.

The whisper, though low, carried across the sweeping drive to Mirabelle's ears. The two, so engrossed in the pleasures of the flesh as they were, had no time for other things.

The groom had disappeared, beyond the end of the sprawling and ancient building. Mirabelle was sure that she knew that confident swagger; the broad shoulders, the slim hips and the way he handled the horses. It was him! She was certain, but what was he doing here?

Sir Everard, his arm around the deep dip of Hatty's waist and fingers groping down the steep slope of her tightly corsetted hip, was already entering the great vaulted hall of the manor house.

'That man! The groom!' repeated Mirabelle.

'Man?' queried Sir Everard, bellowing over his shoulder. 'Choose anyone you like, m'dear!' guffawed the knight magnanimously. 'Got some splendid chaps here on the estate!' He turned towards his younger guest, his eyes glinting with mischievous thoughts and his broad chest puffed out with arms spread expansively. 'Anyone who takes your fancy,' he continued as Aunt Hatty looked up at him adoringly, 'just tip him the wink. He'll know what it's all about.'

Turning to Hatty May he chucked her chin and gave her rosy cheek an affectionate pinch which made her giggle delightedly. 'Like this little minx here,' he continued, 'my chaps know what life at Mountjoy Manor entails!'

'The groom,' repeated Mirabelle, joining Sir Everard and Aunt Hatty at the massive oak double doors. 'Has he worked for you for long?'

Taking both their arms he led them through the great hall with its hanging banners, gallery and enormous stone fireplace. 'Got several of those blighters,' he said vaguely.

'The handsome one who took the carriage,' said Mirabelle, gazing around her quite astounded at the magnificence.

She had to admit that the Manor was very impressive. A long oak table set with many places was positioned in the centre of the hall.

Sir Everard laughed heartily. 'All handsome, m'dear,' he told her. 'Every man jack of 'em! Chosen for their looks for my little games, d'ye see?'

'Oh, goodee!' exclaimed Aunt Hatty. 'Isn't that nice, honey?' she added, leaning across Sir Everard to touch Mirabelle's arm. 'We can choose anyone we like. Any!'

Mirabelle was interested in only one. 'Did you recognise him, Aunt Hatty? Did you?' She looked at her aunt intently. 'Was he the one?'

They were making their way down a stone staircase and

Mirabelle shuddered as the damp air from the depths enveloped her. Aunt Hatty gave a nervous giggle.

'You're going to show us the dungeons!' she exclaimed.

'Aunt Hatty!' whispered Mirabelle hoarsely. 'The groom! Did he seem familiar?'

Sir Everard chuckled, rather an evil sound in the dimly lit dankness, Mirabelle thought. 'A peep at the dungeons,' he said, 'no more. Give you gels the full treatment after dinner!'

'Oooh!' cooed Aunt Hatty, shuddering deliciously. 'The full treatment! Hear that, Mirabelle? The full treatment! My buttocks are glowing already!'

Mirabelle silently admitted that she felt a certain flutter in her cunney, but was it a flutter of fear or of anticipation of forbidden pursuits, she asked herself. Or was it thoughts of the groom? Could it possibly be . . . ?' She shook her head, trying desperately to clear her mind of thoughts which made her head ache.

Another scream of delight echoed through a chamber which they had, only a moment ago, entered. Aunt Hatty was dancing along the damp walls, touching a variety of instruments of flagellation.

'Some of them are so big and fat!' she squealed.

'Well, those are not actually whips, m'dear,' Sir Everard imparted.

With a playful slap upon his ruddy jowls and a light laugh, Aunt Hatty assured him that she knew exactly what they were.

'Ah! Excellent!' He took a thick and solid piece of leather from its hanging place, slicking it lovingly with his fingers and holding it out to Mirabelle.

Juices seeped across the delicate folds which surrounded her clitty and she, too, nodded, feeling a flush suffuse her pale cheeks.

'Ah!' murmured Sir Everard again, giving the thick tube a final stroke before replacing it on its hanging place. 'This is my *pièce de résistance*!' he added proudly, holding out a hand to an iron maiden.

'But . . . but . . .' Mirabelle felt the blood leave her head and her face pale to chalk whiteness.

'No, no, no!' assured Sir Everard. 'Not at all!' The front of the maiden opened, not without a squeak or two from the rusty hinges, and the two ladies looked inside. What they saw brought a squeal of delight from Hatty May and a mew of ecstasy from Mirabelle.

Instead of the iron spikes designed to pierce any poor creature incarcerated in the devilish device an exceedingly lifelike phallus was positioned at precisely the right height to intrude into a lady's willing cunney. It was moulded to the inner side of the door. It was smooth and coloured in such a way as to look like masculine skin filled to turgidity until the tortuous veins which clambered the length bulged. Surging in a very upward direction it terminated in a globe which was as smooth as the finest silk and shone wetly in the dim light.

'How very familiar!' murmured Mirabelle. The remark passed her lips unbidden and she felt her ivory complexion set aflame in embarrassment. Her eyes were focused intently upon the organ which seemed to quiver in a most lifelike manner. Surreptitiously, she looked at Sir Everard who made no attempt to hide a smile.

Aunt Hatty May was not so entranced with the device. Her interest seemed to be converged upon the chains and silken ropes designed to tether a willing victim to the walls or to a bench set in the centre of the chamber.

'But there will be more time for inspection later,' said Sir Everard cheerfully.

'Oh!' pouted Aunt Hatty May. 'Such a spoil-sport!' She threw herself upon the bench, spreadeagled in such a way that her skirts were thrown about her ample hips.

Sir Everard laughed delightedly, caressing the plump cunney which pouted for his pleasure. 'Dinner,' he said firmly, 'which I am sure you will enjoy, will be served directly. The gowns I wish you to wear are laid out for you upon your beds.'

Mirabelle and her aunt gave each other puzzled frowns as they were ushered hurriedly from the chamber and to their rooms.

A scream was heard from Aunt Hatty. Mirabelle's startled eyes were drawn to her bed and, almost immediately, her chaperone bustled into her room holding up a gossamer fine muslin dress which dated from the last century.

'It's disgusting!' squealed Aunt Hatty, holding the high-waisted gown out from her body as though the touch of it would taint her.

Mirabelle was already hurrying out of her travelling suit to try on the transparent gauzy creation laid out for her.

'It's pretty!' retorted Mirabelle.

'I know what he's about!' said Aunt Hatty. 'The Hell Fire Club! He's recreating it!'

Mirabelle plucked at the tightly knotted laces of her corsets. 'Help me, Aunt Hatty!' she pleaded.

'You're not taking off your corsets?' Hatty was horrified that an Edwardian lady should be seen without her corsets. 'Whores and servants . . .'

'Don't be so old-fashioned and stuffy!' interrupted Mirabelle. She stood there, defiance and excitement making her pretty face glow and her eyes shine, her dimpled hands resting on the sharp shelves of her hips created by the corsets. The bush of her cunney gleamed darkly beneath the rim of the tightly confining corset and her full breasts were thrust upwards by the device. 'Help me, Aunt Hatty.'

Reluctantly, Mirabelle was unlaced from her corset and she, immediately, picked up the muslin gown from her bed, holding it against her.

'Oh, I can't wear such a thing!' groaned Aunt Hatty, watching her niece slip the gossamer over her dark head.

'You must!' said Mirabelle huskily. 'It's part of the game!'

The gown now worn by Mirabelle was so fine, so delicately transparent, that she might have been wearing nothing at all. She felt so free, so uninhibited that she danced around the room.

'Come along, Aunt Hatty,' she urged. 'It feels wonderful! They used to wear them damp, you know, so the dress clung to the curves!'

Aunt Hatty sniffed meaningfully, tossing her blonde curls in disdain at such a thought.

With a few deft changes Mirabelle re-arranged her hair to suit the dress and eyed herself critically in the mirror. The high waist and low cut of the neckline were a perfect foil for her pouting breasts which were thrust like pale pillows from the translucent cloth. From the waist the gown fell in fine folds which drifted back and forth as she walked. Her long shapely legs were further enhanced by the flimsy gauze.

Without enthusiasm Aunt Hatty May was preparing herself for dinner. Mirabelle helped her from her corset.

'I can't go down looking like this!' cried Aunt Hatty. With horrified eyes she gazed into the long mirror.

'You look pretty, Aunt Hatty,' assured Mirabelle and it was true. In the almost *au naturel* state required by the muslin gown, her aunt looked buxomly attractive. Her fair skin and fluffy curls gave a bubbly effervescent appearance which Mirabelle was sure would be enthusiastically received by Sir Everard. The splendid buttocks were especially enhanced by the floating gossamer.

'Hm,' agreed Aunt Hatty, peeping over the pale smoothness of her shoulder to admire the sweep of her barely concealed backside with its creamy hillocks cleft by the deep, dark valley. 'Perhaps I might tempt him,' she added reluctantly.

Mirabelle smiled and they left the room together, giggling like girls released from the school room.

'Ah!' greeted Sir Everard, watching the two almost naked figures descend towards him. His handsome, although plump and ruddy, face was wreathed in smiles. He touched his crotch and thrust it upwards in an inviting manner, making Hatty giggle uncontrollably.

A figure stood in the shadows behind Sir Everard. Dressed in shades of grey and black the man, and Mirabelle was sure it was a man by the height and breadth of him, blended into the gloom of the great hall.

'It's him!' shrieked Hatty May, pointing to the shadow.

'Who?' Mirabelle continued to walk down the huge staircase, but her legs felt stiff and awkward. She shivered involuntarily for when she looked again at the dark figure she saw him peering at her, behind a mask. He was looking at her with great intent. She knew there was something familiar about him. It was the same familiarity instilled by the groom. She looked again and he was gone.

'Oysters!' exclaimed Sir Everard, taking their arms and leading them to the great table. 'Brought directly from Colchester this morning.'

Mirabelle and Aunt Hatty were placed in chairs, one beside the other. The chairs were unusual in that they invited the sitters to swing their legs into stirrups fashioned upon the arms.

'How odd!' remarked Mirabelle, finding her legs sliding automatically into the stirrups, thrusting her dainty little ankles into the air and the gossamer of her gown high about her thighs.

Aunt Hatty May giggled as her fluffy blonde cunney lips were opened by the design of the chair. 'But how can we eat our oysters?' she asked as her giggles subsided and Sir Everard arranged the two young ladies to his liking.

'Ah!' he exclaimed, touching the plump lips of Mirabelle's dark-fringed cunney, caressing and moulding them with tender fingers. 'I shall partake of my portion first, dear ladies,' he advised them, 'so that I can more generously service you.'

'Of course!' realised Mirabelle. 'Oysters are an aphrodisiac, are they not?'

Sir Everard smoothed his whiskers in a suggestive upward motion. 'Indeed they are, my dear,' he agreed, 'and I must be Colchester's best customer, second only to King Edward!'

'I still don't see . . .' murmured Aunt Hatty.

'Silly goose!' Mirabelle pointed to her perfectly displayed cunney with its shining pink folds splayed so sweetly and the clitty pert and erect amid it all.

'Oh!' giggled Aunt Hatty May. 'But they'll be cold. The oysters, won't they?'

'Brought from this bed of ice,' said Sir Everard, pointing to a great silver salver upon which lay a layer of crushed ice dotted with freshly cracked oysters.

Mirabelle shuddered and felt her cunney quiver with anticipation of the strange sensations to come. She felt trapped in this extraordinary manor house with its odd devices designed to titillate the sexual parts and yet, she told herself, she was perfectly free to leave.

Sir Everard tipped back his head, holding a large crusty oyster shell poised above his mouth. Mirabelle saw droplets of the oyster's juices shimmer in the candlelight and saw the slippery edible flesh slither into Sir Everard's mouth.

'Hm!' He swallowed the mollusc with some relish and washed it down with champagne. 'Now who shall be first?' he asked with a grin.

He held an opened oyster in his hand and, teasingly, held it within an inch of, first, Mirabelle's cunney and, second, Aunt Hatty's trembling, blonde-fringed little entrance.

'Oooh!' sighed Aunt Hatty. 'I can hardly bear the waiting!' Her plump thighs, splayed so prettily in the blue upholstered stirrups and framed so delicately with the diaphanous muslin, quivered delightedly as she watched the chilled oyster in its open encrusted shell be presented to each girl in turn.

With a delighted cry Mirabelle accepted the slippery cold of the mollusc, feeling the icy moistness of the fish lying in the dish of her cunney.

'What a pretty sight! groaned Sir Everard, kneeling before her.

'One for me!' pleaded Aunt Hatty.

The knight patted her fluttering hand. 'I like to savour my meals, my dear,' he told her, 'rather than bolt them down.'

Aunt Hatty May pouted, slumping down in the strange chair as Mirabelle quivered, waiting for the scoop of Sir Everard's tongue. When it came it felt warm and caressing. The touch was featherlight, slipping moistly into her depths to spoon out the delicacy of the oyster spiced by her musk.

The very thought of the process brought Mirabelle to the edge of a spend and as the knight's tongue eased deeply beneath the oyster to slither into her depths she found herself shuddering to an ecstatic peak.

'Me!' cried Aunt Hatty impatiently, on seeing how very gloriously Mirabelle reached her spend. 'Please, me!'

Mirabelle felt the glorious bounty of her barely clad breasts shudder as she herself shivered from a wonderful spend. Only vaguely did she notice their host treat Aunt Hatty in a similar manner; allowing the chilled oyster juice to drool upon the very openness of her cunney before the mollusc was scooped into the dish of the quivering folds.

From the corner of her blue eyes, still heavy-lidded from the spend, Mirabelle saw again the shadowy figure, padding silently about the great hall.

# Chapter 15

Joshua Hackensack drew the black hood from his handsome head.

Wearing only the briefest of leather cod-pieces, he threw his long muscular legs upwards and rested them, polished boots included, upon the huge scrubbed deal table.

'Joshua!' The cry of anguish at her freshly-scrubbed table being used so ill was drawn from the pretty raven-haired maid busy in the big kitchen.

With naked biceps bulging, the big man folded his arms behind his head in an attitude of relaxation.

'Sir Everard bin working me hard at his dungeon games,' he explained.

He focused his dark eyes upon the shapely bottom swaying from side to side as the girl riddled the kitchen grate furiously. 'Hm, sure do need some relief!'

A large hand was lowered to adjust the leather cup which confined his bulging manhood so tightly.

The girl turned, her face glowing from the heat of the range and wreathed in a dimpled smile. Her large, firm breasts were slicked with a film of perspiration from her labours and he watched a trickle of it shimmer as it ran down the deep valley between the flushed mounds.

'Come here!' he said hoarsely.

'Don't you come in 'ere and order me about, Joshua Hackensack!'

She slammed the cast iron door of the grate shut with a foot clad in a high-heeled button boot.

'T'ain't right! I'm Sir Everard's housekeeper and you . . .' She paused, grinning. 'Well, I don't know what I can call you!' she continued.

'I was hired as a groom,' he reminded her.

Milly laughed uproariously. 'And is it grooming you do with Miss Hatty May in the cellar?'

'Dungeon,' he corrected, his eyes not missing a detail of her curvaceous, luscious figure.

Joshua loved the way her smokey-blue eyes shone as they twinkled at him; loved the way her rosy cheeks glowed from the heat of the kitchen. He felt his cock jerk painfully in the tight pouch as he watched her capable hands rest on the swell of her ample hips as she grinned down at him.

'I won't have you thinking that you can use me at a whim!' she said defiantly. 'When you fuck me I know you're thinking of Miss Hoity-toity Mirabelle Washington!'

Her work-roughened hands fell to a crisp white cotton apron and she smoothed it down, the smokey-blue eyes glittering at him mischievously. The large breasts, pouting over the low-cut black taffeta gown, heaved as she breathed fast and deep.

Giving a wry grin, Joshua let his long legs fall to the ancient flag stones of the manor kitchen. The pain of need in his groin as he looked at Milly was becoming unbearable.

The girl turned from him, stirring a huge pot on the top of the range. Her smooth shoulders were bare, shining in the sunlit kitchen.

'I know you won't stay here forever. You'll go back to America soon,' she reminded him, 'and I won't never see you again.'

He watched the raven curls, dampened by the heat of the kitchen, lower in an attitude of sadness. He jumped up, wincing at the urgency in his groin. Folding his bare arms around the neat waist he felt his own breathing become deeper, harsher as he allowed his hands to stray upwards to cup the firm pillows of those lovely breasts.

'Come with me!' he urged. Why did he say that when he loved Mirabelle as much as ever? Underneath the worn taffeta dress he could feel the unfettered nakedness of Milly's body. No corsets, no bodices, no drawers or any of the rest of the feminine frippery spoilt the curvaceous little maid's body. His manhood told him that this body more than pleased him. But it was simply a body. There was no fire as there was in Mirabelle.

'Me?' she murmured, allowing herself to mould against his almost naked leanness. 'Go to America?'

Joshua let his hands slick lightly over the bounteous fullness of her breasts, slipping over the slight film of perspiration which glossed their upper slopes. He felt the large nipples harden to erect pips under his touch.

'Why not?' he rasped, taking the soft lobe of one of her shell-like ears between his lips, lapping at it softly with the tip of his tongue. 'Sure! Why not?' he repeated more forcefully.

Milly leaned back against him, swaying the firm fullness of her buttocks against the leather-confined bundle, making him groan.

'You don't want me!' She made the denial softly, Joshua felt, and without total conviction.

He placed his big hands on her naked shoulders, gripping them forcefully and whipping her around to face him. She made a feeble attempt to escape, but Joshua felt that it was a token gesture and thrust his bulging leather pouch between the shapely pliancy of her thighs.

'What you been doing with Miss Hatty May this morning . . .'

Joshua placed a big hand over her soft lips, halting the envious tirade. 'Ssh!' he whispered. 'You know I was only doing what I was ordered by old Mountjoy!' He released his fingers from her sweet chin and rosy cheeks. 'Same as I do with all his little fancies.'

The smokey-blue eyes glittered up at him, anger as well

as passion making them wide within the thick circle of dark lashes. 'But you like it!' she accused. 'Makes that big cock of yours full of itself and don't you deny it, Joshua Hackensack!'

The leather pouch which Sir Everard made him wear on these occasions became tighter. His ballsack felt full to bursting. The tension in his cock was unbearable.

He couldn't deny that it was even worse when Mirabelle had taken her turn in the Iron Maiden. Fitting her into the contraption, wearing only strips of leather bindings which hid nothing but made each part seem more prominent and pert, had been sheer torture for him.

Sure that Mirabelle knew that he was the one beneath the hood only made the tension in his cock worse. He remembered the agony of imagination; seeing the inanimate phallus on the inner side of the iron door fitting into Mirabelle's cunney. A groan, which he could not control, rose up from his chest.

'Stop it, Milly!' he moaned. The reminders were too vivid. He pushed at her full thighs, parting them with his naked knee. There was little resistance. Her legs parted willingly and he could feel the heat of her sex mound through the folds of her skirt; could feel the plumpness of her sex lips and a slight dampening of that wonderful flesh.

'I only do as I'm ordered,' he said again, his voice hoarse as he breathed the light perfume of her curls and spoke against the softness of her neck. 'I work at Mountjoy Manor. Same as you.' He gave another involuntary groan as he butted the full pouch against her mound.

Milly gave a disdainful toss of her head. ''Cos you followed Miss Mirabelle,' she snapped, but she didn't struggle and Joshua noticed how there was slight, but eager, parting of the luscious thighs. 'Followed her all the way across the sea.'

That was true, admitted Joshua, his hands toying with the thin leather thong which held his pouch in place. He felt the pain that he'd felt when he saw Mirabelle willingly lie beneath the stoker, but he still wasn't sure whether it was the pain of envy or stimulation. The memory stirred his manhood yet again and he tore the brief triangle of leather from his crotch.

'Oh, Joshua!' murmured Milly, feeling the iron-hardness of his manhood, free at last, press into the folds of her skirt. She succumbed eagerly to the forceful domination of his lips.

His arms swept her up, swept her easily as if she was no weight at all, to lie at his mercy on her precious table. He bent his muscular neck and his mouth burrowed into the deep valley between her breasts to taste the slight saltiness of the slick of sweat. He heard her murmur with pleasure and he nibbled lightly at the tender smooth flesh. He heard her gasp as he held her, helpless and vulnerable, upon the huge deal table.

A joyful giggle hinted to him that there would be no resistance to his new advances. He saw her fingers twitch at the hem of her full skirt to bare neat ankles still clad in boots. She was watching him, with those laughing eyes, between her spread and raised knees.

'Tell me that you like to fuck me,' she ordered huskily, the full skirt staying firmly at ankle level.

Joshua, his dark eyes feeling heavy with longing, allowed a finger and thumb to slide back and forth along the huge length of his cock.

'You know it!' he grunted.

'Tell me I'm good as Miss Mirabelle!' Milly persisted.

The pad of his forefinger smeared the droplet of pre-issue across his globe as he thought back to that one time in his hut on the Plantation. Mirabelle had been a virgin who wanted him desperately. As much as he adored little Milly there was no comparison; could not be.

'You're better,' he muttered.

'And you're lying!' snapped Milly, closing her legs and smoothing down her skirt with an angry rustle. Supporting herself upon her elbows, she glared at him crossly. The creamy mounds of those lovely breasts strained the thin covering of her gown. He could see the hardness of the excited nipples probing against the black cloth.

One of his big hands reached out, grabbing the straining cloth, ripping the tight bodice downwards to free the glorious flesh.

Milly screamed at him. 'What you doing, Joshua?' There was something in her tone which told him that she knew exactly what he was doing and she loved every second of it.

Roughly, he pushed her skirt to her waist. This time there was no cry of horror; no resistance. He stood there, at the end of the table, between her silky smooth thighs. She spread her legs further and, somehow, pouted her plump mound, a nest of lush dark curls and above this was a belly which was not flat, but had a comforting swell which beckoned him to lie upon it.

Joshua's thickness was throbbing unmercifully. He positioned himself, his big, smooth globe only inches from the inflamed folds which Milly was offering to him.

'Well?' she prompted. 'Tell me that you love to fuck me.'

'I love to fuck you,' he said truthfully. He loved the way Milly's cushiony passage drew him in, pampered his length, squeezed it so pleasurably.

Milly held out her arms and embraced him, her smokey blue eyes soft and warm, her lips parted to welcome him.

Eyes closed, he saw Mirabelle lying beside him on the narrow truckle bed in his overseer's hut, but that was then and Milly was lying beneath him now. He thrust into the pliant moistness and heard the girl mew with pleasure.

He thought, when the ship carried him across the Atlantic, that he could not live without Mirabelle, that she was his one and only love, but now . . .

He thrust again, feeling the jerking hardness of Milly's clitty welcome the chafing of his cock. He remembered his disappointment when he found he'd followed the wrong vehicle from Liverpool. He'd followed Hatty May instead of Mirabelle.

Supporting himself on his big hands he looked down at Milly, smiling into the smokey blue eyes. The maid had a look of Mirabelle, he realised.

'You thinking about Miss Mirabelle?' asked Milly, a sharpness giving an edge to the question.

'Maybe,' he replied. His lips fastened upon the hardness of a nipple.

'Stop it!' ordered Milly, pinching the hardness of one of his buttocks and pushing him from her.

Joshua was puzzled. 'What's wrong with you?' he asked, frowning. His cock, slick with Milly's juices, throbbed painfully.

Milly tried, unsuccessfully, to cover the bursting fullness of her breasts with the torn gown. Her skirt lay about her belly, a silky framework to a cunney which was, clearly, more than ready for a thick, long cock.

'It ain't right!' murmured Milly unhappily. She still struggled to close her torn bodice, but made no move to cover the open wantonness of her cunney.

'What you talking about, girl?' Joshua's voice rasped with need.

A hand strayed between the pink folds to touch the sensitive tip of her clitty. The hood was drawn back to reveal the burning scarlet of that tiny part. Joshua watched eagerly as Milly's finger slid swiftly from side to side to finish what he had begun.

'You!' Milly hissed breathlessly. 'Thinking about those beauties when you have me!'

'Oh, girl!' exclaimed Joshua. 'You don't understand me! Don't understand me at all!'

Sinking to his knees and pulling Milly closer to the edge of the table, Joshua, licking his wide sensuous lips, parted them and pushed out his tongue to join her finger, pushing it away to replace it with a moister, lighter flicking organ. He heard Milly sigh pleasurably and felt, rather than saw, her lean back, giving herself up to the sensations which he was creating.

'Is it me?' whispered Milly. 'Do you really love me?'

Joshua said nothing. The time was not quite right, but maybe one day soon... One day soon he could truly commit himself having travelled all this way and found... What?

His tongue slid between the silky portals of her entrance. He stiffened it, making it a cock to invade her passage. His big hands drove into the pillows of her buttocks, pulling her closer to him, until his face was all but enfolded within her flesh. The tip of his nose butted at the hardness of her clitty, making her mew with ecstasy and thresh against him. Finally, he allowed his tongue to lash against her clitty, triggering an explosive climax which seemed to continue for long minutes.

'Fuck me now, Joshua!' begged Milly.

Handsome face slick with her love dew, Joshua rose slowly, to stand between her trembling thighs. With both hands he held his thickness, cradling its stiffness, feeling its throbbing power.

'Beg me,' he said softly. 'I like it when you beg for me to take you.'

'I... need... it!' Milly's words were barely audible and her breathing was ragged. He watched her tear at her tight bodice, pressing her breasts up and together, making them look more enticing than ever. Then he knew. He knew that Milly was spiralling into a spend which she could not control. That she would do anything to please him. That she wanted to display herself for him.

With a grin, he lay upon her, fitting his throbbing heat into the pale hillocks of her breasts.

'Gonna come, Milly,' he grunted.

'Yes, Joshua!' The smokey depths of her eyes seemed to draw him in and she gently pampered her full breasts along the length of him.

It was as if he'd been starved of relief for a long time; as if he'd stored his love sap for years especially for this moment.

When the first wave washed over him, he knew what he had to do. He spilled himself in wonderful pearly fountains over Milly's waiting breasts and, somewhere, far away, he heard her moan her joy at his offering.

It was then that he knew. Knew for sure.

When it was over, when they'd calmed and their breathing was slower and more regular, he stood up. He searched for his breeches which he knew he'd tossed carelessly over a chair when Sir Everard called him earlier that morning.

Without a glance at Milly he began to pull them up his long legs. She was looking at him, lying where he'd left her upon the table. Her pretty face had that glow about it; the glow of fulfilment. Her eyes seemed darker, the lids were lowered with dark lashes thick on the rosy cheeks. He could see the silvery stream of his seed trailing between the twin creamy hillocks and he sighed.

'Where you going, Joshua?' she asked, raising herself on one elbow. Even this entranced him for the heavy breasts fell together, making them look more enticing than ever, but he turned away, bending to pick up a full-sleeved shirt which had been tossed carelessly upon the ancient flagstones.

'Joshua!' She was beside him now, her breasts bare, smeared liberally with his issue, swinging heavily, the nipples taut and inflamed. It made his cock twitch.

'Why won't you speak to me?' The smokey-blue eyes were no longer heavy and languid, but flashing dangerously. A lowly housekeeper Milly might have been but she was no slave to be ordered and bullied.

'Something to do,' he said, knowing that his voice sounded guilty. He busied himself, fastening buttons.

'What?' Milly snapped. Her hands flew to her hips. The tumbled raven curls shook as she tossed her head back proudly. Her breasts, bare and shimmering with his juices, shook with her growing temper.

'You wouldn't understand,' he said, striding across the

worn flagstones, hearing the strident noise of his heels echo hollowly through the vast kitchen.

'Try me!' She was leaning forward aggressively, making her breasts more alluring than ever. How he would have loved to grasp them, bite them cruelly, make his mark upon the pale flesh! But there were other tasks to claim his attention.

A cloak and wide-brimmed hat hung on a rough wooden peg by the door. He reached for them, but she was there before him.

'No!' Milly screamed the negation. Her shapely arms were spread across his belongings. Once again the action focused his attention upon the glorious pillows of her breasts, thrust from her torn black bodice with apparent unconscious wantonness.

'Whaddya mean "no"?' He pushed her roughly, making her stagger and fall. Joshua wasn't a violent man, but it was wrong that she should try to rule him.

The silky stiffness of the black taffeta rustled as it slithered about her bare limbs. He could see the smooth arc of a hip, the more delicate curve of a thigh, the pout of her mound. How easy it would be to throw himself upon her and stay, to take her again, roughly this time.

A deep breath made his chest broaden and press against the tiny pearl buttons. He reached over her to take his cloak and hat. He felt the touch of her hand on his boot, grasping, pleading.

'It's no use, Milly,' he said kindly, folding the cloak over his arm and bending to touch her cheek. 'There's something I've gotta do. If I tell you, you won't believe my motives.'

The smokey blue eyes were tear-filled as she gazed up at him. 'Miss Mirabelle . . .' she began.

He nodded, wishing that he was far away from the manor. He stroked the velvet roses in her cheeks with the back of his big fingers, but she shrugged away, averting his gaze. With a sigh he stood. If he didn't go now he would be lost and so would his love.

With a fierce gesture he threw open the door and left the sunny kitchen. He didn't look back as he flung the swirling cape about his broad shoulders. A smile, a rueful quirk of the sensuous lips, split the handsome tanned face. Was it any wonder that word was out that he was a highwayman? Swirling cloaks and broad-brimmed hats were common enough in winter in Georgia, but not so around the English countryside.

'Mirabelle,' he muttered to himself as he saddled his horse.

He tightened the girth maybe a little too much and the big mare whinnied plaintively. 'Sorry, girl!' he muttered, patting her neck.

'This thing 'tween you and me gotta be settled, one way or t'other,' he muttered to an absent Mirabelle. 'Your pa . . .'

He remembered that Mirabelle's father passed to that Great Plantation in the sky at the discovery of the two of them and he shuddered guiltily.

'Not sure your pa was right or wrong.' He looked over the misty fields as he prepared the horse. 'Sometimes I think you and me don't belong together and others I think we're a matching pair. Gotta find out which it is.'

He swung himself into the saddle, tugging the brim of his hat low over his eyes. 'I know I've been following you and kinda stirring up a whole mess of trouble,' he said, wheeling out of the manor stable yard, 'but you gotta understand, I truly thought I couldn't live without you. Couldn't live without the softness of your cunney around my cock. Well, honey, maybe I can and maybe I can't.'

The horse slipped easily into a gallop as they reached the open road. 'Maybe you'll understand,' muttered Joshua, still practising his speech to the absent Mirabelle, 'and maybe you won't, but remember I still care for you and will always be near if you want me.'

Will she understand? he asked himself. He nodded to himself, reassuring the mind which was in such turmoil. 'Sure she will,' he murmured. 'She's met her own kind; felt how they could satisfy her and she'll be accepted wherever she goes.' A wry grin twisted his mouth. 'But she knows she gets the best with me!'

With the final statement he spurred the huge animal on.

# Chapter 16

Rolly Carshalton was in no end of a good mood!

'By jove!' he murmured, pulling off the road and parking his very new motorcar in a pleasant courtyard outside an even pleasanter inn. 'Why shouldn't a chap have a day off from one's wife now and again?' he murmured cheerfully.

He sighed. Much as he loved Lily she was jolly demanding and a chap had other things to do besides languish in bed all day even though the woman beside him was the most glorious creature ever born.

The engine of the little Clyno sputtered. He patted the steering wheel lovingly. 'Going to have some refreshment, old girl!' he promised the car as though it was a living, breathing creature. 'Expect the landlord will give you water and all those other things you seem to need at such frequent intervals.'

The Clyno was Rolly's most recent acquisition. He'd always stuck to horses in the past, finding them much more reliable and trustworthy than motorcars. 'They smell a jolly sight better than those infernal machines,' he'd always said, but when his friend, Vitus Wyndham, had shown him how much freedom of spirit a motorcar could give him he had relented and purchased the little Clyno.

At a leisurely speed, Rolly unfastened his driving helmet and whipped off his goggles. He eased himself from the driving seat and sniffed the summer air. 'Nowhere as lovely as East Anglia on a beautiful day,' he murmured, placing his gauntleted hands upon his quite ample hips.

'Psss!' he heard.

Rolly stopped sniffing the air and looked around, startled. All he could see was a bank of scarlet tea roses looking and smelling quite beautiful.

'Psss!' came the sound again. 'Over here!'

Rolly's helmetless head whipped round to an abandoned farm cart loaded with hay.

'Yes!' came the voice again. 'In the cart!'

The voice was definitely female and had a strange twang to it in Rolly's opinion. It was sort of foreign, but then again it was definitely speaking English, even if it wasn't the King's variety. 'But then the blighter is more German than most!' he reminded himself, thinking of his monarch, Edward.

'Who are you?' asked Rolly, taking a stride or two towards the farm cart as his curiosity got the better of him.

'I need your help!' said the voice quite plaintively. 'And your coat!'

Rolly looked down at his very new leather driving coat which enveloped him from neck to foot.

'My coat? Dash it all . . .' Rolly wasn't averse to helping a maiden in distress, but giving up a chap's brand new togs was beyond a joke.

'What's wrong with what you've got on?' he asked, shoving his hands deep into his coat pockets as though this would save it from being taken from his very shoulders.

'That's the trouble!' A head of blue-black hair suddenly appeared, a little marred, it was true by the odd straw or two, in the middle of the pile of hay. In the midst of the tumbled jet mass were two of the bluest eyes Rolly had ever seen. 'What I'm wearing hides hardly anything.'

Rolly's eyes widened and he stared at the beautiful head rising from the heap of hay.

'Still can't see why you need my coat,' said Rolly, gazing into the blue eyes. He was hard pressed to keep himself from leaping on to the cart to join the lovely creature for all that he was out for a womanless day. 'All I can see is your lovely black hair, your flawless complexion, the most kissable lips and the bluest eyes I've ever gazed upon.' He gave a sigh and a winning smile.

The vision raised further from her makeshift covering. Shoulders as pale as ivory and as smooth as that wonderful substance rose from the hay. Following the shoulders were the most perfect breasts Rolly had ever seen, apart from Lily's, of course, which were quite on par. What made these particular breasts rather different were leather strips artfully arranged around the globes, making them especially pert for all that they were firm and full.

'Good grief!' cried Rolly. He should, he supposed, be quite disgusted that any fiend should treat a girl in such a fashion, but he wasn't. His gear stick sprang to attention in his motoring trousers and probed, quite uncomfortably, against his fly buttons.

'What dastardly monster bound you like this?' he said, trying to sound cross, but his voice cracked with excitement in the middle of the question.

The vision shook her head, spraying little golden twigs of straw over Rolly. 'He wasn't a monster,' she said.

'He wasn't?' Rolly felt quite breathless with desire and wondered whether dear Lily would mind if he was the tiniest bit unfaithful since, as his father often said, a change was as good as a rest. He leant on the back of the cart, looking up with blind adoration at the ivory shoulders and the leather-stripped breasts.

'Oh, no! Sir Everard is a dear man but his cock isn't ever hard as I hoped, so I decided to let Aunt Hatty May have all the fun,' explained the glorious creature.

'Old Mountjoy?' questioned Rolly, his face beaming with a grin of understanding.

The blue-eyed beauty nodded. 'We played some fun games before I left the manor.'

'Jolly well seems so!' said Rolly, hoping that the lovely

one would rise yet further from the hay like Venus from the waves. 'Is that all you've got on – er – down below?' he asked hesitantly, eyeing the carefully designed leather strips about the glorious breasts.

The blue-black head nodded once more. 'So will you help me?'

Rolly's breathing was becoming awfully laboured, he noticed, and his gear stick was positively throbbing. He knew how he'd like to help the beautiful creature, but if she'd been incarcerated, however willingly, in Mountjoy Manor she'd probably had quite sufficient of all that sort of thing for the time being. He decided to play for time. Give her a chance to recover.

'Who is what's-her-name?' he asked, smiling his most ingenuous smile.

'Aunt Hatty May?'

Rolly nodded, his hands itching to feel those pert mounds, leather strips included.

'My chaperone,' he was informed.

'Good grief!' exclaimed Rolly. 'Must be the dashed worst one ever!' The poor creature had obviously not been at all well-looked after and what on earth were her parents doing letting her get into such scrapes with Mountjoy?

An engaging giggle issued from the sweetest rosebud mouth Rolly had ever seen. 'She's a dear, really! She's just rather fluttery and fluffy and needs to be taken care of, which is another reason why I'm dashing to London.'

Rolly tapped the hay cart. 'Not a vehicle for dashing,' he assured her.

'Well, I was hoping . . .' The lovely voice trailed away quite piteously to Rolly's way of thinking. He felt that he couldn't possibly refuse the beauty anything.

'Yes?' he prompted, leaning further into the cart and not caring a fig if his brand new leather coat became scratched. His fingers, which seemed to have developed a will of their own, delved into the hay searching for Lord-knows-what.

'That you might . . .' The shimmering mane of jet curls was shaken back from the smooth slope of the beautiful shoulders which had the effect of making the leather bound breasts poke out at Rolly in an inviting manner.

It was all too much for the young heir to the Carshalton estates. His legs gave way and he found himself face down in the hay, his wayward hands scrabbling for purchase. When his fingers landed upon firm, but pliant, thigh flesh he felt himself soar to the very brink of a spontaneous spend.

'Oooh!' cried the beauty, for Rolly's fingers progressed through the hay to the lush curls of a pussy mound.

It was then that he realised that they had not been formally introduced. 'Rolly Carshalton,' he panted, delicately fingering two very plump labia liberally garnished with lush curls.

The glorious creature slithered back down into the hay and sighed prettily as Rolly's fingers petted each chubby lip. 'Mirabelle Washington,' she answered huskily.

'You're that dashed lovely American I keep hearing about!' exclaimed Rolly perceptively. He used one hand to swish away the hay from Mirabelle, the better to admire the whole of her loveliness.

'How clever of you!' flattered Mirabelle, stretching on the bed of hay, arms above her head and legs splayed. 'How did you know?'

Rolly gulped. The lower part of Mirabelle's body was decorated with narrow leather strips similar to those about her breasts. 'I suppose . . .' he gasped, 'the accent gave me . . . a bit of a clue.'

With trembling fingers he traced the tight thong which enhanced her tiny waist. Further thin filaments of leather flared out over her hips to be joined between her thighs. Her lush mound pouted at him through an intricate network of bindings which served to magnify its beauty.

'By jove!' he remarked. 'Old Mountjoy has been busy.'

He cupped the fullness of the leather bound cunney and was delighted to feel the warm moistness seeping between each plump lip.

'He had a helper,' sighed Mirabelle, bending her knees and allowing them to drift outwards. Her periwinkle-blue eyes looked dreamy as they gazed beyond Rolly to some distant horizon.

'Another perverted member of the Hell Fire Club, I suppose,' he said, his voice tainted with disgust, although, if he was truthful, the hint of disgust was rather an act on his part. He found the leather bindings quite fetching.

Mirabelle shook her head. 'No, I don't think so.' She bore down upon the finger, now bare of gauntlet, which Rolly had absently slipped into her clutching female passage.

'No?' Rolly used the ball of his thumb to agitate her pert little clitty. The pippin was hot as fire and probing upwards in a most eager fashion. 'Not a member? Some sort of servant, I suppose.'

The curvaceous body arched urgently and Mirabelle's hips did a graceful circling motion and she pumped upon Rolly's finger very temptingly. 'He had a very large cock!' she revealed breathily as she reached a spend.

'Ah!' This disclosure reminded Rolly of his own organ which was fairly battering upon his trouser opening. Mirabelle's love dew was trickling quite copiously over his fingers and he allowed himself the luxury of bathing his digits in the silky stream. 'One of the society set, I expect,' he surmised. 'Some of them are wonderfully endowed and they like nothing better than to exercise their organs.'

The wide blue eyes, heavy with the lethargy of restitution, turned to him, making his own battering ram throw itself upon the enclosure of his motoring togs. 'Do you think so?'

'No doubt in my mind!'' said Rolly, removing the finger from Mirabelle's warm passage to caress the tightly trussed breasts and belly. The nipples, he noticed pleasurably, were as hard and hot as chestnuts taken directly from the fire and he took one little morsel between his lips.

'It was so huge and so hard . . .' she murmured.

The description was causing Rolly considerable discomfort. His own hugeness was not inconsiderable and he began to fumble inside his voluminous leather coat.

'I do wish I knew who he was,' sighed Mirabelle and her curvaceous hips, which seemed to have a will of their own, made an upward arc. 'He wore a hood, you see.'

'That sort usually do,' murmured Rolly, frantically trying to open the yards of leather. There was this lovely girl practically begging him to penetrate her with his hugeness and he seemed to be swamped in leather.

'I wondered if he was the highwayman who frightened Aunt Hatty May,' murmured Mirabelle, swaying the tightly trussed titties from side to side, brushing the erect teats back and forth against Rolly's questing lips.

'Heard about him,' mumbled the younger Carshalton. 'Should be hung!'

He had finally swung his coat open and was tackling his trouser buttons.

Mirabelle's luscious body stiffened and Rolly, not unnaturally, thought that it was an action caused by a need for penetration of the juicy receptacle between her splayed thighs.

'Hanging is rather drastic,' she remarked.

'Just like that Turpin fellow. Blackguard! Galloping about the place as though we were back in the eighteenth century. Not on, you know. Not on at all,' Rolly continued, finally releasing his cock and waving it proudly over Mirabelle.

'No,' she mewed.

'No?' he repeated with some dismay. That was a bit much after all the trouble he'd had extricating the thing.

'Don't hang him,' she continued. 'I've got a feeling I know him, you see.'

'Ah!' The sound was a sigh of relief as he positioned the silkiness of his globe at the pulsing entrance blended with a cry of understanding.

'A feeling that I know him intimately,' the lovely girl whispered as Rolly slowly thrust forward into a softness which was quite blissful.

'One of the Set,' was all Rolly could manage in the immediate circumstances.

Mirabelle's cunney grasped Rolly's length in a wonderfully petting manner which made him feel that his length of pleasure stick was being caressed by the softest of velvet waves.

'I wish I knew,' she murmured, undulating the whole length of her leather bound body under him.

What did it matter, thought Rolly, plunging ever more vigorously into the glorious creature. Masked sorcerer's apprentices, galloping highwaymen were all part of this beautiful girl's life, it seemed to him. Part of her rich pattern of experience, like he was himself. He hoped to goodness dear Lily wouldn't find out about this part of the pattern. That would cause no end of trouble.

'You're very vigorous,' cooed Mirabelle, throwing her agile young legs about his waist.

'And you are deliciously receptive!' he grunted breathlessly.

'Oooh! Can you feel me flutter about your length? I do that when . . . a spend . . . comes upon me!'

'Jolly nice!' puffed Rolly. 'And I . . . I . . . aaagh!' It became more than obvious what he did as gush after gush was swallowed by Mirabelle's cunney.

'Oi!'

The pleasantly relaxing aftermath of conjugation was marred as the owner of the cart staggered from the inn to continue his progress along the lanes of East Anglia.

Rolly, his gear stick steeped in Mirabelle's luscious body, dazedly lifted his head.

'Oi!' came the cry again, followed by the sound of running feet in stout boots.

Hitched to the cart was a shire horse, stout of heart and limb. The cries of dismay from the farmhand and the stumbling clatter of boots, not to mention the trauma of grunts and vibration which the shire had endured for most of the afternoon was beyond a joke for the old mare. With a disapproving whinny and a pawing of the front legs she set off down the road.

'Oi!' cried the farmhand once more.

Rolly found himself sliding towards the rear open end, still attached to Mirabelle at his pertinent part.

'What about my hay?' came the cry along the Essex lane.

Desperately clinging to the side struts of the cart with one hand and Mirabelle with the other, Rolly was in no mood to discuss hay, no matter to whom it belonged. He was barely able to catch his breath such was the jolting of the cart caused by the quite amazing speed the old mare was managing.

'Oooh!'

'Sorry . . . my sweet!' he apologised, tucking his fingers under one of the leather bindings. 'Where . . . does . . . it . . . hurt?'

'It . . . doesn't,' supplied Mirabelle, her voice breathy and excited. 'I am . . . reaching another . . . delightful spend!'

Rolly, daring to lift his head to watch the hedgerows rush past, inadvertently thrust further into Mirabelle.

'Oooh!' she cried again. 'That's it, you wonderful man! What marvellous staying power you have!'

Despite the jolting of the cart Rolly found himself responding quite deliciously to the lovely girl's compliments and found himself thickening rapidly. An urge to thrust once more was also hard to resist and this, plus the rhythmic bouncing of the cart, brought about a speedy spend.

The old mare, sensing that she was missing something, suddenly dug in her iron-shod heels and skidded to a stop. This had the effect of shooting Rolly and Mirabelle, together with a golden shower of hay, through the end of the cart and into the dusty lane.

The old mare turned her head to look at them and gave a snort of disdain.

'Ouch!' Leather strips fastened in tender places were no protection from dusty, stony Essex lanes and Mirabelle's buttocks were on the receiving end of the punishment.

'Look at my hay!' The farmhand was running, somewhat haphazardly from the quaffing of too many pints of lunchtime ale, towards the spillage. 'All over the lane, it is!'

Rolly, still winded and needing a respite, lowered his head upon Mirabelle's breasts, seeking succour and comfort.

'Ought to be ashamed of yourselves!' grumbled the farmhand, standing over the tangled pair. 'Good mind to report you to the squire!'

The Carshalton estates covered a vast area of Hertfordshire and Essex and Rolly was not quite sure if he'd reached the eastern boundary when he stopped to give refreshment to the little Clyno. He buried his head yet further into the bounteous Mirabelle, chance the farmhand was from the estate.

'Aye!' confirmed the farmhand. 'And the vicar too, more 'n likely. Ought to be ashamed. And what about my hay? That's what I'd like to know.'

All this talk of hay and snitching to the vicar and the squire was getting on Rolly's nerves. He lifted his head and turned it, glaring up at the hayseed who dared to threaten him.

'Oh, sir!' The hayseed touched his forelock, not once but several times. 'Oi never meant . . . ! Oi never thought . . .'

'Shut up, you dashed idiot!' Rolly whispered the command as though expecting his father, Lord Carshalton, to come galloping round the bend at any moment with the hunting pack hard on his heels.

It was difficult to know exactly what to do in the circumstances. The simplest answer, Rolly supposed, frowning into the glorious depths of Mirabelle's bosom, was to simply stand up, hauling Mirabelle with him. However, how to do it while still maintaining one's dignity was an entirely different matter.

'Oi never thought it were you, you see,' continued the hayseed, twisting his smock nervously.

'Well, it is!' said Rolly somewhat tetchily. He fumbled in the region of his open fly buttons, but managed to stroke Mirabelle's leather trussed sensitive parts in the process.

'Oh, Rolly!' she cried with obvious enjoyment. 'Again! You are quite insatiable!' She arched her lovely body in a lithe, strong movement.

'Oh, bother!' exclaimed Rolly. The sudden activity tossed him skywards, to land in a heap, naked cock upwards, on the dusty lane.

The hayseed gulped. His bloodshot eyes bulged alarmingly and darted from Rolly to Mirabelle where they remained, totally fixed. His smock took a sharp upward drift, rather like a scout tent being erected by an efficient master.

Rolly buttoned his own tent pole safely away and jumped athletically to his feet. Mirabelle smiled in a friendly fashion, although she did, at least, manage to blush a shade pinker than her normal creamy ivory.

'It's rude to stare!' commented Rolly, slapping the hayseed with a gauntlet which he whipped from his pocket. 'Shockingly rude!' He continued to wallop the farmhand's ruddy cheeks, but nothing would make him avert his gaze from Mirabelle's pertly trussed mounds which were so decoratively held firm by the leather thongs. Since this seemed to have no effect he booted the corduroy breeches, sending the hayseed sprawling upon Mirabelle's prone body.

A lightweight in boxing terms, Rolly judged the hayseed, so no doubt the mishap would not cause very much further damage to Mirabelle's bare buttocks. Interesting how he just lay there upon the beauty, seemingly frozen by her loveliness, mused Rolly. The rough labourer's hands did not stray to the pouting breasts as Rolly's did in a matter of seconds. And there seemed to be no thrusting of the pelvic region or fiddling with trouser openings.

'Perhaps hayseed's sexual drive was not as strong as one's own,' mused Rolly to himself.

'Oooh!' murmured Mirabelle. 'You're very thick!'

Rolly smiled smugly. 'Of course, he's thick! Hayseeds tend to be thick. Don't have the same advantages as us public school chaps, don't you know?'

Mirabelle gave him a delightful smile, sort of dreamy and heavy-lidded and she licked her parted lips, breathing rather heavily, Rolly thought. Couldn't be sure, but he had an inkling that she was tantalising her own erect and rosy nipples. Bit off, that, thought Rolly fleetingly. Could make the hayseed think that she had taken a shine to him.

'Good grief!' he exclaimed suddenly. 'That's not on! Not on at all!' The corduroy buttocks were jolly well pumping up and down. What's more they were pumping up and down swiftly, much as Rolly's had before that dashed mare had run amok.

Rolly's driving boot lashed out once more and landed heavily upon the corduroy buttocks, depositing the hayseed smack bang in the middle of his own hay.

'Pick the dashed stuff up yourself since you're so concerned about it!' he ordered, his confidence returning. 'Come along, my dear,' he said turning to Mirabelle and holding out his hand to her prone figure. 'We shall repair to London in my motorcar and you can tell me more about yourself on the way.'

Without a backward glance at the hayseed Rolly supported Mirabelle as they walked slowly to his waiting vehicle.

'Some of these labourers can be dashed forward, you know,' said Rolly conversationally, stroking a hand over one of Mirabelle's breasts. Once this progress had started it was difficult to stop it. His fingers drifted, almost unconsciously, down over her belly and didn't stop until they reached her cunney. There they stayed for some few moments, feeling the trussed plumpness of the lips, the erect pertness of the clitty and, most particularly, the quite excessive outpourings of liquid from her heated depths.

'My spend must have been more copious than normal,' he remarked, smiling down at her proudly.

'Hm,' she murmured noncommittally, smiling up at him with those innocent periwinkle-blue eyes. 'Do you think I could borrow your coat?' she added, changing the subject rather quickly.

'My coat?' Rolly looked down at the garment in question which was brand new when he left the house that morning. He frowned. It looked decidedly the worse for wear after being rolled in the hay and the dust of the lane.

'Please!' The periwinkle-blue eyes widened in a most engaging manner. They were almost irresistible. 'I can't go to London like this!'

'Rather!' agreed Rolly. 'Catch the most ghastly chest cold riding in an open car wearing nothing but leather thongs. Have to do something about that!' He grinned at her encouragingly.

'So you'll lend it to me?' Mirabelle circled his neck with her long slim arms.

Rolly frowned, deep in thought. 'Er – no!' he said after a moment's pondering.

Mirabelle's eyes filled with tears and if there was one thing that he could not bear it was a woman weeping. Gave a chap the willies!

His face brightened suddenly. 'Hang on a tick!' Pulling Mirabelle's arms from his neck he ran back to the hayseed who was painstakingly picking up his load a handful at a time. It was a struggle, but in the end he achieved his purpose.

'Here we are!' he cried triumphantly, waving the hayseed's smock aloft. 'You can wear this!'

# Chapter 17

'Had to call,' said Viscount Vitus Wyndham. 'Heard how very beautiful you were, you see and, by jove, I'm not disappointed!'

The two young people sat in the orangery of Peacham Place, enjoying the sub-tropical warmth and the scents of the exotic plants.

Mirabelle gave the Viscount one of her most winning smiles. 'Such a shame you're married!' she murmured softly, accepting a kiss on the very centre of the palm of her hand.

Mama would have been delighted to make a young man like Vitus welcome on the Washington Plantation and she had heard that the Wyndhams had a wonderfully large country seat. She pulled a face. Unlike that dank place of Sir Everard Mountjoy's. She shuddered and Aunt Hatty was still there!

Vitus gave her such a sensual kiss. It sent shudders to her very core, melting her from the inside out.

'Dash it all!' he exclaimed, sweeping the lovely Southern belle into his young arms. 'Much as I love Poppy, my wife, don't you know . . .'

Mirabelle dabbed at her eyes with a lace handkerchief.

'Have I upset you?' said the young viscount. 'Didn't mean to. Dash it all, wouldn't do that for the world. No, not at all!'

'It's just that . . .' sobbed Mirabelle.

'Yes?' breathed the Viscount.

Mirabelle felt the Viscount's hand snake up the diaphanous silk of her stocking, feeling the dimpled beauty of her knee and the shapely contour of her thigh. 'Do go on!' he begged. 'It's just that what?'

'I had a love like yours once,' Mirabelle said, allowing her lovely head to droop in a gesture of tragedy. Everything was becoming so horrid and London did not have the class of people she was told to expect.

'Did you really?' murmured the Viscount, absently allowing his fingers to cup her mound. 'And got killed in some ghastly duel or shoot out or whatever you call them in the Colonies, I suppose.'

Mirabelle stiffened. 'Georgia isn't a colony,' she said coldly and she had half a mind to slap the Viscount's hand, but he was doing such delightful things about her drawers. 'And as far as I know he wasn't killed.'

'Oh, jolly good!' said Vitus, looking genuinely pleased. 'Good news, eh?' The skilled fingers had somehow managed to ease her drawers down about her ankles. 'Good news about the Colonies, too. Had some sort of a bloodless coup, I suppose.'

Mirabelle, although enjoying his attentions between her thighs despaired about his lack of historical knowledge. 'There was a Declaration of Independence in 1776,' she managed breathlessly.

'Dash it all!' gasped Vitus. His eyes looked glazed as he parted her lovely folds and felt the moist warmth between them. 'Was there really? Was it reported?' He sank to his knees before her, pushing up her skirts and petticoats. 'That sort of thing ought to be, you know.' He gazed at the glorious parted thighs, the lifted and spread knees and sighed with delight. 'You're the most delightful girl. Very accommodating.'

'I had to leave my love,' continued Mirabelle, her voice choking in sadness. The choke would have been more intense had it not been for the wonderful things Vitus was doing between her thighs.

The Viscount lapped at Mirabelle's clitty, a soft gentle lapping, rhythmic and regular, taking her inexorably to soar above the mundanity of her life in Peacham Place. 'How I wish I could marry someone like you!' she sighed.

'Where did you leave him?' asked Vitus sympathetically. 'Lose him somewhere?' He bobbed up from between her thighs, conveniently forgetting her wish.

'I've come all the way from Atlanta to meet the right man,' she continued. Her lovely little bottom bounced upon the sofa as she rubbed her moist flesh against the Viscount's lips.

'Well, you dashed well shouldn't have lost the one you left there, should you?' Vitus was not a chap to get in such a to do, but he felt that Mirabelle had been very careless to lose a perfectly good fellow.

Sobbing began in earnest, despite the fact that Vitus had changed the method of consoling her. Her upset had quite touched him and touched him where it mattered! His large and much thickened cock slunk into her open and willing cunney.

'Ah!' she sighed, quite forgetting to sob after the initial insertion.

'There!' exclaimed Vitus. 'That's better, isn't it? Made you quite forget about the loss of your chap, hasn't it?'

'No,' sighed Mirabelle. 'I could never forget Joshua. He was my first love; my only love.' She clenched her cunney muscles in a softly cossetting way about the young Viscount's cock.

Vitus groaned for the sheer pleasure she created, thrusting slowly back and forth upon her. 'Lucky chap, eh?' he managed to grunt.

'Joshua Hackensack was a wonderful lover,' she sighed, her eyes closed and eyelashes fluttering against the smoothness of his cheek.

'Hackensack?' grunted Vitus. 'Unusual name that and dashed if I haven't heard it somewhere quite recently.'

The blue eyes snapped open and Mirabelle's body stiffened under the young viscount's. The strong cunney muscles contracted wildly about the thickness which intruded so pleasantly.

'Oh, I say!' exclaimed Vitus. 'Have a care, old girl! My self-control ain't what it was!'

Unheeding Mirabelle contracted her muscles more wildly in her surprise. 'You've heard of Hackensack? Here in London?'

Vitus pumped upon the lovely Mirabelle's body in an involuntary fashion, thrusting up and down, allowing her cunney to caress him in the strongest manner possible. 'Can't be helped!' he cried. 'The spend overcomes me!'

Feeling Vitus pound into her made Mirabelle, momentarily, dismiss memories of Joshua from her mind and concentrate upon the viscount's ministrations. A fluttering, a pre-spend palpitation, began in the most sensitive flesh at her entrance. She sighed deeply, causing more sensation to transmit itself to Vitus.

'Aaah!' he groaned huskily.

'Hackensack?' Mirabelle said urgently, but Vitus was too engrossed in his ecstasy to reply.

'Here in London?' she attempted again as the passion surges swept over her.

'Can't . . . remember . . . where!' groaned Vitus.

'Think!' persuaded Mirabelle urgently.

'Dashed difficult when a chap's . . . aaah!' Vitus irrigated Mirabelle with a copious fountain and was unable to continue his confession for some moments.

At last he collapsed upon her, his young body shaking with the tremors of the aftermath.

'Well?' said Mirabelle sharply.

The heat was heavy upon them. The scents of the exotic plants were all-pervading and Vitus frowned as he relaxed upon the cane sofa, his young cock twitching with anticipation for further stimulation.

'Hackensack?' reminded Mirabelle.

Vitus looked at her, his heart turning over in response to the look of longing in those blue eyes. 'I am trying dashed hard, Mirabelle,' he promised her. 'Truly.'

She felt that she had come a long way and was so close to her goal that it would not be fair if she was foiled at the last fence.

'White's!' said Vitus suddenly, his eyes bright with inspiration.

'Surely not?' questioned Mirabelle. 'Isn't White's a gentleman's club? Mr Hackensack is an overseer and, possibly . . .' She paused. No, it was unfair to accuse Joshua of being the highwayman. More possibilities cropped up every day.

'Aaah!' agreed Vitus, a finger raised to make his point. 'Perhaps not then.' He looked at her, admiring the graciousness of her gown, the neatness of her figure, the careful coiffure which crowned her head. 'Ascot? I was there yesterday.'

'The race track?' Mirabelle became very excited. It was certainly a possibility since Joshua loved horses.

'Lost a packet on a little filly . . .'

'You wouldn't know if the Hackensack you know . . .' Mirabelle paused, thinking about the groom at Sir Everard's manor. He did look tremendously familiar and then there was that little episode in the dungeons with the hooded executioner. Mirabelle shuddered, half in disgust of that dreadful place and half in delight at the memories of the quite delicious spends she enjoyed there. 'No,' she said, mostly to herself. 'It couldn't be!'

'Pater's not going to be at all pleased when he discovers what I lost,' continued Vitus, shaking his head. 'Should be used to my delving into his coffers. Keeps threatening to disinherit and then where shall I be, eh?'

'Will you take me there?' said Mirabelle, her periwinkle-blue eyes as shining and lustrous as a sweet cherub's.

'How could I refuse you?' said Vitus, taking her hand and grazing her dimpled knuckles with the softest of kisses. Then he frowned. 'Would I take you where?' he asked, puzzled.

Mirabelle sighed heavily. Perhaps it would not be such a good idea after all to marry Vitus, if ever he was free to marry someone other than Poppy Field. He could be such a scatterbrain at times!

'Dear Vitus,' she addressed him. 'Be an angel and take me to Ascot!' She spoke patiently and slowly as to a backward child.

'Capital idea!' agreed Vitus. 'Why didn't I think of that? Marvellous! Recoup my losses, eh?'

Mirabelle, with considerable fortitude, held back another sigh. Poor Vitus had not discovered that the only true winners at the racetrack were the horses!

'Shall we go now?' she asked. 'When I put on my newest hat and gown?'

'Rather!' agreed Vitus. 'I'll help, shall I?' His handsome face was split by a happy grin while his eyes glinted mischievously. His hands reached out, the fingers twitching as though to claw at her gown.

Mirabelle laughed, dancing away from him. 'I think not, Vitus! We shall never go beyond the door of Peacham Place if I allow you into my rooms.'

Laughing, Vitus sat back on the cane sofa, his arms stretched casually across the back. 'Perhaps you're right, old gel,' he agreed, 'never could resist a lady in her boudoir.'

On the arm of Viscount Vitus Wyndham, Miss Mirabelle Washington caused quite a stir. While other ladies wore the high necks made so fashionable by Queen Alexander, Mirabelle had chosen a most daring *décolletage*.

'Disgusting display!' remarked the dowager Duchess of Barkington.

'Who does that American filly think she is?' murmured Lady Merchington.

'A contender when Mrs Keppel becomes out of favour, I shouldn't wonder!' replied the dowager Duchess.

Oblivious to the glares and stares of the established members of the set, Mirabelle was entranced by the glamour of this most famous of racecourses.

'There's the Marquess of Buttcester!' cried Vitus, waving his race card. 'Just entering the Royal Enclosure. We'll join him.'

The two hurried over, Mirabelle's short train swishing the closely cropped turf. The Marquess spied them immediately and his eyes lit up at the sight of the black haired beauty with the creamy expanse of breasts bearing down upon him.

'Buttcester, old chap,' greeted Vitus. 'Marvellous to see you. May I introduce Miss Mirabelle Washington over from America?'

The Marquess thwacked his riding crop against his thigh and grinned broadly. 'Certainly may, old fellow!' he chortled.

'Hi, Buster!' said Mirabelle in her friendliest manner, but her eyes darted about the enclosure. Didn't Vitus say that the groom who Mirabelle was sure was Joshua might be here?

'Mirabelle's just returned from a few days in the country,' supplied Vitus. 'Mountjoy Manor.'

The Marquess's eye brows shot up and he licked his lips lasciviously. 'By jove! Nothing I like better than a filly who enjoys a bit of slap and tickle!' The riding crop which the Marquess carried was stroked very surreptitiously across the lower margin of Mirabelle's corset.

'Talking of fillies,' said Vitus suddenly waving his race card in the air, 'got to place a few crisp white notes on my fancy.'

'Good show, old boy!' said the Marquess, practically pushing him out of the Enclosure. 'Mustn't miss an opportunity!'

Mirabelle, intent upon looking for Joshua, barely noticed the Marquess guiding her to a small tent which seemed to be his private domain.

'So you've been to Mountjoy's, have you?' The Marquess stroked the riding crop through his hands lovingly. 'Like that sort of thing, eh?'

Remembering the huge variety of sexual tantalisers which were housed in Mountjoy Manor Mirabelle was at a loss to understand exactly to what the Marquess was referring.

He twitched her gown with the crop, lifting the short train to give him sight of her dainty ankles encased in those dear little button boots.

'What sort of thing?' she asked huskily, genuinely puzzled.

'You know!' groaned the Marquess. 'Don't pretend you don't, you teasing little minx!'

The crop caressed the pouting mounds of Mirabelle's buttocks, sawing across the fullest part which imparted a warmth, not only to those glorious mounds, but also to the soft moistness of her cunney.

The Marquess was breathing heavily and the crop hooked Mirabelle's gown high. She knew that her sheer silk stockings were clearly in view all the way to the very taut suspenders which held them in place.

'Oh, my dear!' rasped the Marquess. 'I can quite see the attraction for that old rascal Mountjoy.' He grasped her about her tiny waist and pulled her down across his lap upon a low chair.

'Do you wear open drawers, my dear?' whispered the Marquess, bending close to her shell-like ear. She could feel the warmth of his breath upon the peach of her cheeks and she could not help the shudder of pleasure which ran through her body at the Marquess's query.

'Yes,' she whispered, pouting her lower body in invitation.

Inexorably, she felt the touch of gentle fingers lifting the hem of her elegant gown and the frills of her petticoats until her drawers were revealed. Naughtily, she parted her thighs to give the Marquess full view of the open nature of that garment.

'Beautiful!' sighed the Marquess. A very long and elegant hand smoothed across the silkiness of her buttocks, feeling the swell of each hillock and the heat emanating from the deep cleft between them.

Mirabelle could not help but open her elegant thighs allowing the Marquess to enter the moist heat of her cunney.

'Marvellous!' murmured the Marquess on the completion of his investigation. 'Ever thought of marriage, Miss Mirabelle?'

Mama could not fail to be impressed with a marquess, thought our heroine, pouting the ivory hillocks yet higher, but would this suitor measure up to Joshua? Mirabelle questioned.

'Sometimes,' murmured the Southern belle.

The elegant fingers slid deeper into the moist cleft while the crop stroked tantalisingly over the upthrust ivory smoothness of the buttocks. An involuntary shudder ran through Mirabelle's shapely form, splayed in such an ungainly manner upon the Marquess's lap.

'To me?' he asked, still teasing the bared hillocks.

'I must know . . .' she said hesitantly.

A finger and thumb pinched the hard, moist pip of her clitty, making her jerk pleasurably. 'You were saying, my sweet girl?'

Mirabelle breathed hard, fighting and yet wanting the enjoyment of a spend. 'I . . . must . . . be . . . sure that . . . you can satisfy . . .'

A band of heat suddenly burned the upthrust hillocks. Mirabelle gasped at the suddenness of the crop descending upon her creamy flesh.

'And do you think that I must not!' growled the Marquess.

Thwack! The crop beat down again, heaping fire upon fire and yet Mirabelle, after the training at Mountjoy Manor, welcomed the tantalising tickle. 'Oh, Buster!' she sighed delightedly. 'Again, my sweet man!' She kicked her shapely limbs up and down in sheer delight, making the pretty buttocks all the more tempting to the taste of the Marquess's crop.

'How wonderful to meet a game gel!' chortled the Marquess. 'Love to tickle the flanks of such a one!' With this joyful whoop the high-ranking aristocrat brought down the whippy little tickler upon the merry wriggling hillocks of flesh.

'We are a perfect pair!' exclaimed the Marquess. 'Surely you must agree?'

Buttocks striped scarlet by the taste of the crop and cunney swollen beyond measure with desire, Mirabelle mewed softly through her parted rosebud lips.

'Was that a "yes"?' groaned the Marquess, flipping the lovely girl upon his lap to face him. 'Please say it was!'

Mirabelle looked up at him, not at all ashamed to have her skirt and petticoat in such disarray. Her blue eyes were misty and wistful, while her lips were curved and generously parted in such a sensuous smile. There was no further need for words. Within moments the Marquess was upon the giving girl, covering her luscious body upon the turf which formed the carpet of the little private tent.

'Oh, you lovely creature!' he murmured.

The gracious gown formed a froth of lace to frame the perfect picture of the shapely legs splayed for the very purpose of receiving the Marquess. At the very centre of the inviting body was the gloss of pure black which was Mirabelle's bush. Swollen pink lips pouted from the curls, slick with love dew and quivering allurement for the suitor.

'Aaah!' he groaned, kneeling before her as if in homage. 'Are you ready to receive me?' His voice was husky with passion.

Mirabelle could only nod, for she could not help but wonder if the Marquess would measure to her standard.

The riding crop was tossed aside as he fumbled hastily with his trouser suiting. Mirabelle watched with baited breath, her cunney tense with apprehension and her little clitty aching for real stimulation.

'Not what one's got,' murmured the Marquess by way of persuasion, 'but the way one uses it, I always say!' The haughty nobleman was an unconscionable time unsheathing the weapon in question and Mirabelle, ever the impatient little minx, touched a dainty forefinger to the inflamed tip of her clitty.

'Ah!' sighed the Marquess, watching with interest, 'I see what you're about.'

Mirabelle paused, not shamedfaced but annoyed that he had noticed. It was his cock which she wished to see and taunt with the cossetting walls of her ready cunney.

'I am so very ready for you, my lord!' she persuaded, arching up from the springy turf to show him exactly how she was prepared for him.

'No!' he insisted. 'Always like to pleasure a gel in full measure!' One of his large fingers was touched to the very tip of his tongue and Mirabelle watched the passage of the finger bearing down upon her.

'It's not that I dislike the touch of a digit upon my very private little pippin . . .' she murmured.

'Should hope not indeed!' remarked the Marquess. 'Glorious little pippin! Obviously aching for attention!'

Mirabelle gave a barely audible sigh. 'But I was rather hoping for your monster . . .'

Aristocratic eyebrows shot up in surprise. 'My monster, eh?' The Marquess of Buttcester gave a wry smile. 'That what you were expecting? A monster?'

'You do have one?' Mirabelle wriggled under the skilled touch upon her clitty. The little bud seemed to rise from its flushed bed and jerk quite alarmingly. Whether this was from need of stimulation from a masculine appendage or from simple frustration, Mirabelle could not be sure, but the Marquess, thoughtfully making sure, rubbed all the harder.

'Hm,' murmured Mirabelle, her splendid buttocks pumping up and down upon the springy turf, 'that's extremely nice but . . .'

A gloriously consuming climax overtook Mirabelle and somehow, without her quite noticing the exact size, the Marquess inserted his injecting equipment. He was extremely adept at the thrusting action and the turgid length remained of mysterious size.

'What d'ye think then?' he grunted, gyrating and pumping at one and the same time.

Mirabelle remained silent.

'Understand,' panted the Marquis. 'Got to give the matter some thought. Important decision.' He thrust ever more eagerly.

Another spend washed over Mirabelle and had she been questioned on the issue of marriage at precisely that moment she could well have been persuaded that it was a good idea.

'Ahhh!' said the Marquess profoundly and Mirabelle gave a loving caress of her soft, but skilled, walls.

The nobleman jumped deftly to his feet, tucking his trouser suiting neatly with his back turned towards her.

'What d'ye think?' he repeated, jumping to face her.

It was certainly enjoyable, she admitted and gave him one of her most radiant smiles.

'You're saying "yes"! A girl after my own heart, someone who enjoys the tickle of the cane and crop and . . .'

'Hey, Buster!' she interrupted.

The Marquess halted in his monologue, his eyes wide and questioning. 'Yes, my pet?' he murmured sinking beside her upon one knee.

'Didn't say "yes" and didn't say "no",' explained

Mirabelle. She lay casually, leaning on one elbow, her low *décolletage* revealing the most enticing of mounds, pressed most prettily together to form a deep valley.

'You didn't?' said the Marquess, deeply puzzled.

'Staying power,' she reminded him. 'If I'm to love you, you must have staying power.'

'Must I?' The Marquess looked much downcast.

Mirabelle pulled herself to kneel beside him, looking deep into his dark cinnamon-brown eyes. 'May I put you on my short list?' she said, her voice as caressing and deep as velvet.

The eyes sparkled and the finely etched eyebrows rose steeply. The full, wide mouth curved upwards and showed splendid, even, white teeth. 'Would you really?' he gasped excitedly.

Mirabelle nodded, echoing his smile.

Moments later, looking her most dazzling, she strolled alone among the crowds looking for Vitus. Gentlemen stared admiringly while ladies whispered behind their fans. Entranced by the magic of the racecourse Mirabelle noticed little of this as she made her way, at last, to the stands.

Suddenly, and most frighteningly, she found herself being taken roughly by the arm. Before she could turn to see her attacker a hessian sack, smelling of oats, was forced over her head and shoulders.

'Joshua!' she cried, her voice muffled by the sack. 'I know it's you. I've been following you, you wretch!'

There were sounds of a scuffle and Mirabelle screamed in the hot darkness of the sack. She heard a blow and a grunt of pain.

'That'll teach the blighter!' said a hearty voice. 'Believe you know my daughter, Bertilla Sayer?'

The sack was pulled from her head, leaving particles of oats in the blue-black locks and a cartwheel hat much the worse for wear.

# Chapter 18

The Earl of Westchester clutched Mirabelle, very protectively, to his broad and manly chest. Put in such a fright by the attack, our heroine clung, trembling and breathless to his tall, powerful frame.

'Is he dead?' quavered Mirabelle. She hid her tumbled coiffure against the Earl's reassuring frame. She couldn't bear it if Joshua was dead; couldn't bear it if her handsome lover was no more, if she would never again feel the fullness which only his cock provided in her cunney.

'Dashed well deserves to be!' exclaimed the Earl, with considerable feeling.

Hiding her eyes with her little hands, Mirabelle ventured a peep between her dimpled fingers. She saw long muscular legs clad in shabby trousers sprawled upon the Ascot turf.

'Oh, no!' she murmured fearfully.

The figure on the grass was face down, arms outstretched in a very lifeless manner.

'Did you hit him with something very hard?' she asked, her dimpled hands still partially hiding her blue eyes.

The Earl was gazing down at her, his eyes fixed upon the creamy expanse of her lovely breasts so sweetly exposed by her *décolletage*.

'A block of wood,' admitted the Earl. 'No more than a splinter to my way of thinking. No need for the fellow to make all this fuss!'

Mirabelle took another surreptitious look at the sprawled figure. A thin trickle of blood seeped from the scalp and down a tanned neck. 'That thick hair probably protected his head,' she murmured, mostly to herself. She gazed down affectionately at the dark curls which her little hands had grasped so adoringly as he kissed the very depths of her cunney in far off days back in Georgia.

'Can't have bounders like that throwing sacks over ladies' heads!' exclaimed the Earl, pulling Mirabelle towards him in a manner which could have been protective, but could have been a more lustful action.

Mirabelle murmured softly as she felt the manly arms surround her, plucking at vibrant chords within her slender body.

'He still has not moved,' she said anxiously.

'Doesn't deserve to, the blackguard!'

The Earl bent his head and kissed the silky skin at the base of Mirabelle's neck where it joined her glorious breast.

'But I'm sure it's Joshua Hackensack!'

'No doubt!' cried the Earl, spanning the tininess of her waist with his big hands. 'Hackensack by name and Hackensack by nature!' He hooked the sack, with which Mirabelle's attacker had pinned her arms, with the toe of his highly polished shoe.

To have searched for Joshua all these weeks only to have him killed in her defence! Mirabelle gave a little hiccoughing sob.

'There! there!' soothed the Earl, somehow managing to allow his caress to sweep down to the splendid pout of Mirabelle's buttocks. 'Don't take on so! Chap's nothing but a footpad when all's said and done!'

'A highwayman,' corrected Mirabelle, wriggling with enjoyment under the Earl's softly investigating gesture.

'So that's the bounder who's been flitting about London terrorising the ladies!' The Earl's maturely handsome face became a mask of disgust. 'Dash it all! 'Bout time the fellow was put behind bars!'

Mirabelle could feel the strength of the Earl's feelings

through her gown and petticoats and it made her feel vastly more protected to nestle against it.

'I think he's a fellow American,' whispered Mirabelle.

'Ah! Be deported, no doubt!' said the Earl triumphantly. 'Can't have that sort of thing going on in these islands, m'dear!'

With the nearness of Joshua, lying just a yard away upon the turf, so close that if she bent her dimpled knees she could touch him, Mirabelle had to admit to a certain dampening of the cunney. What with that and the cunning caresses which the Earl was managing about her buttocks, her clitty began to butt eagerly through the slit in her frilled drawers.

'Got rid of highwaymen nigh on a hundred years ago,' murmured the Earl, allowing a long finger to dip into the pale valley between Mirabelle's breasts. It was gesture of friendship, rather than intimate investigation. 'And now this fellow comes dashing over the Atlantic and thinks he can start up all the thievery which those fellows got up to!' He tutted loudly. 'Ain't on, I tell you. Ain't on at all!'

'But they're very romantic, aren't they?' murmured Mirabelle, looking up with wide blue and ingenuous eyes. 'Very dashing and swashbuckling!'

The Earl did not appear to hear her comments about romance and swashing, probably dismissing it as silly feminine nonsense picked up in a female weekly paper.

'And this young bounder thinks he can canter about the English countryside unhindered! Dash it all! Something's got to be done!'

The Earl shook his head wondering that such a thing should have occurred in the Home Counties. He swayed his lower body across Mirabelle, allowing her to feel how deeply he felt about the whole thing.

The figure sprawled upon the grass moved. It tried to lift its head, but the effort seemed too much and the head was lowered much quicker than it was lifted.

'He moved!' gasped Mirabelle, taking a tiny step towards the figure. She felt a tenderness towards the man, the same feeling which she experienced when she lay beside Joshua on the narrow truckle bed. Closing her eyes she felt his hard lean body, naked and unashamed, glossed with sweat in the Atlanta heat, felt his hand cupping the plumpness of her cunney, driving a caressing finger into the entrance which he had so recently opened.

'If the blighter moves too quickly,' rasped the Earl, 'I'll give him another dose of what-for!'

The Earl, like Mirabelle, had allowed his thoughts to drift. In his mind's eye he could see himself in the great hall of his country seat with Mirabelle naked and more than willing lying upon his table. The picture was much as he experienced with his former housekeeper, the buxom and just as willing, Liddy.

So vivid was the picture that the Earl could smell the rabbit stew which was Liddy's answer to haute cuisine. He pictured himself flinging his huge body upon the delicious Mirabelle at the expense of scattering rabbit bones and tin plates about the ancient stone floor.

'How beautifully your titties fit in my hands!' The milk-white globes were cupped in his huge hands, while his thumbs flicked the young pink buds which were centred on each mound.

Mirabelle, in the vision, smiled mutely, curving the soft moistness of her lips, showing the perfect teeth. Those same lips parted to enfold the thickness of the Earl's charger.

'Oh, marvellous!' said the Earl thrusting hard since this seemed to be what this wonderful girl required of him. He could feel the gentle caress of those luscious lips and a lap of a warm wet tongue all along his length. The girl did not seem able to have enough of him since she sucked him in quite to the hilt.

'Such technique!' he complimetned. 'My globe is butting your very palate!' He gave another little thrust to bring the point home and heard Mirabelle murmur her joy. 'My spend cannot be controlled!' he gasped, squeezing the lovely cushions of the breasts which he still held in his big hands.

The gorgeous Mirabelle drew back in the Earl's imagination to allow the jets of his issue to splatter the loveliness of her perfect ivory features.

'It's so silky!' she murmured, allowing her pretty tongue to take a pearly droplet from her cheek. 'It tastes so salty; so delicious! Hm!'

In the aftermath of his spend the Earl opened his eyes and was brought back to reality. He was at Ascot, but the lovely Mirabelle was truly in his arms.

A groan emanated from the prone figure upon the turf and it moved, slowly and cautiously, sliding snakelike across the grass.

'And where d'ye think you're going, you blackguard?' boomed the Earl, adjusting his racing tackle in his trousers. The vision of Mirabelle placing her rosebud lips upon his globe had barely left him and he did not take kindly to having this villain intruding upon his daydream.

The figure froze, the broad shoulders quivering in shabby suiting.

'Oh, Joshua!' murmured Mirabelle. 'How could you!' She looked over her smooth shoulder, so creamily displayed by the low-cut gown, her face a picture of anguish.

'He's an out-and-out bounder,' declared the Earl. 'That's how he could give you such a fright! London's full of such scoundrels and getting more so by the day, seems to me.'

He took Mirabelle's sweet little face in both his hands, turning her pretty head away from the very sight of such a person.

'Answer me, Joshua!' she pleaded plaintively.

The figure continued its progress, adder-like, across the turf. All the turmoil had created quite a stir and a sizeable crowd had gathered around the culprit.

'At least speak to me, Joshua!' begged Mirabelle to the miscreant.

The dark head, set on the muscular neck and shoulders, turned, just a fraction.

'Oooh!' cried the lovely girl, her soft lips forming the most perfect 'O'. The blue eyes widened in alarm and the dimpled hands flew to fling the Earl's huge ones from her cheeks.

'You're not Joshua!' she cried, throwing herself upon the figure which was so stealthily trying to escape.

The man, who was not unattractive in Mirabelle's eyes, gasped as he was attacked by what appeared to be a ferocious wildcat with slashing talons.

'How dare you allow me to think that you were Joshua!' she snarled. Having sheathed her claws she began to pummel the man with clenched little fists, sitting astride his prone body and clutching his lean loins with her dimpled knees.

'I never!' he protested weakly. 'It were you that kept saying I were the Joshua cove!'

The Earl, noticing how extremely well Mirabelle was handling the situation, punched the air in seeming great anger. 'Should be hung, sirrah!' he cried. 'Fellow like you! Highwayman terrorising ladies!'

'I ain't a highwayman!' gasped the fellow in question, quite enjoying the feeling of heat seeping through Mirabelle's tumbled petticoats and skirts and transmitting itself to his bulky masculinity.

'You're not?' murmured Mirabelle, finding great difficulty in keeping her own loins perfectly still for, having so long persuaded herself that the man was Joshua, an urge was upon her to lift her skirts and insert his stiffened manhood within her extremely ready cunney.

'Then what are you, sirrah?' questioned the Earl. 'To go about making ladies helpless with sacks?'

'Well I were given a guinea, see?' murmured the man, finding it ever more difficult to tame his loins. Mirabelle, was no longer pummelling the man's chest in quite the same way, but was slyly plucking her skirts upward for the purpose of freeing her cunney of clothing.

'A guinea?' she repeated, finding her dark lashes becoming heavy as they were prone to do under extreme sexual provocation. To make her seeming anger more believable she gave her captive the odd prod with the finger.

'By a gentleman,' went on the man, who under cover of Mirabelle's skirts had freed his urgent steed.

'What sort of gentleman would arrange such a dastardly deed?' asked the Earl, an expression of total disbelief upon his face, not to say disgust.

'Dunno,' grunted the man, thrusting his loins in an upward direction. No doubt it appeared to the watching crowd that he was attempting to throw Mirabelle from his body.

Mirabelle for her part was bouncing up and down, plunging ferociously upon her captive, making certain that he could not escape.

'What was this so-called gentleman wearing?' persisted the Earl.

'Funny get-up!' The captive could barely speak, such was Mirabelle's savage attack upon him.

'What say?' The Earl frowned as he watched the struggle taking place between Mirabelle and her captive.

'A cloak . . . and a . . . wide-brimmed hat!' the man managed breathlessly.

'Oooh!' murmured Mirabelle. 'A . . . highwayman!'

'Aaagh! groaned the man, not in pain, but seeming pleasure. 'Could 'a bin!' he agreed.

'Joshua!' cried the lovely girl in apparent ecstasy. No doubt the very name of her lover caused this emotional outcry.

'I ain't Joshua!' The man had finally managed to escape from Mirabelle's clutches, rolling onto his stomach.

The Earl clutched the man's shoulder, hoisting him upright, causing immediate horrified screams of dismay from the ladies in the gathered crowd.

'Dash it all!' cried the Earl, bending to retrieve his shooting stick which he had earlier thrown upon the grass. 'What is this, sirrah?' the shooting stick was used to lift the man's tackle which, for some strange reason, was protruding in a manner which made it obvious that it had, quite recently, been put to good use. It had a warm, moist appearance and that was a silvery pearl at its slowly shrinking zenith. The Earl growled and booted the fellow across the turf.

'Birching!' he exclaimed to Mirabelle, but she was heading off on some errand of her own. 'Birching would be too good for a fellow like that,' he continued, mainly to himself.

Looking over the heads of the crowd he spied Mirabelle's damaged hat bobbing hurriedly into the stands. The Earl followed eagerly.

'Oh, Vitus!' cried Mirabelle. 'Thank goodness I've found you!'

Viscount Vitus Wyndham was feeling rather pleased with himself, having recouped the portion of his father's estate which he lost the previous day.

'Mirabelle!' Vitus staggered into her arms. 'Gosh, you're devilish pretty! Will you marry me?'

Mirabelle sighed, tumbling backwards under the young viscount's tipsy stagger. 'You're married, Vitus!' she reminded him.

They rolled, in sweet harmony, beneath the stands, hidden from the prying eyes of other racegoers. What with the caresses received from the Earl, the tussle with the man who was not Joshua and now the tumble with Vitus, Mirabelle's elegant gown became more low cut by the second.

'Oh, dash it all!' cried Vitus. 'Am I really? Had too much champagne, I expect. One forgets about such things.' He was desperately attempting to stuff a veritable haystack of crisp white five pound notes in every pocket of his Saville

Row racegoer's suiting, but somehow he mistook openings and his shooting stick sprang eagerly into the summer air, shadowed conveniently by the tiers of seats.

'You told me you loved Poppy desperately,' murmured Mirabelle.

It would not surprise her one iota if Vitus was the highwayman after all. He was surely the most swashbuckling of all the gentlemen she had met. Perhaps he simply threw in the name Joshua Hackensack to put her off the scent.

'Poppy is a dear girl,' agreed Vitus, tucking away the last of the fivers but somehow quite forgetting that his shooting stick protruded mightily from his immaculately tailored trousers. 'But I do believe that if I had met you first I should have fallen in love with you.' His smile was boyishly affectionate, but the recently consumed champagne caused a certain mischievous twist of the lips.

Those same lips suddenly pressed against hers and gently covered her mouth. Mirabelle, feeling the sweetness of the kiss, could not help herself but take his stiffness in her hands, feeling the wonderful warmth and power which emanated from it. The moist smoothness of the globe made her shudder with pleasure and a renewed heat made her plump little cunney swell with eagerness. Mirabelle could not hold back a sigh of longing.

'Something has upset you,' whispered Vitus, giving the pink shell of her earlobe a nibble.

Slicking a thumb over the delicious slipperiness of the viscount's globe, she sighed again, making her full breasts swell with the swift intake of breath. Her gown, the elegant cut much weakened by the many happenings since she left Peacham Place earlier that day, gave up the ghost, baring the delicious breasts. Vitus, with a mighty whoop of joy, fell upon the creamy mounds as upon culinary delicacies, but still Mirabelle sighed. Busy as he was in tasting the considerable pleasures of the milk-white globes, Vitus was much concerned by the unhappy exhalations whispering from his lover's breasts.

'What is it, my dear one?' he said softly, having satiated himself for the moment with the sweet-tasting flesh.

'That's just it!' gulped Mirabelle, caressing the handsome young man's pulsing probe.

Vitus, ever the gentleman, rolled her over to save her the effort of the manual tenderness. Her gown, tattered in all the most convenient places through the events of the day, allowed him access to her feminine chamber.

'Don't understand,' he murmured, thinking that the amount of celebratory champagne he had consumed must have been more than he first thought. 'What's what? What's making you so dashed sad?'

Another sigh, timed to the very second that Vitus placed his plump and slippery knob at her willing portal, caused his length to be drawn in with such force that he thought he would be totally ingested. The young couple were locked in a close embrace.

'Tell me!' pleaded Vitus breathlessly.

'You said you would find my love!' Mirabelle complained, her sweet little lips pursed in a dainty pout.

'Well,' panted Vitus, supporting himself as a true gentleman should upon his elbows, 'one cannot do these things to order.' He kissed the heaving slope of a beautifully bared breast, hoping that this would prevent further complaint.

'Joshua Hackensack!' reminded Mirabelle, not to be put off by the heady sensation of his lips against her neck.

Vitus could feel the pulsing of his length throbbing against the moist cushion of Mirabelle's passage. It was causing a muzziness within his brain, quite apart from that already caused by the champagne he had quaffed earlier.

'Who or what is a Hackensack?' he said, hardly missing a beat.

'Joshua!' cried Mirabelle, quite distraught, even though

Vitus, expert lover as always, was causing her to reach an especially delicious peak.

'Still at a loss, my pet!' pumping from a greater height as he leaned upon his hands to give him purchase.

'You said you'd seen him!' The soft lips although still deliciously pursed and kissable began to look quite petulant.

'Did I?' Vitus frowned. 'Then I suppose I must have,' he added trying to appease the unhappy girl. His spend was very close now and there was nothing worse than having it spoilt in this manner.

Mirabelle sighed once more, causing the same swift intake of breath which drew Vitus into the pit of ultimate delight.

'Aaagh!' he groaned.

Mirabelle felt the sudden hot gush of the viscount's spume and this, in turn, sent her soaring into Elysian fields. Everything was so perfect for those few seconds but, with a bump, she fell to earth.

'You didn't see him, did you?' she sobbed unhappily.

Vitus grunted, drawing her lovely face towards his in a renewed embrace. 'The Hackensack cove?' he murmured sleepily.

Mirabelle nodded.

'Heard the name at Ascot,' he said. 'Jolly well sure I did.'

Unable to resist yet another sigh, Mirabelle heaved her lovely breasts in a truly engaging manner. If Joshua was in London he was very elusive, but that was always supposing that he was also the highwayman. It was all very confusing and, to add to her worries, she had lost Aunt Hatty May and was no further towards finding a titled husband than when she first arrived in London. She sighed again and goodness only knew what Mama would say if a titled husband did not come her way.

'Could you sigh a few more times, my pet?' pleaded Vitus, his lips bobbing from one scarlet little pippin to the other. 'It is the most glorious sensation to feel the silkiness of your flesh against my lips.'

Mirabelle obliged for such were her anxieties that she could do little else. If Joshua was in England, he could only have come to find her, but Mama had already made it quite plain that only a rich and landed gentleman would do for her daughter. Did he mean to abduct her? Was that what he was about when he abducted Aunt Hatty? Was he planning to make his fortune by such a means? Her head ached with the deluge of puzzles which beset her.

Vitus, burrowing into the deep valley between her breasts, grunted with pleasure. 'Sigh away, my sweet,' he pleaded happily, allowing his lips to graze the steep, soft mounds.

'There you both are!' said a familiar booming voice.

Mirabelle took a startled look through the struts supporting the stands. The Earl of Westchester's handsome face peered into the gloom.

'By jove, young Vitus!' continued the Earl. 'Been a bit rough with our young filly, eh?' He prodded the tatters of Mirabelle's gown with the point of his shooting stick.

She, so numb with the many events of preceding days, scarcely noticed.

'No!' denied Vitus, attempting to cover the loveliness of Mirabelle's bared breasts with a couple of large crisp white five pound notes. 'No, dash it all! Not me! She was like that when I found her!' Tenderly, he wiped a tear from the creamy peach of her cheek. 'Something seems to have caused her quite an upset, too.'

'If you've hurt the filly . . .' The Earl prodded Vitus hard enough to make him grunt.

'No! Told you! Not me! Something to do with a Hackensack!'

'The highwayman?' queried the Earl, frowning.

Mirabelle found her voice. 'Joshua may not be the highwayman. It may be all a mistake. The only one who would know is Aunt Hatty May since she had intimate dealings with him, but she's still at Mountjoy Manor!'

* * *

'None of you!' said Mirabelle, looking with tear-glazed periwinkle-blue eyes at the array of gentlemen exposed in the drawing room for the past several minutes. 'None of you measure up!'

The beauty threw herself across Lord Reginald's lap and buried her pretty little face in the approximate region of his vitals. Far from being disconcerted, the peer seemed to have other matters on his mind.

'Dash it!' he rasped, stroking Mirabelle's tumbled curls abstractedly and coming to a firm decision. 'Something's got to be done about Hatty May. That old rascal Mountjoy doesn't seem to have any intention of releasing her.'

Looking up and dabbing a snippet of lace to her tears, Mirabelle saw how very dejected he was and snuggled into his still exposed person.

'Perhaps she likes being imprisoned,' suggested the Earl of Westchester.

'T'ain't on!' exploded Lord Reginald. 'She's engaged to me!'

'Aunt Hatty is most fearfully fond of being tied up,' Mirabelle supplied, looking up with ingenuous blue eyes, 'and Sir Everard has the most marvellous imagination.'

'I want her back!' said Lord Reginald staunchly. 'And immediately! Don't know what London's becoming! Hell Fire club, highwaymen dashing about the place! Are we in the eighteenth century, dash it, or the twentieth?'

The Earl couldn't, for the life of him, think what that silly old dolt saw in the fluffy aunt person, but, helpful as always, suggested: 'What do you propose, old chap?' 'Send in troops? Get Vitus to rustle up a few Hussars among his chums?'

'Rather!' agreed Vitus readily.

Lord Reginald found it all too much and made a hiccoughing sob into Mirabelle's bosom.

Prince Adolphus von Schittler had been silent for some time, standing with his back to the room and silhouetted against the long window. He was a man of mystery to Mirabelle. Invited to Peacham Place with the other gentlemen he had made no attempt to join in the proceedings.

'I shall rescue Miss Hatty May,' he said in his intriguing Prussian accent.

Mirabelle's heart gave a little lurch at the sound and it was as if the Prince had caressed her with those long aristocratic fingers. Admittedly, his kingdom, Schlossburg, was so small and vulnerable against the might of the other members of the Austro-Hungarian Empire, but it was a kingdom and it attracted Mirabelle's imagination mightily. Mama would be pleased at last if . . .

'By yourself?' asked Mirabelle in a small voice.

The Prince whirled around upon the heels of his highly polished boots. Mirabelle's blue eyes were drawn to the muscular thighs clad in fine white buckskin and the taut bundle of manhood which nestled so neatly between the parted legs.

'I have the means to take the lady by force,' he said in a terse threatening tone, but his tortoise-shell eyes belied his voice. They gazed down at Mirabelle, full of hot promises which she knew he would fulfill.

All the men in the room looked at the Prince with new respect. Mirabelle found herself walking with slow steps towards him, her peignoir fluttering loosely at each side of her naked body. It was as if those deeply set eyes had mesmerised her and were drawing her ever closer to his tall, imposing figure.

'And what means would that be?' asked the Earl, watching Mirabelle's progress across the room.

'An airship,' he said succinctly.

Mirabelle could not prevent her little feet from taking tiny steps towards the Prince. Her little cunney, too, was ready for him, despite the hectic game devised by the Earl.

He held out his arms to her, smiling a knowing smile with wide and sensuous lips.

'But have you got the fire power, old boy?' asked the Earl.

The Prince, holding Mirabelle close, looked at him with something akin to disgust. 'I have all the fire power I need,' he snarled and Mirabelle could attest to that fact as she squirmed close to the lean hardness of the buckskin clad body. 'Come, my dear,' he purred to Mirabelle, 'prepare yourself for the conjugation of a lifetime.'

Said in that deep, guttural Prussian manner the command seemed to have very special significance to Mirabelle. She was powerless to resist him.

'Vee shall soar high above ordinary mortals,' he continued, looking at them with particular disdain.

'But will you rescue my darling Hatty May?' queried Lord Reginald.

Prince Adolphus von Schittler looked at the concerned owner of Peacham Place with haughty contempt. 'The Mountjoy person vill cringe before the might of my airship,' he promised looking like the handsome figurehead he was.

'But will you rescue her?' repeated Lord Reginald quite querulously.

'Of course, dolt! I have already promised you!' He turned to Mirabelle, patting the fullsome beauty of her buttocks. 'Run, my precious, and prepare yourself!' It was said in a way to touch the cunney.

'But how does it stay up in the air?' asked Mirabelle, looking at the strange-looking object glittering in the sunshine just beyond Rotten Row.

'Iss very simple, mein liebling,' explained Prince Adolphus von Schittler. 'Iss filled mit the gas called hydrogen.'

Mirabelle suddenly found her tiny waist encircled by strong arms. The Prince's lean, hard body felt hot for her through the confinement of her corset and the long velvet dress and coat which she had chosen for this strange adventure.

'Such beautiful breasts,' murmured the Prince, trying to burrow into her outer garments. Her soft curves seemed to mould to the contours of his lean body despite the polished black leather coat which he had chosen to wear for the rescue attempt.

'It may be simple,' frowned Mirabelle, taking a cautious look at the huge shimmering thing as the Prince whispered against her neck, 'but I still find it difficult to understand how it stays in the air.'

'You are a woman, liebling!' exclaimed the Prince. 'You do not need to understand! I shall rescue your chaperone from this fiendish Mountjoy and on the way I shall make vunderful love to you! Iss so simple, mein liebling! All so very simple. You have nuzzing to do but enjoy!'

Mirabelle, in the strong cradle of the Prince's arms, was suddenly arched, almost to the ground, gave herself up to the passion of the Prince's kiss. Somewhere, it seemed far away, there was a smattering of applause from the strolling public in Hyde Park. The hard Prussian lips devoured her hungrily. The kiss sang through her veins doing wonderful things to the sensitive flesh of her nipples, making them graze against the cool silk which lined her gown. Her cunney, too, seemed to open like the petals of a flower under his passionate onslaught.

Gasping for breath, still held fast in the Prince's arms, Mirabelle looked up with her periwinkle-blue eyes wide with wonder.

Oh, goodness! she thought. Could this wildly passionate Prussian be the very one she sought? Could he have the staying power to satisfy her hunger? Could she, at last, forget the man who whetted her appetite so long ago in Atlanta? She sighed, but then did she ever wish to forget Joshua?

'Come, liebling,' said the Prince, pulling her upright to walk to the airship. He held her elbow firmly, allowing no freedom of movement. She was propelled with tiny steps to the cabin which was suspended from the belly of the airship. She was a willing prisoner and this very thought excited her tremendously.

Both frightened and excited at one and the same time, Mirabelle allowed her little button boots to trip, one after the other, across the grass. She smiled at the gathered crowd, acknowledging their admiration for her bravery to venture into the dirigible balloon.

'In you go, liebling,' said Prince Adolphus courteously.

Mirabelle hesitated momentarily, button boot poised upon the lowest step of the short stairway which allowed passengers to enter the silver cabin. A seepage of warmth from her cunney folds told her that this was to be one of the most exciting days of her life. The hard butting of her clitty pippin against her lacy cotton drawers made her shudder dramatically against the clutch of the Prince's strong hands.

'Glorious princess . . .' whispered the Prince against the softness of the nape of her neck.

*Princess*, she heard with a gasp. Did he mean to ask her to be his wife? But then she must see how his performance measured against her other suitors'. But princess! How Mama would be pleased with her!

There was a sudden roar as the airship engine was started. The crowd murmured excitedly. Mirabelle felt the echoing throb within her body setting her vitals aflame.

'I am anxious to please you!' whispered the Prince, his arms circling her waist from the rear, pressing her close so that the fullness of her buttocks pressed against a heated bulge under his leather coat.

Amid the cheers of the crowd Mirabelle and her Prince turned to wave as the guide ropes were released and the magnificent machine soared into the blue of the late summer sky.

'Alone at last!' grunted the Prince, leading Mirabelle into the luxury of the cabin. Long, aristocratic fingers slowly released the three buttons which held the neat bodice of her coat closed. She could do little else but shiver with anticipation. She felt a gust of wind buffet the cabin as the airship lifted and, at the same time, she felt buffeted by their own savage harmony.

'I wish to make love to you naked as the day you were born,' whispered the Prince. He lowered her gently to the comfort of a low sofa sprinkled with satin cushions of many hues.

'Yes,' agreed Mirabelle, thinking how romantic it all was. 'Me, too!'

The Prince chuckled softly. 'This time I shall only have time to create your appetite for the future. Allow me to undress you.'

His last words were smothered on her lips and Mirabelle allowed him to explore her mouth with the soft moistness of his tongue. A hand slid along the silk which tightly enclosed the shapely contour of each leg.

At this point in time Mirabelle had experienced many lovers and, it must be said, enjoyed them all, but the Prince was different. His fingers were both firm and gently caressing. His kisses, as he explored her mouth, were as a cock tantalising her cunney. The slowness of his investigation was both irritating and exciting.

A hand slowly released the tiny buttons which held her gown bodice closed over the fullness of her breasts.

'Your arms are as unblemished and creamy white as those of Venus,' he whispered and the whisper blended with the noise of the wind which swirled around the airship. The bodice was peeled from the fullness of Mirabelle's breasts which peeped so enticingly above the corset, and yet the Prince concentrated upon her arms.

The smooth shapeliness of Mirabelle's arms were admired minutely by the Prince. His thumbs grazed over the creamy silkiness of her shoulders. The slowness of the caress drove Mirabelle mad with desire but he would not be hurried. The caress slid to the upper arms and down to the forearms. Suddenly, each was bent to form plump creases. His fingers pressed each crease tightly together and he looked at her, smiling wickedly before he snaked his tongue into each silky valley in turn.

The action was incredibly erotic, making Mirabelle wish that in the smooth creases she sported erect nubbins which could be cosseted by the Prince's agile tongue.

'Oh, Adolphus!' she sighed, but she could go no further. Her mind was numbed by the wonderful feelings which he was creating within her body.

'Each of your breasts is so beautiful,' sighed the Prince, 'as to drive a man mad with desire.' A long forefinger traced the lower fullness of each mound.

Mirabelle gazed into the young Prince's eyes. They were deeply set, mysteriously brown, and flashed with a fire which was almost fanatical in its intensity. A shudder which she could not resist ran through her partially naked body. She was sure that this strange man would, at last, satisfy her to the full.

His mouth, with its wide lips, fastened upon the tautness of a heated teat while his hands kneaded the fullness of breast flesh. Mirabelle, anxious to discover if this was indeed the man of her dreams, slid her dimpled digits into the swinging blackness of his leather coat.

'Nein!' he exclaimed. His voice was rough and hoarse; intimidatingly commanding.

Her hand drew back as though she had touched a hot iron.

'I shall make love to you, liebling,' he breathed, the soft purring quality of his voice evident once more. 'I shall make you quite crazy with desire. You will never know vot I shall do next!'

The very mystery of his threats set Mirabelle's cunney aflame. Love dew seeped from her secret folds to soak the hot little bud which hid amidst them.

The airship swayed beneath the great silver balloon,

making the Prince's every caress all the more sensuous. The wind sang a melody as it stroked the heavy wires holding the cabin safe beneath the great balloon, serenading the two lovers as they plucked their heartstrings.

Petticoats and skirts slithered to the floor, leaving Mirabelle's glorious limbs quite bare but for drawers and silk stockings.

'Ah! What perfection!' cried the Prince, splaying her thighs upon the sofa with such vigour that the cabin rocked violently on its hawsers and Mirabelle's soft cotton drawers were split asunder. The very violence of the movement sent searing shudders through her tantalised body.

'Magnificent!' crowed the royal plunderer, cupping the darkness of her mound in a most possessive manner.

Mirabelle urged upwards, arching her shapely legs to take full benefit of his caressing fingers, one of which dipped into damp silkiness of the jet curls.

'Tear my drawers from my body, Adolphus,' murmured Mirabelle. 'Free my cunney for you!'

'Ah, my princess,' groaned the Prussian. 'How I have longed to hear such a plea!'

Mirabelle heard the metallic clink of metal as Adolphus drew his sabre from its sheath. She allowed herself a slight murmur of fright, a kittenish mew heard only vaguely above the singing in the hawsers and the steady hum of the great engine.

'No need to be afraid, kleine mädchen,' assured the Prince, but Mirabelle was not so sure. There was something very daunting about the tall, dark-haired Prince with the smouldering eyes standing over her in the all-enveloping black coat with sabre drawn glinting in the sunshine beaming through the cabin windows.

The sabre slashed down, hooking the delicate cloth of Mirabelle's drawers, cutting them to flimsy ribbons which fell from her corseted body. The wickedly polished sword swished once more and she felt a sudden loosening of her stays which fell heavily from her naked body.

'There!' cried the Prince triumphantly. 'You are completely naked for me, but soon you will not wish to be anything else for I shall arouse such passion within you . . .'

Mirabelle took a surreptitious peep below as the Prince was sheathing his sword.

'We're there!' she cried, pointing excitedly through the cabin window.

'Pshaw!' exclaimed the Prince. 'I have instructed the flier to circle. I have not finished with you yet!'

The statement was both threatening and exciting and she looked up at the leather-clad Prince with sparkling blue eyes. He obviously intended to ravage her with his mighty flesh sabre just as he had her drawers with the cold steel weapon. He sank beside her, stroking the silky milk-white flesh above the welt of her stockings.

'Open to the utmost, meinen mädchen!' he ordered, encouraging the shapely thighs to split asunder.

Mirabelle felt the muscles strain with effort to please him, knowing that the puff of jet curls would be pouting upwards, the plump curly lips would be parted to divulge the pink folds beneath.

'So sweetly vulnerable for me!' sighed the Prince. 'A delight to behold!'

Feeling so helpless Mirabelle knew that her cunney was fully exposed. An unbidden surge of excitement made the flushed and swollen pink folds flutter pleasurably, much to the delight of the watching Prince.

Two thumbs pressed open the plump and willing lips with the dark frosting of jet curls.

'Such pretty petals,' sighed the Prince, delicately stroking the velvety moistness. 'Do you feel me opening them to find the bud within?'

Mirabelle nodded mutely.

'I shall pay homage to the dear little bud,' sighed the Prince, not looking at her but keeping his eyes firmly fixed on the flushed folds within her plump dark lips. 'And, in doing so, I shall make you beg for mercy; relief from the pleasure dome in which I shall place you.'

Such was the excitement created in Mirabelle by the Prince that she had, unknown to him, reached several glorious spends.

The tip of a silken tongue intruded into the dewed cavern beneath the inflamed little bud which was his quarry. Mirabelle mewed and wriggled her buttocks, causing the Prince to sip the bounteous sap.

'How you crave for my tongue!' he noted, looking up with a smile from between her thighs.

Mirabelle wriggled afresh. It was true. His tongue was delightful. It gently parted the flushed and puffy folds. It opened them with particular gentleness. It stroked the tiny slopes of the inflamed peak and pressed back the fragile skin of the minute hood to bare the very tip of the extremely sensitive nubbin, but . . . Mirabelle sighed.

The Prince, with those startlingly intense brown eyes, peeped up from the milky frame of Mirabelle's thighs. His handsome features were shining with the gloss of her juices. He smiled proudly, spreading the plump darkness of her outer lips, to lap at the bud which he had so carefully sensitised.

'It iss vunderbar, my Princess, is it not?'

Mirabelle was incredibly aroused. Never had she felt such sensations without the aid of a masculine thickness. He tormented her by prolonging the climax which she knew would peak at any moment.

'Please!' she gasped.

'What iss it, mein liebling?' he said huskily, looking up along her squirming body.

Mirabelle felt that she could hardly breathe from the waves of glorious perception circling out from her tiny hub and yet the Prince always knew exactly when to stop before she reached the ultimate peak.

'You . . . are . . . the . . . greatest lover!' she gasped.

There, she told herself. She had found what she sought, hadn't she?

The Prince, his leather coat slicking over her nakedness, shining with the gloss of her excitement, covered her. The caress of his lips on her mouth, allowing her to taste the headiness of her own musk, set her body aflame once more.

'Will you marry me?' he said softly.

Mirabelle hesitated, her mind a jumble of thoughts. At the front of those thoughts was Joshua and the single time they lay together on the rough narrow bed, his body so sweetly joined to hers. If only she had found him again so that she could know for sure whether or not she truly loved him, but it seemed that he was forever out of reach.

The airship rocked violently as it landed, startling Mirabelle but renewing the wonderful sensations engendered by the Prince. It seemed that with his instigation instant spends could be a part of her way of life.

'Dumbkopf!' exploded the Prince, shouting to the flier at the bow of the cabin.

'My darling!' she whispered, reaching out to him with a pale and dimpled hand. He sat up, an angry expression marring the handsome features, but perhaps it was only natural that he should be infuriated, being tossed from his loved one so rudely.

The flier turned around. He wore a long leather coat which enveloped him from head to toe. He wore a leather helmet and goggles which hid most of his face leaving only his wide sensuous lips visible below the tip of a straight nose.

'Apologies, sir,' he said softly, but the expression of regret for the mishap was overlaid by a hint of insolence.

Mirabelle looked at the broad shoulders, the way they were set, so straight and square. She shuddered and reached out with a trembling hand to her gown; anything to cover her nakedness. She was sure she saw a glint of amusement behind the goggles.

'Vot are you staring at, dumbkopf!' spat the Prince, pulling himself to his feet and dusting down his immaculate black leather coat to brush away invisible specks of grit gathered from the luxurious carpet on the floor of the cabin.

'Was I staring, sir?' said the flier, still with a vague hint of amusement in his voice.

Again Mirabelle shuddered. Those shoulders, the handsome features behind the mask, the flash of lust in the dark eyes only partially hidden by the goggles! She was sure they were familiar and then there was the slight accent!

'By gad!' exclaimed Sir Everard. 'It was the oysters.'

Mountjoy Manor dozed in the early autumn sunshine, its peace only shattered by this cry of utter agony. Sir Everard, after a surfeit of oysters, was suffering the effects of his over-indulgence.

The swathe of green lawn fronting the manor was broken by the shimmering giant of a silver airship. A small group of people stood over Sir Everard.

Clutching his middle, when he was not clutching her dainty ankles, he rolled in agony at Mirabelle's feet.

'Where is Aunt Hatty May?' she asked in a tone which was not in the least sympathetic. She strode, in a very determined fashion, across the lawn. 'You've kept her imprisoned long enough. We have come to rescue her.'

'Me, madam?' queried Sir Everard unhappily.

'Ja!' agreed Prince Adolphus giving the stricken squire a taste of leather boot where the pain was greatest. 'It iss not a gentlemanly thing, keeping ladies bound in leather and manacled in iron.'

'Dash it all!' grunted Sir Everard, squirming upon the gravel drive. He gasped for breath between bouts of extreme pain. 'That what you think? Not true! Not true at all!'

Mirabelle, still dishevelled and only partly clad from the flight in the airship, looked quite stunned. She pulled what was left of her gown about her and shivered in the chill of early autumn.

'What do you mean?' she murmured, bending down to hear Sir Everard's mumbled excuses. Uncaring that her lovely breasts were fully displayed and popping from her torn gown, she stroked the squire's sweating brow.

'Aaagh!' groaned Sir Everard. The sound could have been one of ecstasy or agony for all we, dear readers, shall ever know.

'Speak, dolt!' commanded the Prince, giving the squire a further prod with his highly polished boots.

'Dashed woman wouldn't . . . leave . . . my house!' With that sentence uttered in pain and anguish, Sir Everard Mountjoy expired.

The airship's flier hurried towards the stricken group. 'It's true!' he exclaimed in a deep and very familiar voice.

Mirabelle gasped, her pretty little dimpled hands clasped tightly to her heroically bared bosom. 'Joshua!' she sighed. 'Joshua – at last!'

The very same took the lovely girl in his arms, holding her close in a very intimate manner. 'Sir Everard tried many times to persuade Aunt Hatty to return to London,' said Joshua as Mirabelle lay her dark curls upon his broad chest. 'But she would not leave. She thought Mountjoy Manor so cute and quaint that she could not bring herself to leave the variety of toys and little diversions, as she called them.'

Roughly, Mirabelle was wrenched from Joshua's arms. 'Unhand this girl!' exclaimed the Prince, pulling her to his chest.

Joshua pushed up his goggles with an easy, unhurried manner. 'Says who?' he queried, his rugged jaw thrust out threateningly. Eye contact was made and Mirabelle was pulled back into his arms, where she snuggled sweetly.

'Ich!' spat Prince Adolphus. 'You are nuzzink! You have nuzzink!'

Joshua threw back his handsome head and laughed

unroariously, quite taking Mirabelle by surprise. Only moments before her breasts were cupped lovingly in his big hands and she could feel the thick evidence of his arousal beneath his flying clothes.

'Why are you laughing, my darling?' she ventured.

He kissed her with slow, drugging kisses. 'Some weeks past,' he said slowly, 'Sir Everard showed me his will.'

'Vot does it matter, dolt?' said the Prince, attempting to take Mirabelle into his own arms once more, but Joshua held her protectively, allowing a hand to slip between the tatters of her gown, to clutch her about the plumpness of her pussey mound.

'I now own Mountjoy Manor and all it generates in income,' he told her.

The periwinkle-blue eyes stared at him in disbelief.

'It's true,' Joshua confirmed. 'Poor Sir Everard has left me everything.'

Today, thought Mirabelle, there are no shadows across my heart. A warm glow flowed through her as she looked up at Joshua and felt the hard leanness of his body.

'But you do not have a title!' said Prince Adolphus triumphantly. 'Ziss little liebling vill not marry you!'

All the wonderful warmth which Mirabelle had felt for that brief moment; all the sweet torment about her erect clitty and the seepage around it were all dispelled as she admitted the truth of the Prince's statement. She slumped against Joshua unhappily, the glow flowed from her as quickly as it came.

Pulling her yet closer, Joshua touched the high coiffure with his lips. 'I have a middle name,' he said enigmatically.

'Pshaw! What of that?' scoffed the Prince. 'I have several names.'

'My true given name is Joshua Duke Hackensack,' he said, looking down so lovingly at Mirabelle.

Prince Adolphus von Schittler gave Sir Everard's portly body a peevish shove with his polished boot. 'Iss a name, nuzzink more!' he said crossly. He whacked his thigh with a